THE JOURNAL
OF
EDWIN CARP

By Richard Haydn

Published in the USA by:
BearManor Media
P O Box 71426
Albany, Georgia 31708
www.bearmanormedia.com

ISBN: 978-1-59393-396-8
Printed in the United States of America
Book design by Robbie Adkins

THE JOURNAL OF EDWIN CARP

NEW YEAR'S DAY, 1936

I experienced a small wave of excitement as I penned the inscription above. It is natural I suppose in view of the fact that, hitherto, I have ventured but gingerly into the field of literature. My dictionary, given me in 1915 by my dear Mother in commemoration of my twenty-first birthday, defines the word "literature" as follows:

> Writings in which expression and form, in connection with ideas of permanent and universal interest, are characteristic.

That definition accounts, I am certain, for my exhilarated state of mind. I am determined to spare no pains to ensure that the entries in this journal be both permanently and universally interesting.

Without wishing to appear immodest, I do not think it will be too Herculean a feat. That I have a natural flair for words has been proven by the reaction of my intimates to the few poems I have composed in the past. This gift, combined with a keen sense of humor and an avid interest in one's fellow creatures, both mute and voluble, equips me superbly, I am convinced, for the task at hand.

The first interesting thing I should like to record is the fact that this journal is a gift from the lady of my choice, Mrs. Maude Phelps. She is a widow. Incidentally, I fear the actual paper is of rather poor quality. Already I notice that some of my heavier pen strokes are beginning to blur. However, this minor flaw is more than compensated for by the exquisitely hand tooled leather jacket which Maude has made for it. She is exceedingly clever with her fingers and, even though the workmanship is not quite as deft as in some of her earlier pieces (my coon purse for instance), it is nevertheless a fine example of her artwork.

Perhaps the few minor imperfections are accounted for by the fact that on Christmas Eve, so she tells me, while hurrying to finish the binding, Maude struck her ring finger quite severely with the repoussé mallet.

On the cover, in deeply incised Gothic lettering, are my initials E.O.C. Beneath, in Roman numerals, my birthdate, "March 10th,

1894" and then the two word—"HIS BOOK." Over these inscrip-
tions there hovers a remarkably lifelike reproduction of a bee. This
is a private between my affianced and myself and has to do with
my being, by nature, exceedingly industrious. The bee's wings are
made from fragments of the mother o' pearl brooch which I gave
Maude as an engagement present eight years ago. She subsequently
crushed it on the rail of a steamer during a river picnic she is, I fear,
a poor sailor.

I only hope that, when this journal is completed, its contents
will be worthy of the hours of loving industry that went into the
making of its cover.

New Year's Eve at our house is always a scene of great festivity
and last night was no exception. Mother was feeling much better
and did not retire until 9:30 P.M. Miss Costaine, a maiden lady and
one of our two paying guests, was with us, as of course were Maude
and her son Harrison. He is the result of her previous and otherwise
childless marriage.

I am deeply concerned about this boy. In spite of my understanding of human nature, he becomes more and more of an enigma
to me. He is fourteen years old and, I consider, far too plump for his
age. This is a touchy subject with Maude. I have done my utmost to
win his confidence, but to no avail. He is also becoming increasingly
ill-mannered. To cite the latest instance: Last evening, after supper,
Miss Costaine asked me to sing. Naturally I was happy to indulge
her love of music and, with Maude at the piano, I commenced rendition of "The Indian Love Lyrics" which showed promise of doing
more that justice to this delightful work of Miss Amy Woodford
Finden. During the first song of the group, "The Temple Bells,"
Harrison consumed, very noisily, an entire box of figs. In view of
the gala occasion and his tender years I overlooked this. However,
no sooner was I well launched into "Less Than the Dust," a favourite of my Mother's, than he exploded a toy balloon behind Miss
Costaine, who suffers with nerves.

Of course he was reprimanded by Maude, though far too gently
I thought, and we recommenced the song. During the first verse he
was silent though restless. During the second verse, in spite of my
repeated look of censure, he seemed to lose all control and finally

left the room whistling "Three Blind Mice." Undaunted, I continued singing, only to hear him go upstairs where he proceeded to flush the toilet five times in rapid succession. Ours is a small house and sound carries. I did my best to drown out the noise of rushing water, but after my heavy meal I was, I am afraid, in rather poor voice. My Mother, who is inclined toward deafness, did not help matters by shouting "Louder, louder," from time to time.

It was all very disconcerting and I am afraid I disappointed Miss Costaine by being unable to sing "Pale Hands," which is her favourite. However, perhaps it was all for the best because, owing to Maude's crushed finger, the accompaniment was by no means up to standard.

It was my intention to raise the subject of Harrison's behaviour when I had seen them home. They live three doors away. Unfortunately he had been in bed only a few minutes when he was violently sick, so the opportunity did not present itself.

Once again I noticed that, when I kissed Maude good night, our pince-nez met and made a slight tinkling sound. I find it embarrassing. I wonder if Maude does too?

I did not reach home until almost 1:30 A.M., where I found Mr. Murke, our other paying guest, seated on the doorstep. On seeing me he began to sing "Auld Lang Syne" very loudly and very emotionally. The New Year festivities had led him to indulge too freely I fear. I managed, with some difficulty, to get him halfway up the stairs when he, too, was violently ill. In spite of this misfortune he seemed very happy and, on reaching his room, went to sleep immediately on the floor.

I did not retire until 2:30 A.M.

Luckily Mother heard nothing.

January 8th

Today, in our drawing room, The Society of Health through Sanitation held its first bi-quarterly meeting of the year. This organization was founded in 1902 by my poor father as a protest against our community's then inadequate plumbing. Although

Civic Authority has always refused to recognize it, our Society has, from time to time, made its voice heard. This mainly through dint of trenchant letters to the Press and carefully planned demonstrations. Indeed it was while gathering data, in a branch sewer beneath the Town Hall, for one of these demonstrations, that my poor father contracted the case of pleurisy which, Doctor Triggs is convinced, contributed to his demise four years later.

On his death, in 1926, I automatically donned his robes of office and, since that time, have enjoyed a certain prestige as President of the Society. In recent years, because of what I can only attribute to a lamentable atrophying of public spirit, the Committee has dwindled to five members. They are:

President—Myself
Vice-President—Mr. Vernon Rolfe, our local plumber
Joint Treasurers—Mr. and Mrs. Claude Tisdale, who own con
    siderable property on the river
Secretary—Miss May Throbbitt, B.M., Teacher of Pianoforte

Good citizens all, although Miss Throbbitt, since the loss of her twin sister in 1928, is given to bouts of hysteria.

Today's meeting was not a success. To begin with, Mr. Rolfe insisted on smoking. Secondly, the Tisdales, because of a conference with the newly appointed Sewage Commissioner regarding one of their houses as Gravesend, were unable to attend. And finally, Miss Throbbitt omitted to bring the Minute Book. Being aware of her highly strung temperament, I took great pains in rebuking her to be as gentle as possible. In spite of this, and to my great dismay, she began to sob uncontrollably. Both Maude and I are convinced that the root of Miss T.'s trouble is anaemia. In an attempt to distract the poor creature I recommended Dr. Bland's Iron Capsules. At this she became completely distraught and seemed to have such difficulty with her breathing that I was forced to ask Mr. Rolfe to extinguish his cigar. Why he should have taken umbrage at so humane a request is beyond my comprehension. Nevertheless, he did, and after several inappropriate and tasteless references to people who do not pay their bills, he stormed from the room, slamming the front door so violently that my Mother, who does not wear her hearing aid when alone, hurried downstairs in a state of extreme *dêshabillê*.

Although as a general rule we do not serve refreshments at our meetings, I sensed that tea might help matters. Mother kindly made it and after two cups Miss Throbbitt became so much more composed that I offered to accompany her to the bus. As we left the house she inadvertently stepped on a flower bed, completely crushing one of my "alpines." I controlled myself, as one must with Miss T., but in spite of my dissembling I fear she was aware of my inner disapproval. With an odd snorting noise she hurried past me and ran up the street as fast as her rather thin legs would carry her.

I am afraid that the weaker sex is a riddle which I shall never solve.

While writhing the above a drop of moisture fell upon my journal from the damp spot on the ceiling. I am more determined than ever to withhold payment of Rolfe's bill until he rectifies this condition. His explanation, that it is condensation caused by the inferior construction of our house, I find not only ridiculous, but insulting.

January 15th

At times the idiosyncrasies of one's fellow creatures are strangely illuminating. I am thinking, in this instance, of our paying guest, Mr. Murke, and his reaction to a certain picture which hangs, above the mantel, in our dining room.

The work is by Mr. Maxfield Parrish. It is entitled "Dawn" and is, of course, a reproduction. In this pastoral scene the artist has unleashed the entire wealth of his palette and the picture is a riotous blending of those vigorous hues which have brought its creator world-wide acclaim. It is a source of constant stimulus to me: particularly at breakfast time on those grey days when Jupiter Pluvius is in command of the weather. In the foreground of the work kneels a nude female figure. Mr. Parrish, with his usual impeccable taste, has placed part of an Ionic column in such a position that the lower limbs are shadowed and, to further ensure decorum, the lady has her back to the viewer.

Mr. Murke has always seemed tremendously interested in the model's pose. Each morning, as he pours his second cup of tea, he looks at the picture, winks at me and says, "Think she'll turn round today?" It is an innocuous enough remark coming from one so jovial and full-blooded as Murke. Indeed, on those rare occasions when he and I are alone, I enjoy, to the full, its masculine innuendo. However, when Miss Costaine and my Mother are present, his oft-repeated pleasantry creates an atmosphere of tension. I am beginning to believe that he delights in Miss Costaine's consternation. It can be for no other reason, for my Mother, owing to a mandibular malformation, dispenses with her hearing aid while eating. Miss Costaine does not exactly blush; but considering her years, it is most interesting to watch the rapidity with which her ear lobes redden at this juncture of our morning meal. Murke himself, although vigorous, must be at least two years her senior. I wonder if, possibly, our humble abode is to be the setting for what Mr. Robert Hichens so aptly describes as "December Love"?

January 17th

On arriving home this afternoon, I found, awaiting me, a potted plant from Floyd's Garden Nursery. The accompanying note was from Miss Throbbitt. In it she further apologized for her recent depredations in the front garden, and trusted that the attached would be a suitable replacement.

I am truly delighted. It is a small, but sturdy, specimen of the *Dryas Octopetala,* or Creeping Wood Nymph.

January 20th

At the Public Library today I lit upon a new book on sewage disposal. It is called *The Activated Sludge Process* and is by Mr. A. J. Martin. I have marked, with blue pencil, one passage which I intend to read at the next meeting of The Society of Health trough Sanitation. It is intensely instructive and deals with the respective merits of both the Horizontal Agitator Type Activated Sludge Channel and the Fill and Draw Sedimentation Tank with Continuous Filter.

January 22nd

Twelve years ago today Maude's husband, Mr. Frederick T. Phelps, passed into limbo. I regret to say that the anniversary had completely slipped my memory. When Maude called for me this morning, suitably dressed for our annual visit to the cemetery, I was gardening. She arrived to find me, on my kneeling mat, preparing to plant the Creeping Wood Nymph. That she was irritated by my forgetfulness, and justifiably so, was apparent immediately. However, her patent annoyance with Miss Throbbitt's gift I could not justify until later. Her deprecatory remarks (she called it a weed) seemed, at the time, unaccountable.

Her son Harrison was with her. He was wearing roller skates, which, in view of the solemn occasion, struck me as inappropriate. I mentioned this to Maude, whereupon, with a terse remark to the effect that she was perfectly capable of raising her own child, she brushed past me and entered the house to visit my Mother. This too surprised me for, unless it is unavoidable, social intercourse with her Mother-in-law-to-be is not one of Maude's customs.

No sooner were we alone that Harrison began to skate on the lawn. Owing to the resilience of the turf I could see that this afforded him little pleasure. I therefore remonstrated with him, but, in spite of my carefully chosen words, he continued his vandalism. To avoid completely losing my temper I hurried upstairs to change.

It was while donning my black suit that I was struck by a possible explanation for Maude's odd behaviour. It occurred to me that perhaps Maude was jealous of Miss Throbbitt's gift to me. So invigorated was I by this flattering thought that I inadvertently put on my pale blue tie (a gift from Mother and hitherto unworn) and hurried downstairs.

Maude was shouting at my Mother in the drawing room when I joined them.

I was about to suggest to Maude that, although aurally afflicted conversation with my parent could be achieved with much less volume, when I remembered that I had forgotten to buy new batteries for Mother's hearing aid. I apologized for m omission to them both. Mother, of course, did not hear me and Maude, with the same terse inflection she had used earlier, remarked, "Forgetfulness seems to be your middle name." she then enquired if it was my intention "to wear that tie to the cemetery?" Naturally I hurried upstairs and changed the offending neckwear for one more in keeping with the sad pilgrimage ahead. While so doing I evolved a plan. A plan which, I hoped, would prove to Maude that her jealously—if such it was—had no foundation. Descending the stairs and after hurriedly writing "Good-by" on a notepad which I handed to Mother, I rejoined Maude in the front garden. She was watching Harrison's skating prowess with considerable pride and complete disregard for the havoc it was creating on my small lawn. I dissembled bravely and commenced putting my little plan into commission. I will try to recall the conversation that ensued. I remember I spoke first.

"It occurs to me, my dear Maude," I said, "that perhaps the *Dryas Octopetala* would make an ideal adornment for poor Fred's resting place."

Maude looked a little startled and said, "I beg your pardon?" I indicated the plant on which she was standing. She coloured charmingly. "Edwin," she said, "you mean you don't want it?"

Picking up the broken pot, I looked from it to her. "You must not think me unappreciative of Miss Throbbitt's thoughtfulness," I replied.

Maude placed her gloved hand on my arm. "And you'd really give that beautiful bush to dear Fred?" she asked.

I looked deep into her eyes as I answered her question. "It holds no value for me," I whispered. "Either commercial or sentimental."

That we were both tremendously moved by this verbal byplay was obvious from the pregnant silence which followed. It lasted but a moment however for suddenly, the spell was broken by a squeal of pain from Harrison. His left skate had caught in a syringe root throwing him, face foremost, onto the gaily coloured bricks which I used to edge my garden path. He was quite unharmed, however, although his nose bled slightly after Maude boxed his ears.

It was raining when we reached the cemetery. In spite of this Maude was in high spirits. Even at the graveside she made light of the fact that, since our visit a year before, her husband's headstone had listed considerably. Her enthusiasm over my sacrifice of Miss T.'s Creeping Wood Nymph was most gratifying. The plant is by no means the 'beautiful bush" that Maude insists on calling it, but it has two sturdy leaves and will, I trust, eventually cover poor Fred's resting place completely. I planted it, at Maude's direction, immediately over the spot where she imagined Fred's heart to be. It was during this operation that I snapped the large blade of my pocket-knife. I was most annoyed. Being a gift from The Sons of Temperance (Group 11), it has great sentimental value. However, the small blade is still in working order, as is the implement for removing stones from horses' hoofs.

The walk home was uneventful, although we were forced to stop three times on Harrison's account. For a child, he seems to me to have surprisingly weak kidneys. I had been looking forward to a few moments alone with Maude on our return. My hopes were short lived. On reaching the house it was discovered that Harrison had left his skates at the last port of call and Maude and he hurried off to retrieve them. I learned later that, by the time they reached the convenience in question, the skates were gone.

Harrison's chagrin was, I suppose, understandable in one of his tender years. His tantrum lasted until 9:15 p.m. and caused Maude to develop one of her heads. In view of my ruined lawn and my ruined evening, the boy's loss of his skates leaves me, I regret to say, with a feeling of deep satisfaction.

January 25th

At the Public Library today, when I returned *The Activated Sludge Process* by Mr. A. J. Martin, the attendant drew my attention to the marginal notations I had made therein. He—I will not dignify him by the title of Librarian—refused to agree that future readers might find added interest in my penciled remarks and demanded that I remove them, or pay the fine. It was his manner rather than his argument that nettled me and the ensuing altercation quite spoiled my lunch, I advised him that his mien ill-became a servant of the taxpayer, whereupon he became most abusive. By way of rebuttal, I quoted from the immortal Bard:

...but man, proud man!
Dress'd in a little brief authority,
His glassy essence—like an angry ape....etc.

Unfortunately irritation gave my voice an added ring and, as I declaimed the words "like an angry ape," the readers in an adjoining Silence Room "shushed" me in vehement unison. To find oneself suddenly the object of mass antagonism is a disconcerting experience. In view of this and remembering that "a reed before the wind lives on—while mighty oaks do fall," I attempted to remove the pencil marks with my pocket eraser. I must have borne down too heavily for the page detached itself from the book. This, the attendant informed me, came under the heading of Malicious Desecration of Public Property.

With as much urbanity as I could summon, I capitulated and paid the requisite fine. Unfortunately my purse contained only bank notes of high denomination. I tendered one of these and was given my change entirely in pennies. Their weight must have been at least two pounds and as I exited, with them rattling in my pocket, the Silence Room, like a venomous reptile, hissed at me for the second time.

The foregoing is I fear, a sad example of the small-mindedness I find in certain of my fellow men. Of course there are others whose intelligence is great enough for them to be above Life's trivialities. That the Universal Architect saw fit to cast me in the latter mold is a blessing for which I am constantly grateful.

January 20th

Mr. Murke has presented me with tickets for a theatrical presentation. Neither Maude nor myself can be described as inveterate theatre-goers but, once a year, on the occasion of her natal day, we do indulge in this form of entertainment. By some fortuitous chance, the date of the performance coincides with Maude's fortieth birthday—the 20th February.

Our mutual preference is for some musical type of production in which romantic and comic songs abound. However, since Harrison has been of an age to accompany us, we sometimes cater to his taste, which, as in all young people, leans toward the mysterious or bloodthirsty.

Not being a student of the drams, I have not heard of the play we are to see. Murke tells me that it is a "revival." This I understand is theatrical jargon and means that the piece has been acted at some previous date. Without, I hope, appearing unappreciative of his kindness I enquired if this particular play had a good story. He assured me that it would make me "sit up." From the title I imagine he is quite right, although it suggests that perhaps it will be more to Harrison's taste that his mother's or mine. But the tickets are free and we are all looking forward to a jolly evening and our full quota of thrills. The play is called *Ghosts*.

January 29th

Man is the hunter. Woman the hunted. Since the beginning of time this law has been irrevocable. Although modern civilization has expunged barbarity, The Chase still goes on. Today, subjugation of the beloved may be achieved with a poem rather than a pike; but, beneath the flimsy habiliments of convention, the only uniform Society will countenance, there lurks in every man a primitive monster. I speak from experience. However, unlike some of my less fortunate brothers, I have a weapon with which to combat this savage beast. That weapon is Self Control.

The foregoing is the result of my restless musings since leaving Maude's house this evening. Although we are in the ninth year of our betrothal, our moments alone together are precious to us both and occur far too infrequently. The upbringing of her son Harrison, demands a great deal of Maude, although not as much as my Mother's ill health demands of me. Only twice, since Maude consented to be my wife, have I broached the subject of my marriage to Mother. On the first occasion she lost consciousness immediately and even the expert ministrations of Doctor Triggs took two hours to revive her. The second occasion was on Good Friday of last year. Maude had joined us for tea, which we were enjoying by the rockery in our modest garden. Before commencing the short speech I had prepared, I waited until Mother had consumed three Hot Cross Buns. She is very partial to them and, I have noticed, is invariably good humoured after such a *bonne bouche*. Such was not the case that day. Hardly had I mentioned the word "marriage," before a crumb became trapped in her glottis. Maude, by striking her repeatedly on the back, finally managed to dislodge the obstruction, but during the process my poor Mother's countenance turned an almost gentian blue.

To recall what followed distresses me even now. Suffice to say that Mother took to her bed for five days. Doctor Triggs diagnosed her indisposition as nervous shock, in conjunction with an over laden esophagus.

Whenever Maude performs her piano arrangement of selections from Grieg, as she did tonight, she invariably plays "The Death of Ase," at least twice and with considerable relish. I wonder whether, in view of Ase being the hero's mother, this has any significance.

Maude's finger is still bandaged, but in spite of this handicap, her attack on some of the more trickily fingered bass passages was brilliant and I told her so. My compliment was repaid with a look of such devotion that I could not continue turning the pages for her and was forced to sit down. Thanks to my Self Control, the battle with my base alter ego was soon won and, in order to prevent any further eruption, I suggested cocoa.

In the kitchen, while watching the milk boil, we discussed the cruel circumstances which make the consummation of our love impractical. I kissed her cheek before partaking of the modest repast and, as Maude filled my cup with the comforting brew, I quoted a verse of *Omar Khayyâm*:

> Ah! Fill the cup—what boots it to repeat
> How *Time* is slipping underneath our feet:
> Unborn *Tomorrow* and dead *Yesterday*,
> Why fret about them if *Today* be sweet.

I love Maude very deeply.

February 1st

Being due for my bi-monthly trim, this morning I dropped into "Harket et Cie, Hairdressers." Joseph Harket, the proprietor, has ministered to my tonsorial needs for the past fifteen years. He is a good fellow and always has a tale or two with which to titillate the more broad-minded of his special customers.

Although I pride myself on a keen sense of humour, I derive little pleasure from the average smoking room yarn. Due, perhaps, to a greater degree of sensitivity than is usually found in men of my station, I find the early Anglo-Saxon terminology, on which most of such stories depend, vaguely embarrassing. Harket's anecdotes, I am glad to say, are never in this category. Though amusing, they are never vulgar. Though risqué, never crude. Besides which, he tells them with so much finesse and is such a fine mimic. (I believe he was connected with a circus as a boy) that I always look forward to my visits to his establishment.

His response to my cheery greeting, as I took the chair this morning, puzzled me. It was off-handed and had none of the warmth due to an old and valued patron. My enquiries as to the welfare of his business and his family (he has many children) were met with impolite grunts. His unaccountable despondence saddened me and, being something of a raconteur myself, I decided to regale him with an anecdote. I know two excellent ones. I told him the one about the short-sighted midget at the Zoo, who shakes hands with one of the monkeys and says, "Good morning, Angus." (She is a Scotch midget and imagines the anthropoid is her brother.) As can be imagined, it is uproariously funny and I have never yet been able to relate it without rocking with laughter. Poor Harket must have been in very low spirits; with no vestige of a smile, he kept right on cutting my hair and advised me not to roll about unless I wanted to lose an ear. He then, with a certain delight it seemed to me, predicted that within a year I should be as bald as a bladder of lard. This displeased me. I do not think I am a vain man, but I am, I must admit, sensitive about my receding hairline. Although my reply to his prediction made i8t very clear that I considered his smile unnecessarily flippant, he grunted and muttered something about the Truth always hurting. From then on conversation languished and on the completion of his work, Harket raised the chair-back to the vertical position with such violence that I bumped my knee on the washbasin quite forcibly.

A strange young woman, with very bright hair, was at the cashier's desk. I was surprised not to see Mrs. Harket in charge of the money and enquired after her. I was informed that she was in the hospital. This sad fact explained to me at once the cause of Harket's ill humour and I harried back to him. I apologized for my testiness and offered my wishes for his wife's speedy recovery from whatever ailed her. My words affected Harket oddly. His breathing became irregular and his face slowly turned a deep magenta. Then, with the wail of a soul in purgatory, he turned to the wall mirror and grasping the frame with great force, began shouting hysterically at his reflection. I gathered from his quite terrifying ravings that *he* was the one in trouble, not his wife. She, I managed to understand , was fine: always had been fine and always would be fine. Then he turned and, thrusting his face very close to mine, asked me if I didn't think that the nine children he had already were enough for one man to raise and educate. The subject, being rather outside my province, found me at a loss for words. What followed was most embarrassing. Poor Harket collapsed into the chair and sobbed in the most heartbreaking fashion. For his sake I was thankful there were no customers. I patted his shoulder, rather ineffectually I am afraid, and left him. The bright-haired lady explained matters to me as I made a quiet exit.

This morning, at 3:25 A.M.., Mrs. Harket presented her husband with triplets.

February 3rd

Harrison is confined to his bed with a bilious attack. Therefore, this evening, after first settling Mother before the fire with her new book (*Wormwood,* by Miss Marie Corelli), I sped along to Maude's. Time is all too fleeting when one is happy and the hour we spent alone together seemed but a mere moment.

---

*Floors are "pugged" or packed with slag wool between the joists to render them sound-proof. R.H.

Maude is learning "Hiawatha's Wedding Feast," from *The Song of Hiawatha*, by H. W. Longfellow. It is her intention to recite it, on the 18th, at Miss Throbbitt's musicale. Tonight we had, what I believe is called, a rehearsal. That Maude has a retentive memory I know from various incidents in the past. In spite of this, however, I was deeply impressed by her brilliant memorization of this extremely long poem. (If poem it can be called, for it does not rhyme.) Not only is she almost word perfect, but the assurance of her delivery could not be bettered were she, by profession, an orator. It is true that she has certain difficulty with some of the American Indian proper names—such as "Maskenozha,' "Nagoo Wudjoo," " Chibiabos," "Nokomis," "Iagoo," "Yenadizze," "Mondamin" and "Shaugodaya"—but her pronunciation of "Pau-Puk-Keewis," which occurs seven times, is flawless. I am convinced, and I told Maude so, that if, on the night of the party, she hurries over the trickier names, none of the guests will be any the wiser. While we were discussing these things, I was struck by an idea which, I am certain, will make Maude's performance at the musicale the success of the evening. She is going to wear, together with her fawn lace evening dress, the Red Indian feather headdress which her grandfather purchased at the Earls Court Exhibition.

After cocoa, as I was leaving, Maude presented me with a fine a specimen of the *Dryas Octopetala* as I have ever seen. It must be at least three times as big as Miss Throbbitt's.

This sweet and subtle gesture of Maude's left me quite inarticulate. It is further proof, if proof be needed, that a man's most cherished prize is the unselfish love of a good woman.

February 5th

Some men, on leaving this vale of tears, are fortunate enough to leave behind them tangible and lasting evidence of their greatness. Their memories are perpetuated in the minds of generations to come by, perhaps, books they have written, discoveries they have made or edifices they have designed.

What man, living today, can pick up a copy of *Oliver Twist* without the magic name of Dickens immediately springing to mind? Who can look at an apple without thinking of Sir Isaac Newton

(Discoverer of the Law of Gravity) or, perhaps, William Tell? A dullard, too, must he be who, on looking at a postcard of the Taj Mahal, does not remember Shah Jehan and his wife Mumtaz. On every side, as we go about our daily tasks, the reminders of genius, that is now dust, are legion.

Conversely, some men leave little behind them for posterity to revere. Though they have the attributes of greatness, a capricious Fate weaves into the fabric of their lives a pattern of stultification, so enervating that they die with the arrow of their ambition fallen, humiliatingly, short of its mark.

Such a man was my poor Father, Thomas Anselm Carp: Building Contractor. "Tacky" Carp, as he was known to his intimates (his initials being T.A.C.), showed promise, in his youth, of leaving an indelible mark on History's page. He was a natural carpenter and, when only seventeen, won a much coveted Inter-Borough Medallion for his mortice jointing. This handsome trophy still hangs above my Mother's bed next to her marriage certificate. The frame for the latter is also Father's work and contains such exquisite examples of his "joggle," "tusk" and "birdsmouth" jointing that it induces a reverential awe in the most expert of cabinet makers. At an Ideal Home and Building Exhibition, at the age of nineteen and in competition with twenty-three other contenders, my Father won a sterling silver egg-warmer for his Slag Wool Pugging.*

I will never forget how choked with pride I was when, at his funeral during a memorial speech made by Mr. Mead (proprietor of The Crown and Quiver and Tacky's closest friend), my Father was referred to as The Cellini of the Adze.

Although a somewhat humourless man (my love of fun I inherit from the distaff side) my Father was, because of his industriousness and ability, respected by all. Soon after his twenty-first birthday, while erecting a King Post Trussed Partition in her father's house, he met and subsequently espoused the lady who was later destined to give me birth. Miss Gertrude Ivy Gubbion. After their marriage he went into business with my maternal grandfather, Tobias Gubbion, who owned a brickyard. It was the firm of

Gubbion and Carp that erected all the villas which now stand, so proudly identical, on either side of Gubbion Avenue.

Our house is number thirty-five. At my Mother's insistence, my Father named it IVY HOUSE and deeded the freehold to her along with that of two other dwellings: MON REPOS, number thirty-three, and DUN ROVIN, number thirty-one. Maude resides at THE NEST, number forty-one, which we do not own.

It is from the rental of these properties, together with the fees received from Mr. Murke and Miss Costaine for their board and residence, that I derive m income. Although no fortune, it is sufficient for my modest needs and enables me to live with dignity.

There are those of his relatives who place the blame for my Father's ill fortune at my Mother's door. Aunt Hilda and Uncle Saul in particular: they say she drove him too hard. Their accusation is, of course, the foulest slander and we have not spoken since 1916. (I make a point of cutting them whenever we meet.) I am willing to admit that my Mother has a dominant personality, but the true cause of my Father's downfall was intemperance. How dread is this disease and how tragic its victims. They resist all attempts at rehabilitation and Reason is a useless weapon with which to combat the demon that rides them.

I discovered this fact in 1923. My Father was recovering from his first attack of delirium tremens. On the May morning in question, I placed on his breakfast tray, next to the porridge, a poem I had composed. The content of it would, I prayed, by the very sordidness of the picture it painted, goad him into making a fresh start. Ascending to his bedroom and after arousing him with some difficulty, I placed the repast on his lap. He played with the porridge for some moments before his rheumy eyes lit upon my brain child. Although his grip was extremely palsied, he managed, finally, to hold and read my work. I waited, breathlessly, for his reaction. It was not at all what I expected. Luckily I was near the door and was able to leave the room just as he threw the tea-pot. The architrave (a fine example of his earlier work) bears evidence, to this day, of the impact. In the nick of time I managed to lock myself in the bathroom, where I remained until noon, while my poor Father had his worst attack to date. Had his disintegration been less far advanced, I am certain the sincerity of my composition would have affected him quite a different way.

The poem, written when I was only twenty-nine, is of course, immature and by no means epic; but the tragic circumstances by which it was inspired give it, I think, a certain plaintive ring. It runs as follows:

MY FATHER
By

Too often he looks on the wine when 'tis red
And many a day he will lie in his bed;
With nought but foul oaths for his kith and his kin,
A pitiful sight with his unshaven chin.

Please try to remember the Dad you once were
Ere Bacchus, with alcohol, made you a cur.
Oh! Turn to the fam'ly who hold you so dear
And please, Father Mine, do not drink so much beer.

It was my intention, in the foregoing, to record only how great an artist my Father was. I fear that memories of the poor man have caused me to digress from the subject at hand. It concerns our tenants, Mr. and Mrs. Luby, of DUN ROVIN, 31 Gubbion Avenue.

Snobbishness is a failing, of which, I am thankful to say, I have never been guilty. Therefore, the distaste I felt for the Lubys, at our first meeting, can only be ascribed to some sixth sense which warned me of the poorness of their fibre. That they are not the type one expects to find in a neighbourhood such as ours was immediately apparent to me when, some eighteen months ago in answer to my advertisement in *Dalton's Weekly*, I interviewed them. My Mother had allowed them to view DUN ROVIN the day before.

A huge man, Mr. Steven Luby, as he introduced himself (he had no card), appeared to be in his middle thirties. He had black hair, white teeth, a florid complexion and very dirty shoes. Mrs. Luby impressed me as being some years his senior. I could have been wrong however: so heavily smeared was her face with red colouring matter and rice powder that her true age could only be conjectured.

No sooner had I ushered them into the drawing room that Mr. Luby, after flicking his cigar ash into the bowl of artificial sweet peas, seated himself, without invitation, in my Father's armchair. It stands to the right of the fireplace and has never been used since his death. Mrs. Luby giggled and, after remarking that Steveyboy always made himself at home and so did she, sat on his lap and giggled again. It was then I decided that nothing would ever induce me to rent any house of mine to people such as these.

If only I had had the strength of character to abide by that decision.

While trying to formulate a plan wherewith to rid myself of this uncouth pair, I made sundry apt comments regarding the weather. Mr. Luby rudely interrupted me to enquire whether I had heard the one about the monkey and the giraffe. Once again my sixth sense warned me instantly that this would be an off-colour story. The telling of it in front of Mrs. Luby, who, although not a lady, is after all a woman, would, I knew, lead to nothing but embarrassment. My attempts to veer the conversation into other channels were futile. I could think of no way to stop Mr. Luby and so, at great length, with incredible barrack-room minutiae and the most disconcerting gestures, he related his anecdote. The point of the story, which, incidentally, is biologically impossible, brought squeals of delight from his wife and beads of perspiration to my brow. Mrs. Luby then jabbed her elbow in my ribs and told me to cheer up as I was among friends. She started to giggle again and Mr. Luby, after slapping her posterior and telling her to "cut the cackle," suggested that we get down to business. In order to gain a moment's respite and so compose myself, I suggested tea. Mrs. Luby waived my hospitality aside and said that Steveyboy had something much tastier in his hip pocket. Her husband told her to shut up and seating himself on an occasional table at my side, leaned over me. He asked me what rental I had hitherto received for DUN ROVIN. I told him. He smiled at me widely and offered to pay me ten per cent more, take the house on a year's lease and give me six months' rental in advance. I was completely bewildered. I did not want the Lubys as tenants at any price. But there exuded from this man, with his gross face directly above mine, a quality so overpowering that I was rendered speechless. There was a moment's silence and then, placing his arm round my shoulders (it was very heavy), he asked me if I knew the one about the chorus girl and the chimney sweep. Mrs. Luby started to shriek with laughter again and screamed, "Tell him,

Steveyboy. Tell him. It'll kill him." I cannot explain my emotions. I felt as though I was suffocating and knew that I must get away from them. Making the excuse that I heard Mother calling, I hurried from the room. In spite of a drizzling rain I went into the garden and walked round the rockery several times. This brief communion with nature revivified me and I returned to the house, determined to refuse Luby's offer and bring the interview to a close as quickly as good manners would allow.

When I entered the drawing room, Luby was wiping his mouth with the back of his hand. His wife, her head tilted back, was drinking from a small pocket spirit flask. On seeing me, Luby strode across the room, pounded my back and indicated the table. On it were a pile of treasury notes, a pen and a sheet of paper. "There you are, Carp old boy," he said in a voice much too loud for the size of the room. "Just sign the receipt and we'll wander off." ("Wander" was not the verb he used.) I stood quite still. Mrs. Luby stopped drinking, winked at me and gave a short giggle. "Better sign it, Mr. Carp," she said. "Otherwise Steveyboy might get nasty and he's not nice when he's nasty, are you, Steveyboy?" Luby took the flask from her and grinned at me. "Don't mind her, she's stinko," he said. He handed me the pen. I signed the receipt.

Placing the paper in his pocket, Luby picked up the bundle of notes and thrust them into my hand. "Come on, Dot," he said and, grabbing his wife's arm, they took their leave. Mrs. Luby patted my cheek as she passed me and said, "See you in church, ducks." I did not move from the drawing room and, as they went down the hall, I heard her speak again. "Mind my arm, Steveyboy, you know how easy I bruise." Then the front door slammed.

During their first nine months as tenants of DUN ROVIN, Police Officer Coggins visited the Lubys twice. The first occasion was necessitated by Mr. Luby's refusal to accept my polite suggestion that Sunday, being the seventh day, he should rest, rather that throw bottles at his wife. The next occasion was after Mrs. Luby refused, point blank, to remove the six empty beer crates and the dozens of rain-sodden racing forms, which littered the front garden of DUN ROVIN, turning it into an eyesore. I do not think I would have enlisted the aid of Officer Coggins the second time had my remarks as to the general condition of the house been received with better grace.

I have never been able to see the advantage of keeping coal in the kitchen sink and I have yet to be convinced that the water closet is an ideal means of disposal for corset stays and old socks. (Which is what Mr. Rolfe found on exploring the upper conduit.) When I voiced these thoughts, Mrs. Luby said I had better leave before her Steveyboy got back from the race-course. I attempted to explain my point of view, but she raised her voice and shouted, among other things, that the house was a jerrybuilt pigsty, that I was a mealy-mouthed humbug and that I would be wise to "wander" off. It was then I went home and telephoned Mr. Coggins.

The cruel things she said about the house my dear Father had built and the sad state of disrepair into which his handiwork had fallen haunted me for days. Doctor Triggs prescribed his usual tonic, but it took two bottles before I felt completely recovered.

Six months ago, at the expiration of their lease, I notified the Lubys, by letter, that I was desirous that they vacate DUN ROVIN at their earliest convenience. My letter was ignored, as were eight subsequent communications. The house has been extremely quiet of late and I have seen neither of its occupants for some time, although once since last October I got as far as the front door. I had determined to take a firm stand and to be very businesslike. Just as I raised the knocker I saw, through the front window, Mrs. Luby asleep with her upper body sprawled awkwardly across the dining room table. Although it was 4 p.m., she was wearing a soiled dressing gown. Her mouth was ajar, her face had a puffy, unhealthy look and the feather trimming of her garment was soaked with milk from an overturned bottle at her elbow. I lowered the knocker silently and went for a long walk by the reservoir.

For reasons which are not easy to explain, I postponed my next visit until today. It was just 3 p.m. when I knocked on the door. Mrs. Luby opened it. Her appearance shocked me. She was wearing the same dressing gown I had seen her in previously, but her face was bereft of powder and artificial colouring. I noticed, too, that her voice was much more subdued than when last we met. She is much older than I imagined. I was shown into the dining room which, I was surprised to see, was comparatively tidy. She offered me a chair and we sat facing each other across the dining table. I had the impression Mrs. Luby was under an emotional strain of some kind. This made me feel ill at ease and I did not immediately come to the point of my visit. We discussed the weather (it was raining heavily) and then I enquired as to the welfare of Mr. Luby. At the mention of his name, Mrs. Luby began to dab at her eyes with a paper serviette. She then asked me if I hadn't heard? Not having seen her husband for at least a month, her question found me at a loss. It may have been my look of ignorance, but suddenly Mrs. Luby's face crumpled and she began to cry.

If a display of one's feelings is likely to embarrass another, I firmly believe it should not be indulged in. Good breeding is an aid in accomplishing this, of course, but I see no reason why more ordinary people cannot exercise their will power to achieve the same end. Mrs. Luby apparently has neither breeding, nor will power. From 3:15 until 4:30 P.M.. I was made the recipient of the most appalling confidences regarding this poor creature's association with Mr. Steven Luby. I learned, to my horror, that their union had never been sanctified, that her husband (I shall continue to call him that) had left her, that she was too old to go back to "The Game" (whatever that may be) and that she was penniless. I finally persuaded her, with no great difficulty, to drink some whiskey (she used a dirty cup) and her tears ceased. After being told that I was not mealy-mouthed at all, but the kindest man she had ever known, who would never, she knew, turn her out into the street, I managed to get away. I arrived home considerably shaken. There was a tea-spoonful of Doctor Trigg's tonic still in the bottle, but, in spite of it, I am still upset. At the moment I can think of no clear solution to this problem.

One thing is certain. Mother must never know.

I suppose it is asking too much, but I cannot help wondering why all women cannot be more like my dear Maude. Incidentally, she must never know either.

I wonder whether Mrs. Luby has found the two one-pound notes which I placed under the butter dish while she was wiping her eyes?

February 6th

The instances of my Mother's absent-mindedness have been occurring with much greater frequency of late and I am becoming a trifle concerned. Last Sunday, the Shepherd's Pie we had for dinner was hardly palatable, owing to the fact that, in its preparation, she had used sugar instead of salt. This afternoon, when Miss Throbbitt called unexpectedly, I had to entertain her alone, simply because Mother could not find her upper denture and refused to come downstairs. I discovered it late this evening. It was marking her place in *The Sorrows of Satan*, by Miss Marie Corelli, which she is re-reading. I must discuss this matter with Doctor Triggs.

The reason Miss Throbbitt gave for her visit was peculiarly nebulous. She said she wished to reassure herself of my intention to attend her musicale, on the 18th. As I had written her my acceptance, immediately upon receipt of the invitation some weeks ago, I felt rather awkward.

I do not enjoy being alone with Miss Throbbitt. She is not gifted conversationally and is given to sitting and staring at my forehead. I wonder if, perhaps, Maude and I are wrong and whether her nervous manner is due to some cause other than anaemia?

Having received an invitation from Mr. and Mrs. Harket, to visit them today and inspect the triplets, I had arranged to call for Maude at THE NEST at 2:30 P.M., although I had looked at my watch, very pointedly, at least four times, Miss Throbbitt's eyes still remained riveted upon my hairline. There had been a silence of perhaps a minute and, in spite of the chilliness of the room, I had started to perspire slightly. I was trying to rid myself of a strange conviction that we were both gradually turning to stone, when, luckily, Maude arrived to enquire into the reason of my tardiness.

I have noticed on other occasions that Maude's eyes whenever she meets Miss T., acquire an expression which, until recently, I found inscrutable. By no means hostile, her gaze is, at the same time, not exactly friendly. I, myself, have received a similar glance from her on the few occasions when I have ventured a criticism of her beloved Harrison. It is caused, I have come to realize, by the most fundamental of all feminine traits: Protectiveness of the

Loved One. That I evoke such a feeling in my bride-to-be, I find most pulse=quickening. Therefore, leaving the ladies to chat, I went upstairs and changed my boots.

We, all three, left the house together and, as Maude and I bade Miss Throbbitt farewell, an unfortunate occurrence took place. Just as I was shaking Miss T.'s hand, she noticed the clump of Creeping Wood Nymph which Maude had presented to me a few days ago. Mistaking it for her own gift to me, Miss Throbbitt, while still retaining my hand, went into raptures of disbelief regarding the speed of its growth. Instead of enlightening her, I agreed, much more warmly that I should have done, that it certainly was doing very well. I admit it was a lie, but such a harmless one and told only to avoid hurting Miss T.'s sensitive nature that I felt sure Maude would forgive it. I looked at Maude. She was watching Miss Throbbitt's hand in mine. Then she smiled, inscrutably, at us both. "Yes, I bought it for Edwin at Rankin's Nursery," she said. My hand might have been a red-hot coal, so quickly did Miss Throbbitt release it. "Floyd's Nursery had some too," continued Maude, "but they looked more like weeds that *Dryas Octopetala.*"

Before I could explain, Miss Throbbitt drew a deep shuddering breath and, as the first sob shook her, she fled. I looked very sternly at Maude, who, I am glad to say, had the grace to flush guiltily. "That was extremely unkind, my dear," I said and, opening the front gate for her, we made our way to the Harkets. During our journey I could see that Maude was ashamed of herself and so, apart from teaching her the correct pronunciation of *Dryas Octopetala,* I did not refer to the matter again.

The Harkets reside in a rather small flat above their hairdressing salon. Their drawing room is, perhaps, fourteen feet wide by ten feet long. Seeing them in it surrounded by their twelve progeny, is an experience not easily forgotten. While being intrigued by this good couple's fecundity (I doubt if Mr. Harket is more than five feet tall), one is, at the same time, deafened by the noise.

Conversation under such conditions can be quite laborious. Very soon after our arrival my throat was aching. So were my legs, as I did not dare to take a seat for fear of crushing a little Harket. Harket senior seemed much calmer today, although, twice, I noticed a bewildered look in his eyes as he regarded his seething young. He insisted that I hold the new triplets. They looked, I thought, extremely wrinkled and seemed much redder in the face than is usual for babies of their age. This could have been due to the frenzied, passionate way in which all three cried, unceasingly, throughout our visit. Harket's eldest son, Alfred, impressed me as being remarkably well poised and polite. He called me "Sir." I could not help comparing this little gentleman with Harrison, who was not with us, but who is the same age. By shouting, I enquired of Alfred what he was going to be when he grew up and learned that within six months, he will be earning a salary as lather boy in his father's shop.

I am afraid that Maude's upbringing of Harrison has, in spite of her good intentions, retarded his mental development more that she realizes.

While the ladies chatted (figuratively), I accompanied Harket downstairs to the shop where he enjoyed a pipe. (It was early closing day.) He is a remarkably good fellow and was very concerned and apologetic about his emotional outburst when last cutting my hair. I assured him that an apology, if one was necessary, should come from me. I explained how inadequate I had felt on the day in question and added, with a certain profundity I thought, that "there are times when even our closest friends cannot ease our pain." He would agree to none of this however, and insisted that the fault had been his. By way of amends he said that he had a gift for me, which I would receive within a week. I cannot imagine what kindness Harket has in mind, but I always enjoy a good surprise.

Soon after our return to the drawing room, Mr. Bovey of Bovey's Photographic Art Studio, arrived to take a group portrait of the Harket family. He brought with him two assistants and a great amount of apparatus. Because of the smallness of the room and to ensure that we would not appear in the picture, it was necessary for Maude and me to crouch behind the piano. Owing to the inefficiency of the younger of Mr. Bovey's assistants (he knocked a lamp over once and the camera twice), we were forced to retain our cramped positions for almost three-quarters of an hour.

When we finally emerged, Maude was so dusty and felt so faint that we took or leave. The numb sensation did not leave my knees and pelvic region until two hours later.

On the way home we waited, outside his school, for Harrison. When, eventually, he came through the gate he was hand in hand with another student: a girl. She was taller than Harrison, considerably plumper and had, almost completely, outgrown her gymnasium tunic. Maude called to her son, whereupon the girl, after whispering something to him, scampered away. In the bus, I felt rather sorry for Harrison. During the fifteen-minute ride Maude subjected him to a searching cross-examination regarding his playmate. She discovered that the girl's name is Ursula Monks and that she can cross her eyes further than anyone in her year.

This evening, as I was halfway upstairs with a glass of warm Ovaltine for Mother, was thrust into the letter box. It was from Mrs. Luby and read, rather cryptically, "You are a gentleman." It was signed "Dot."

February 11th

In my entry dated January 8th I see that reference was made to the damp patch on my bedroom ceiling and Mr. Rolfe's attitude thereto. Since then the affected area has widened considerably and moisture falls upon my desk beneath, with ever increasing regularity. In order to gather sufficient data wherewith to prove a point to the illogical Mr. Rolfe, I have over a period of four weeks, timed the rate of precipitation. My findings are as follows:

> January 9th: Time lapse between droplets...
> 4 minutes, 5 seconds.
> "   20th: Time lapse between droplets...
> 2 minutes, 59 seconds.
> February 3rd: Time lapse between droplets...
> 1 minute, 12 seconds.
> "   10th: Time lapse between droplets...
> 32 seconds.

At the commencement of these experiments I found that an eye-bath was an adequate receptacle in which to catch the droplets. Last night I had to use a pudding basin and plug my ears to boot.

After a disturbed night, I arose in an exceedingly ill humour and telephoned Rolfe this morning, before breakfast. His attitude was most uncooperative and he refused to do anything until his outstanding account was paid. I pointed out to him that the bill in question is for "Correcting Leak in Attic" and, that as the leak is still leaking, it is, therefore, uncorrected and would he stop being puerile. His reply was obscenely monosyllabic. I replaced the receiver with some force and Mr. Murke, who, at that moment was descending the stairs, said "Temper. Temper." He delivered the irritating rebuke with such jovial patronage that I did not enter the dining room until after he and Miss Costaine had left.

It was 9 a.m. when finally, with my annoyance un-assuaged, I sat down to break my fast. I then discovered that Mother had forgotten to cook my egg at all. When I broke the shell (too vigorously of course), the raw contents splattered all over my face and garments.

It was a simple matter to cleanse my moustache, but my foulard tie (a Christmas Gift from Miss Costaine) is, I fear, irremediably stained with albumen.

At moments such as these I have found that a walk in the garden can be very soothing to jangled nerves. Not so this morning. One turn round the rockery sufficed to show me that an army of snails was devouring all my *Primula Obconica*. I remained motionless for a few moments, watching them. So great was my depression, on seeing such pillage, that my eyes filled with moisture and I sincerely believe that, had I not blown my nose twice in rapid succession, I would have made a spectacle of myself. This display of weakness was but momentary, for, being an avid student of human nature (even my own), I quickly realized that this behaviour was not only unworthy of me but exceedingly stupid. In short order I wiped my eyes and polished my pince-nez. Then after carefully dropping the snails over the back fence (I cannot kill a living creature), I got the ladder and a wrench from the tool shed and went upstairs to the attic.

Maude has told me, on several occasions, that my appearance belies the great tenacity of purpose which I possess and, as I placed the ladder in position, I determined that, even though I spent the entire day doing it, I would locate and correct the leak.

Entrance to the attic is gained through an overhead trap-door. My ladder, being far too short, made this maneuver somewhat hazardous, but I discovered that, by standing on the topmost rung, I could, with an agile leap, spring through the hole. I effected this but, in so doing, the ladder collapsed. I called to Mother and, as I waited for her answer, I remembered seeing her hearing aid in the bathroom and realized that my cries were unheard. I was unconcerned, however, for I knew that she would be coming upstairs to make the beds at 11:30 A.M., and besides I had man's work to do. I established a firm footing in the darkness and, after carefully assuming an erect position, found and switched on the hanging light.

I have not been in our attic for many years. As I looked about me, the leak, the purpose of my mission, faded from mind. The ceiling joists, so symmetrically planed by my poor Father, were stacked high with relics of the past and, as I inspected the piles of sentimental debris, the sluice gates of Memory opened.

To my right, leaning against Grandfather Tobias' night-commode, was the hoop I had bowled when, "with shining morning face I had sped so willingly to school." (I paraphrase the Bard to suit the case.) To my left, rising, Juno-like, from a pile of worn stair carpet, an ancient dress-form of my Mother's towered above me, its wasp waist giving mute evidence of the tortures once decreed by Dame Fashion. At my feet lay a lacrosse racquet. It had been left with us, in error, by my cousin Clara Gubbion in 1920. (She was subsequently drowned while learning to float in the reservoir.) As I stepped cautiously from beam to beam, a host of familiar objects, now dust enshrouded, claimed my attention. A pile of books: *Ida's Secret*, or *The Towers of Ickledale, Life in a Nutshell, Floss Silverthorne*, or *Master's Little Handmaid* to name a few. All written by Mrs. Agnes Giberne. I remembered that she had been my Mother's favourite authoress until the day I found a copy of *Barrabas*, by Miss Marie Corelli, on the beach at Leigh-on-Sea.

I opened a battered leather hat box. In it were the remains of my poor Father's silk hat, a number of dead moths, what must once have been a simulated ermine muff, and a time-stained letter. This last was from a firm of solicitors. The calligraphy, though scholarly, was so faded that I could decipher only "Dear Sir, Unless by the 21st inst . . ." Attached to it was a bill from The Crown and Quiver.

My next find struck a much happier note. A pair of skates which I had not worn since I was twelve. They are rusted, to be sure, but in excellent condition otherwise, for I used them only once. I remember my leg was in plaster for six weeks (it was a clean break of the tibia) and I will never forget the sense of loss I felt on hearing my Mother say to Doctor Triggs, "As long as my name's Ivy Carp, Doctor, that boy'll never put foot to skate again." I think that I shall give the skated to Harrison. They will make a nice gift and I am still a little ashamed of having been so unsympathetic when he lost his own. I put them on one side to take below with me and, as I did so, my eye fell upon a real treasure: my Fono-Fiddle. Why, I cannot imagine, but the playing of this instrument is not as fashionable as in my younger days. I constructed mine myself, using an empty cigar box, a small gramophone horn, and the lintel of a rabbit hutch which was dismantled when Mother disposed of its occupants. The Fono-Fiddle is single stringed and is played with a violin bow. The tone can be superb and I recalled the many times when, as a small boy I had been made to entertain guests with my repertoire. It consisted of "Danny Boy" and part of a Bach Fugue.

I found the bow and, as enough horse hair remained on it, tried out the instrument. My rendition of "Danny Boy" was quite creditable, but I do not know how much of the Bach Fugue I would have remembered, for, as I played the second note (which is pizzicato), the string broke. I placed the fiddle beside the skates and, as I did so, an idea occurred to me which I consider excellent. I am going to put the instrument in order and accompany Maude when she recites "Hiawatha" at Miss Throbbitt's musicale. Two tunes have already come to mind, either of which would be ideal. They are "By the Waters of Minnetonka" and "Little Redwing." I shall let Maude decide.

My next discovery was a bird's nest. It nestled in the crown of a disused Salvation Arm bonnet and, from its empty and friable state, I deduced that many years had flown since occupancy. The twigs and grasses, which had gone into its construction, were intertwined with great care, and I pondered awhile on the skill of the feathered engineers, whose sanctuary it once had been.

It was while doing this that a sudden and terrifying noise all but startled me out of my wits. It was the forty-gallon water cistern emptying and refilling. Only those who have been alone in an attic at such a time can fully appreciate my feelings. My whole frame shook and, in an effort to retain my balance, I put my left foot through a large, posthumous photograph of Aunt Hester. (She was an amateur swimming champion and Clara Gubbion's mother.) On regaining my composure I realized that, for the water level in the cistern to have dropped, Mother must been in the bathroom. Convinced that she had found her hearing aid, I shouted through the trap-door and waited. As there was no answer, I decided to continue my quest for the elusive leak.

The first pipe I attempted to tighten, I inadvertently loosened. This resulted in a quantity of water being wasted on the lath and plaster immediately above my bedroom. Quickly discovering the correct way to use the wrench, I staunched the flow and tested every other pipe I could find. There was no vestige of a leak from any one of them. This fact annoyed me intensely, for it seemed to prove that Rolfe had been right. It was while planning my next move that a drop of water fell upon my scalp and, looking up, I saw, at once, the source of the trouble. It had commenced to rain and there was a hole in the roof.

The sweatband from my poor Father's silk hat made a splendid plug for the orifice and, my work finished, I picked up the skates and fiddle and clambered across the joists to the trap-door. My intention was to attract Mother's notice at all costs. Imagine my consternation when, on looking below, I saw that the ladder, which had been lying on the floor, was no longer there. As desperation mounted, I saw, through an angle of the stairway, my Mother approach the hat-rack in the hall. I called frantically to her, but she was oblivious of my cries. She appeared to be in a great hurry. I called again, this time using full lung power and simultaneously throwing the skates to the landing below. The crash with which they landed was ear-splitting. Mother reacted to it as though they had been snowflakes and, taking her umbrella from the stand, disappeared from view. A second later the front door slammed and I realized that I was alone in the house: trapped in the attic.

The dilemma I found myself in, would, I imagine, throw a man of weaker caliber into a state of panic. I am proud to say that, throughout the interminable ordeal that ensued, my equanimity remained unshaken.

Several hours passed while I crouched there waiting for my Mother to return and, finally, hearing no sound whatever, I succeeded in knotting the broken string on my Fono-Fiddle and passing the time by trying to pick out the melody of "Little Redwing." I played it numerous times and, although usually I can carry a tune perfectly, each succeeding attempt sounded, for some inexplicable reason, more like "Danny Boy" than the last.

It was not my Mother, but Mr. Murke who, returning from his day's toil, heard my cries and, bringing the ladder, assisted me in my descent. Apart from being tremendously parched (I had been breathing a high percentage of dust for six hours), I felt, after slaking my thirst, none the worse for my experience.

My most vital concern was the whereabouts of my Mother. She had left the house, for the first time since my Father's funeral, at 11:15 A.M. and, in view of her recent lapses of memory, I feared the worst. I hurried along to THE NEST to enlist Maude's aid, but it was Doctor Triggs who, upon my telephoning him, decided that we should notify the Law. Maude and I picked him up en route to the Police Station. Unfortunately Officer Coggins was enjoying a leave of absence and the constable in charge was a stranger to all of us. Doctor Triggs gave him a detailed description of my Mother, whereupon, after looking at us rather oddly, he disappeared through a door marked "Private." We, all three, stared at each other, not daring to voice our thoughts and then, in the distance, an iron door clanged. A moment later my poor Mother, incredibly disheveled, was brought in.

The policeman smirked at us. "She came in 'ere of 'er own free will this morning," he said. "Blind drunk." I am convinced that, had not Doctor Triggs restrained me, I would have struck the oaf. Instead I withered him with a glance and said, "I think, my good man, that you are the intoxicated one. My Mother is deaf, not drunk." My contempt stung him and, with his colour deepening, he moved menacingly toward me. Doctor Triggs, with an authoritative tone diverted his attention and Maude and I did our best to soothe my distraught parent. As I went to hail a taxicab, I saw the policeman and Doctor Triggs whispering earnestly in a corner.

Finally, we reached home, but it was not until after two cups of very hot Ovaltine that my Mother recognized me and became, more or less, normal. Doctor Triggs, who had acquainted himself with all the facts at the Police Station, described to me what must have occurred.

My Mother, not realizing that I was in the attic, found and replaced the ladder. My apparent absence from the house had disturbed her and she had gone to the Police Station to report it, without her hearing aid. On arrival there, the resultant confusion had induced an attack of amnesia. Apparently her behaviour had been so hysterical, the good Doctor told me, that it had been attributed to inebriation.

Today, February 11th, has been one of the most harassing days of my life and I am now retiring to my bed with the hope that, while in the arms of Morpheus, its memory will be partially erased. It is 9:15 P.M.

It is now 3:22 A.M. and I am retiring, this time on the sofa in the dining room for the second time tonight. Thirty minutes ago the entire ceiling of my bedroom descended upon me.

February 12th

ODE TO AN EMPTY BIRD'S NEST
by
E. O. CARP

Dedicated

to

Maude

Twigs: Grass: A piece of twine
Torn from a washing line,
Woven in deft design:
      Simple, but sturdy.
Soft lined, this cosy nest
With down from Mother's breast:
Pieces of undervest
      Gleaned by a birdie.

Many a year, since two,
Or three, or four pale blue
Eggs hid inside of you,
    Safe from detection.
No ornithologist,
Groping with bended wrist,
Grabbed you within his fist.
    For his collection.
Four bills, all gaping wide;
Dawn, Noon and Eventide,
Never enough inside
    Fat caterpillars.
Night falls. Wait. Wait in vain,

Mother comes not again
Ever; for she is slain.
    Pussy-cat killers.

Although still depressed from yesterday's ordeal, I called at THE NEST, late this afternoon, to give Maude the above. She was out. Miss Throbbitt was there, however, instructing Harrison in the art of the pianoforte. I have pointed out to Maude, many times, that as the boy is completely tone deaf, his tuition fees are a sheer waste of money. Maude can be very stubborn. Apparently she envisions her son as a future Paderewski. Has she heard his rendition of "The Bluebells of Scotland," this afternoon, she would have reorganized her dreams. When I arrived, Harrison was being his most unruly and Miss Throbbitt, as usual, was on the verge of tears. Thinking to coax the boy into a more docile mood, I presented him with my older roller skates. I have seldom seen a human being (let alone a child) less impressed with a gift. He criticized their rusty condition and, after reluctantly taking and inspecting them, announced that they were useless because "there wasn't no ball-bearings."

I corrected his English, made him wipe his nose and sent him off into the garden. On his way out he threw the skates in a corner. They landed on the fretwork magazine rack, which I had made for Maude four Christmases ago, and splintered a portion of the filigree work irreparably. While I was inspecting the damage, Miss Throbbitt began to snort slightly. This poor creature is becoming a trial. Purely to avert any sort of scene, I allowed her to read my Ode.

Her appreciation was, I must admit, most gratifying and while she was showering me with compliments, Maude returned. As she entered I saw immediately that she was looking inscrutable. I handed her my Ode at once and, upon seeing the dedication, her eyes softened. However, after reading my composition, she asked me, rather belligerently, what it was supposed to be. I attempted to explain that an ode is a form of lyrical verse and that, in the days of ancient Greece, these poems were sung to an instrumental accompaniment. Maude looked at me suspiciously and then said, "What's the tune?" I replied that there was no tune and she said, "But you just said I was supposed to sing it." The ensuing conversation became extremely involved and I was quite unable to convince Maude that by dedicating the Ode to her, I did not mean that its subject was *about* her. She said that she had never been so insulted in her life, that she was not a "birdie," that she didn't eat "fat caterpillars" and that the pussy-cat wasn't born yet who was going to catch her. She said this last, looking very intently at Miss Throbbitt, and then flounced from the room Miss T.'s sniffs increased in volume most alarmingly and, to avoid further contretemps, I came home.

Mother is very much better today. Doctor Triggs has prescribed that she stay in bed until the week end. She not what is known as an "easy" patient and, twice today, has accused me of hiding her hearing aid, which has completely disappeared. I have used an entire memorandum pad, communicating with her since noon. However, my burden is eased, slightly, by our daily woman, Mrs. Grace Ottey, who has agreed, during this trying time to perform certain extra-curricular duties (for and added compensation). Mrs. Ottey takes great pride in her cooking. I do not like to disillusion her.

Mr. Frome, the plasterer, was unable to start work on my bed-room today. I am not looking forward to another night on the dining room sofa. Its upholstery has an unpleasant musty odour and its springs are singularly recalcitrant. Still, "Needs must, when the devil drives." I try to persuade myself that these minor irritations are all part of Life's rich pageant. I am not always successful.

February 13th

Although Miss Costaine has made her home with us for the past four years, she is, by temperament, so reserved that only the most formal relationship is possible with her. That she is a lady is obvious. (Never have I seen a tea-cup handled with more grace.) And that she has sufficient means to live as such is evidenced by her interest in the fluctuations of the stock market. Slender, almost to the point of emaciation, Miss Costaine affects rather flowing garments. Their style is influenced, I am certain, by her devotion to the memory of a Miss Isadora Duncan (on a train with whom she once traveled) and whose picture hangs above her bed. She is a member of the Primrose Hill Folk Dancing Academy, is learning the clavichord and receives quantities of correspondence from the Southwark Psychical Research Society.

These facts, coupled with the lady's age, make it difficult for me to believe that the events of last night actually took place. Were it not that evidence exists to the contrary, I would swear that I had been the victim of some ghastly nightmare.

After making Mother comfortable with *The Mighty Atom*, by Miss Marie Corelli (which she has no memory of having read before) and entering the events of the day in my journal, I retired onto the dining room sofa at 11:45 P.M. Miss Costaine had withdrawn, with a nervous headache, immediately after supper (cold lamb, mustard pickles and rice pudding). Mr. Murke was attending an Odd-fellows Meeting and would not, I knew, return until after midnight.

Before extinguishing the light I read, as is my wont, from the *Encyclopaedia Britannica*. (I am at MUS to OZON, Vol. 16.) I find perusal of these educational tomes a perfect method of wiping from my over-active brain the cares of the day and also an ideal soporific. I had skipped "Obstetrics" and was reading, with a certain interest, that Oconomowoc is a city in Waukesha County, Wisconsin, U.S.A., that it is served by the Chicago, Milwaukee, St. Paul and

---

*see entry dated January 15th. R.H.

Pacific Rlwy., that its population in 1920 was 3,301 and that its name is an Indian word which is said to mean "home of the beaver." Suddenly, a light footstep on the staircase diverted my attention. My first thought was that Mother had arisen. I threw back the bedclothes and, as my feet touched the linoleum, Miss Costaine entered the room. She was, to my acute embarrassment, in her sleeping attire. Her hair was unbound (I was surprised at its length) and, although she did not speak, her arms were outstretched in my direction. She stood, for a moment, in the shadow of the door-way, as though imploring me to go to her and then, slowly, moved toward me. I darted to one side and, as she reached the spot where I had been standing, I noticed an extraordinary thing. Her eyes were closed.

Sleepwalking, the condition under which people walk while asleep, apparently unconscious of external impressions, is a subject into which, until nine years ago, I had never delved. My interest then was occasioned by a confession made by Maude on the day I proposed to her. The dear creature felt it only fair for me to know that, during her marriage to the late Frederick Phelps, she had somnambulated twice. The first time she had come to her senses in the cellar and the second time she awakened to find herself mowing the lawn. Doctor Triggs, when I discussed the matter with him the next day, put my mind completely at rest and, although I bought and read a pamphlet on the subject, I have given it no thought since that time.

Last night, as I crouched by the coal scuttle watching Miss Costaine, one italicized line from the aforementioned pamphlet leapt to mind. *The somnambulist, if suddenly awakened, instantly drops dead.* I dared hardly breathe. The knowledge that one cough from me would dispatch her filled me with a sense of responsibility almost beyond human endurance.

That she was oblivious of my presence was immediately appar-ent, for she crossed the room with a strange floating movement and stood before the picture of "Dawn," which hangs above the mantel-piece.* Her fingertips moved, caressingly, over its surface for some moments and then, kneeling below it, in front of the fireplace, she assumed the pose of the model in the painting. (Not as gracefully, of course, for Miss Costaine is much older.) She remained immobile for perhaps ten seconds, during which I tried not to contemplate her next move. It came soon enough. With terrifying deliberation, she proceeded to unbutton the neck-band of her sleeping garment. It was obvious what she was about to do. Her intention was to disrobe. Slowly, inch by inch, her entire neck came into view. Next, her right shoulder was bared. A moment later, her left. The pounding of my heart seemed to deafen me and, at any second, I felt certain that its noise must awaken her. Gradually the garment slid lower and lower, gathering momentum as it descended. Then, with a quick flutter (thank Heaven she had her back to me), it fell about her waist.

When I regained consciousness, Mr. Murke was fanning me with his bowler hat. I threw a glance of terror round the room, but Miss Costaine was nowhere to be seen. Because of the shock my nervous system had received, my explanation of what had occurred was none too coherent. To my complete bewilderment, Murke received it with hoots of laughter. (I have known for some time that his sense of humour is peculiarly earthy, but never, until that moment, did I realize that it is also tragically warped.) As gales of mirth shook him, he told me to stop gibbering and repeated, innumerable times, that never had he heard, or seen, anything so funny. While wiping tears of merriment from his eyes he told me that he returned to the house at 12:15 A.M. Hearing a thud in the dining room (it must have been my body falling), he entered to see Miss Costaine, stripped to the waist, stepping over my prone form. She had then turned, curtsied to the picture, and proceeded upstairs to her room. I was very "on edge" and I told Murke, in no uncertain terms, that I considered his levity extremely out of place. He then made a remark, the only satisfactory interpretation of which filled me with alarm. He said, "Didn't you about the old bat? Why, she's been up to her tricks ever since I've lived here." I sat down on the sofa and looked him directly in the eye. "What, exactly, do you mean?" I asked. He looked at my face and then gave an inexplicable guffaw. "Don't be a fool, Ed," he said. "I mean that when Miss C. walks in her sleep, she usually does it in my room." Something must have happened to my face, for he added, "You needn't worry, old man: she's safe." I gasped and said, "But Miss Costaine is a lady." Murke threw back his head and laughed again. He then slapped my back. "Ed," he said, "you kill me. Of course she's a lady, but she's also a virgin and she doesn't like it." He slapped me on the back again and, after assuring me that what had happened wasn't the end of the world, bade me good night and went upstairs.

Although I lay down on the sofa, I did not close my eyes for the rest of the night. At 4:15 A.M. I got from the bookcase Volume 20 of the *Encyclopaedia Britannica* (SARS to SORC). From page number 976 I gleaned a modicum of consolation. Under "Somnambulism or Sleepwalking" it said, among other, more disquieting, things: "Although the actions of sleep-walkers may be complicated and bear direct relationship to their daily lives, when awake they have no recollection of any of these occurrences."

If only my mental picture of Miss Costaine before the fireplace could be as evanescent.

I had arranged with Mr. Frome that he commence the repair work on my bedroom ceiling at 8:30 A.M. today. He is an elderly man, immensely tall (six feet five inches) and gives the impression of being far too frail for any type of manual labour. On his arrival this morning (at 10:37 A.M.) he asked if, before going upstairs, he might "catch his breath." I ushered him into the drawing room, where he lay down of the settee and went to sleep. After allowing fifteen minutes to elapse, I coughed loudly. This failed to disturb his slumbers and, as he looked so peaceful, I left him.

I was on my way to the garden, intending to sprinkle Snail Snare around the remains of my *Primula Obconica*, when Mother called to me from her bedroom. It took me twenty-five minutes to minister to her needs and, upon returning to the drawing room, I found that Mr. Frome had removed his boots and was snoring loudly. Holding our family photograph album approximately five feet from the floor, I let it drop close to his head. He opened his eyes and said, "What's today?" I told him, not only the date, but the hour. He said, "I see," and asked me if I would put his boots on for him. While I performed this service, he explained that, during adolescence, he had outgrown his strength and, as a result of this, tired very easily. He then asked me to guess his weight. I failed. He told me that it is one hundred and forty-two pounds and added, with a look of great depression, that three insurance companies fail to understand why he is not in the cemetery.

It took him some time to mount the stairs and, on surveying the wreckage in my bedroom, he sighed deeply and said, "What a pity." I agreed with him. He then looked round for somewhere to sit, but, as the entire room is inches deep in rubble and plaster dust, Mr. Frome was compelled to remain standing. He gazed for a while at what had once been the ceiling. I gazed with him and, after perhaps twenty-five seconds, looked at my watch. He looked at me, sighed again, and went downstairs and out into the street. I accompanied him, intending to assist with the carrying in of his equipment. As none of it was in sight I enquired as to where it was. "At home," he replied and started rubbing his legs as though to encourage the circulation. He then rubbed his arms and his face and, after saying very sorrowfully, "Oh, well," wandered off into the rain.

At 2:30 P.M. I telephoned his house. Mrs. Frome answered. She said that "Dad" had overtired himself, was resting and that I would see him as soon as his strength returned. In reply to my enquiry as to which day that might be, Mrs. Frome sighed and said my guess was as good as hers.

I am disturbed by a further complication in my Mother's condition. As I entered her bedroom this afternoon with tea, she told me, rather excitedly, that she remembered the whereabouts of her hearing aid. I was most relieved until she informed me that she had loaned it to Aunt Ruth. I called Doctor Triggs immediately, but, unfortunately, he was out.

Aunt Ruth died in 1928.

February 15th

Apparently Mr. Frome's strength has not yet returned. Two days have passed and there has been no word from him. My Mother's recuperative powers are, I am glad to say, far superior. She is up and about and, although by no means normal, is at least her old self again. Doctor Triggs is delighted with her condition and is bringing an alienist friend of his, a Mr. Hume, to enjoy tea with us one Sunday. I reminded the good Doctor of my Mother's antipathy for foreigners, but after giving me a searching look, he said I was not to worry.

Happily, I found the hearing aid at the bottom of the umbrella stand and life is much easier now that aural communication with my parent has been resumed. I am feeling rather exhausted however, for, although upon retiring each night I lock the dining room door, the sofa affords me little rest. I sleep fitfully and my knees and elbows, upon arising, are incredibly stiff. Because of this, today I decided to walk briskly to Rolfe's Plumbing Establishment and settle my account there. Having broken my fast in the kitchen (I feel I cannot face Miss Costaine for at least a week), I left the house at 8:34 A.M.

As I passed DUN ROVEN, the door opened and a sleepy-looking infantry corporal emerged and closed the door gently behind him. His uniform was unkempt and he was unshaven. There was no sign of Mrs. Luby. I could hear his footsteps behind me and, wishing to get a closer view of my tenant's visitor, I slowed down and allowed myself to be overtaken. He came abreast of me and I saw that he was young and, in spite of his unwashed condition, a splendid example of the virile manhood which defends this realm of ours. He volunteered a friendly greeting to which I responded and, slowing his gait to mine, asked if I could direct him to the barracks. I did so, whereupon he thanked me politely and strode ahead.

I cannot think why he should have been visiting Mrs. Luby at that hour, unless, of course, he is a relative. The problem puzzles me.

By the time I reached Rolfe's shop my exercise had exhausted me. When I entered he was sawing through a length of gas pipe and the shrill, rasping noise made conversation impossible. Although Rolfe looked directly at me as I approached his work-bench, he kept me waiting, with my teeth on edge, for fully three minutes while he completed his task. Indeed, he appeared to retard his saw strokes deliberately, so that the screeching sound became even more dissonant. I was standing quite close to the vise when the pipe parted and a piece, some two feet in length, fell upon my foot with considerable force. The nail on my great toe will, I am afraid, detach itself eventually and, at the time of writing, the flesh surrounding it is painfully contused. Time will, of course, heal this minor injury. It will not, however, heal the patent leather toe-cap of my left boot, which is grazed and indented in the most unsightly fashion. Rolfe would accept no responsibility for the mishap. He is really most uncouth. I regret to say that my high temper got the better of my good judgment and, without even mentioning the purpose of my visit, I turned on my right heel and limped out. I have decided to have my boot repaired, deduct the cost from Rolfe's bill and send him the remainder by Postal Order.

On my way home I dropped into Bovey's Photographic Art Studio. Maude's birthday is on the 20th and Mr. Bovey has been framing the gift which I have spent several happy evenings making for her. It is a small square of oak board (8 inches by 10 inches), on which I have inscribed, with a red-hot knitting needle, the following verse:

TO MY BETROTHED
by
E. O. Carp

Frail barque, that is my ship
Of Life;
Tho' storms may override
Thee
Hold fast thy course, through
Strain and strife,
Thy Captain's hand shall
Guide thee.

Mr. Bovey had the order completed and waiting for me. The frame is beautifully made, but, somehow, the over-all effect disappointed me. I am my own severest critic and the words of the verse, as I read them aloud today, seemed, for the first time, extravagant and meaningless. To begin with, Maude being a very poor sailor, the line, "Frail barque, that is my ship of Life" sounded, to my acute ear, tactless. I asked Mr. Bovey to give an opinion. He said, "It's very nice if you like that sort of thing. Myself, I prefer limericks." While speaking he avoided my eyes and I knew that, in spite of his politeness, he was not impressed. I asked if I might sit down and, after kindly bringing me a chair, Mr. B. excused himself and disappeared into his darkroom.

While resting my foot (the toe was throbbing most painfully), I considered the problem from every angle. Finally, after remembering how Maude had misconstrued the Ode I had dedicated to her, I decided that, as a birthday gift, my pyrographic effort was completely unsuitable. I continued my rumination until a splendid thought struck me. When Mr. Bovey returned, I asked if he could take and finish a photograph of me in five days. At first he seemed dubious, but, when I explained the imperativeness of the matter, he agreed to do his best and ushered me into his studio.

When it comes to his art, Mr. Bovey is a perfectionist and he took infinite pains to get my head into the position, which, he assured me, would be most effective. My neck is still slightly stiff. The proofs will be ready for my inspection in three days. I am a little concerned as to what my facial expression will be in the photographs for, while adjusting a fold in my left trouser leg, Mr. Bovey unwittingly stepped on my crushed toe. I am almost certain that, when he exposed the plate, I was still wincing.

Later as I passed Harket et Cie, Joseph darted out of his shop and asked if I would call there tomorrow, after closing time, to receive my present. He still refused to give any hint as to its nature, but, from the little man's merry demeanour, I could tell that his joy in giving me the gift will be as great as mine when I receive it.

This afternoon I visited THE NEST to show Maude my toe. As I entered the front gate, fiendish shrieks, issuing from a privet bush, caused me to drop my umbrella. They were emitted by Harrison and his playmate Ursula Monks. I learned that they were playing a game they had invented called "Hospital." I asked Harrison to introduce me to his little friend. He did so, rather sullenly, but, instead of shaking my proffered hand, Miss Monks stuck out her tongue and crossed her eyes in the most startling fashion. I went into the house.

Maude was most solicitous about my injury and insisted on dressing the wound. As she knelt before me, bathing my foot with hot water, I was reminded of a ministering angel. I mentioned this to her and when she raised her eyes to mine, I noticed that her pince-nez were moist. She insisted that it was steam, but I am not so sure, for she if very tenderhearted. She told me that nothing made her happier than taking care of me and that, when the time came for us to be together always, her joy would be complete. After I had put on my boot, I put my arm around her and, with her head on my shoulder, we sat for some time in silence. It made me feel very peaceful and, once again, I realized how fortunate I am. Then Maude, rather haltingly, confided that she regretted her behaviour on the last two occasions when we had seen Miss Throbbitt and begged my forgiveness. Instead of answering, I kissed her temple where her hair, in the last two years, has become flecked with silver. It is most becoming to her, but for some reason, she does not like me to speak of it.

This idyll was shattered by cries of childish rage and Harrison, pursued by a red-faced Ursula Monks, burst into the room. Screaming, like creatures possessed, they circled the settee on which we were seated. Their noise completely drowned Maude's commands for them to cease and, after upsetting the bowl of water at our feet, they fled through the French windows into the garden. My attempts to dry my trouser leg (which were saturated), were curtailed by cries of help from Maude, who had followed the children outside. When I reached her, she was trying, quite ineffectually, to pry the young antagonists apart. They writhed on the lawn, with legs and arms intertwined, shrieking at each other in the most uncivilized manner. Maude begged me to "do something and not just stand there," and I approached the combatants cautiously.

Harrison was at a disadvantage for, in spite of the firm grip he had on his playmate's hair, Ursula, her heavy body astride his, pummeled his face with vicious concentration. Each blow was punctuated with a stream of unbelievably course invective (I understand her father is a longshoreman). At the risk of straining myself, I attempted to lift her off the boy, but my efforts were futile. Indeed, I received a job in the stomach which was so painful that I returned to Maude's side. The dear creature was completely distraught and kept up a wailing cry of "My baby. Oh. My baby," which, while adding noise to the babel, did nothing to bring the melee to a halt. It is amazing how much vitality children possess and I watched the tussle, fascinated. Harrison was soon defeated, but, in spite of his and Maude's screams for mercy, Miss Monks continued to belabour him for several minutes. She lost interest at last, however, and, after giving Harrison's already bloody nose a resounding thwack to consolidate her victory, she stood up, kicked him, clambered over the back fence and disappeared from view.

Maude rushed her howling offspring into the house and I was left alone in the garden. After a moment's consideration, I decided that my presence within would be superfluous and, opening the garden gate quietly, I returned home via the back alley. I shall wait until tomorrow to retrieve my hat and umbrella. I think that Maude will be feeling much better by then.

February 16th

Maude has decided that "Little Redwing" will be an ideal accompaniment to her recitation at the musicale and so, this afternoon, I went along to THE NEST and we spent two happy hours practicing assiduously. Without wishing to sound conceited, I must say that the effect of "Hiawatha's Wedding Feast," as declaimed by my betrothed, is immeasurably enhanced by the melodious tone of my Fono-Fiddle. I also discovered that Maude's mispronunciations of "Maskenozha" and other such tongue-twisters is almost unnoticeable if, as she says them, I play fortissimo.

We were interrupted, at 4:30 P.M., by a knock at the door. The visitor, an angry woman, whom neither Maude nor I had seen before, introduced herself as Mrs. Monks. After throwing a look of hostility in my direction, she said that the matter she wished to discuss was of a private nature. Maude explained that, as her fiancé, she would prefer me to remain and Mrs. Monks, after sniffing contemptuously and muttering "fiancé, at her age," to herself, took a chair. "It's about my Ursula and your son," she said and commenced rummaging in a large paper bag. I looked at Maude. Her jaw was set and her expression inscrutable. From the bag Mrs. Monks took and held up for our inspection a mud-stained gymnasium tunic and a tattered feminine under-garment. "I shall be obliged if you will kindly explain the meaning of these," she said and sniffed again. Maude started to speak, but I interrupted her. I had suddenly remembered my appointment at Harket's shop and, in spite of the look of displeasure I received from my betrothed, I took my leave.

It was a few moments after closing time when my good friend Joseph, agog with ill-concealed excitement, welcomed me into his hairdressing salon. After locking the door and assuring me that we would not be disturbed he seated me before the plate-glass mirror and having said, "Won't be a minute," scurried away. His happiness was infectious and, as I waited for him to return, I felt quite exhilarated. He was soon back, bearing in reverent hands, a small cardboard box. His eyes shone as he laid it on my lap. Then, with his hand affectionately on my shoulder he said, "There, Edwin. I hope that this gift will enable you to forgive the insulting remarks I made when last cutting your hair." In order to prolong the thrill of anticipation I was experiencing, I did not remove the lid of the box completely, but instead lifted one corner and peeped within. I shut the lid down quickly. I had glimpsed something brown and furry and felt sure that Joseph, knowing my love of dumb creatures, had given me a marmoset or, perhaps, a tame squirrel. I looked up into Joe's face, smiling. "What do I feed it?" I asked. Joe threw back his head and laughed heartily. "Edwin," he said, "your sense of humour will be the death of me." I was, I must confess, mystified by this remark, but I remained silent. With a sweeping gesture, Joseph took the box from me, removed the lid and held its furry contents triumphantly aloft. It hung inert and I knew that, whatever its nature, it was lifeless. "What is it?" I asked. Joseph looked slightly annoyed. "A toupee, you damn fool, a toupee," he said and laying the object on my head, indicated the mirror. I was amazed at what I saw.

A sudden, drastic physical change in any familiar face is always surprising, but, when the face in one's own, the effect can be something of a shock. I gazed at my reflection, speechless. After a moment's silence, Joseph said, rather testily, "Well, what d'you think of it?" I found my tongue at last and remarked that "it certainly makes a difference." Suddenly I realized that, so far, I had shown no enthusiasm whatever and so I began to thank my good friend for his kindness. He patted my back and smiled at me again in the mirror. Then he hooted with laughter and slapped his thigh. "What a joker you are, Ed," he said "You've got the damn thing on back to front." I did not like to remind him that he had been the one to place the "gift" in position and so, I let it pass. He whisked it around and, chatting merrily, applied some adhesive substance to my forehead. "Knew you'd like it, old man," he said. "Matched your colour from the sweepings after you left the other day. . . . Just felt I had to make it up to you for saying you'd go bald. . . . Now. . . ." He pressed the rim of the toupee to my head with a damp towel. ". . .you'll be able to go as bald as you like and no one will be any the wiser." Removing the towel with a flourish, he stepped back and assumed a posture of beaming pride, while I examined the result of his handiwork in the mirror.

The effect, now that his creation was properly in place, was, I must admit, remarkable. I looked many years younger and the line, where the truth of my brow met the fiction of the wig, was almost imperceptible. My only criticism, which of course I could not tell Joseph, was that the man in the mirror looked much more like my poor Father than it did me. My good friend was ecstatic over his artistry and I had the greatest difficulty in preventing him from taking me upstairs and showing me to his wife. The man in the mirror made me feel extremely ill at ease and I wanted to get away as quickly as good manners would allow. My escape was quite simply accomplished for, knowing that my Mother had been indisposed, Joseph accepted, without question, my excuse that I had to hurry along. Before donning my hat I attempted to remove the toupee, but my good friend would not allow this. At last, after thanking him sincerely, I took my leave.

On my homeward journey a gusty wind made the going some-what hazardous, but the firm grip I kept on the brim of my hat prevented any mishap. It was very still inside the house when I entered and I thought that, in all probability, my Mother was upstairs, resting. I closed the front door gently, removed my hat and stood before the hall mirror, studying my general appearance. In the dim light and now that I was becoming accustomed to the hairy innovation, the change to my looks appeared much less startling. I rather liked it. Suddenly a piercing scream wheeled me around. My Mother was standing by the kitchen door, her eyes staring. "Tacky ...Tacky," she cried. "You've come back from the dead. I can't bear it." Then she fainted.

By the time Doctor Triggs reached the house I had Mother on her bed and the toupee hidden. I was forced to use Eau de Cologne to remove the adhesive substance from my brow and, in my frantic haste, I removed a portion of the skin as well. Luckily the good Doctor noticed nothing. He cross-questioned me closely regarding what he described as my parent's "attack" and, in replying, I fear I was guilty of evasion. While telling him that my Mother had imagined seeing my poor Father, I did not mention to what extent I had contributed to her collapse. The explanations this would have necessitated were, I felt, far too intimate and embarrassing. He suspected nothing I am certain for, when I had ended my expurgated version of the incident, he nodded his white head sagely and said, "Hallucinations are to be expected in your Mother's case. Keep her off solids, if you can." We shook hands warmly and, as I opened the front door for him, I noticed that he studied me. As he put on his hat he said, "You know, my boy, if you had more hair you'd be the living image of your father." It was just a chance remark, of course, but, after his departure, I sat on the staircase for nearly twenty minutes.

I had supper with Mother in her bedroom (I am grateful for any excuse to avoid eating with Miss Costaine) and, as I descended with the trays, Maude arrived. She sat on the hall chair while I removed her galoshes and noticed that she was in a state of some agitation. Later, in the drawing room, I enquired how she had fared in her interview with Mrs. Monks. Maude blushed and refused to discuss the subject. Women are unpredictable creatures and, this evening, I found Maude's mood most mystifying. We sat in silence for a while, sipping our cocoa and then, while pretending to examine the pattern on her saucer (she has seen it many times), she muttered something about Harrison. Her head was bent so low that I could not catch her words and I said, "I beg your pardon, my dear." Maude put down her cup noisily (she cracked it I discovered later) and looked directly at me. "You heard what I said, Edwin, you know you did. Why must you make everything so difficult?" Her words and manner flabbergasted me. My look of surprise must have told Maude that she was in the wrong for, taking my hand in hers, she apologized for her brusqueness. Then, dropping her eyes, she said, "I want you to have a long talk with Harrison as soon as possible." I was of course agreeable and asked, "What about?" After a moment's pause Maude said, "Oh, you know. Things," and took her hand from mine. "What things?" I enquired. Maude raised her head and in her eyes was a look of extreme irritation. She took a deep breath and, when at last she spoke, she appeared to be exercising great control. "Things, Edwin." She enunciated very slowly and very clearly as one sometimes does to a backward child. "Things—Birds ...LIFE. Oh! For goodness sake, don't sit there looking so stupid. . . .Don't you understand? I want you to talk to Harrison about . . .about

MEN and WOMEN!" In the pause that ensued, I felt my neck turn scarlet.

I firmly believe that the "Facts of Life" are something we must all learn from Life itself. I am well versed in the world and its ways, but this is knowledge I have had to glean for myself. Some of it is beautiful. Some of it is ugly. There are, I understand, certain fathers who discuss these "things" openly with their sons. This is quite beyond my comprehension. Some there may be who, in their worldliness, might consider my attitude unintelligent. On the other hand, my thinking may be due to the fact that, by the time I had reached an age when I could understand "things," my poor Father was in no condition to discuss them. Be this as it may, Maude's request presented me with an extremely difficult problem.

Maude broke the silence by saying, "Well, Edwin?" In order to gain time, I replied, hurriedly, "Of course, my dear, anything you say. Have some more cocoa?" Maude accepted and, later, after we had kissed (our pince-nez tinkled again), she said, "I knew you'd understand, dear. After all, some day you'll be Harrison's father." And, leaving me with this disquieting though, she bade me good night.

I wonder where I can get a book on the subject.

February 18ᵗʰ

At last the repairs to my bedroom have been started. Mr. Frome, accompanied by his grandson, Edgar, arrived this morning only one hour and twelve minutes later than had been arranged. Apparently, Edgar is "learning the trade" and, under the direction of Mr. Frome, who did not once stir from the deck chair he had brought with him, the young man has restored (after two attempts) one third of the ceiling. The newly finished surface is somewhat uneven and I remarked on this to Mr. Frome. After looking sadly at the ceiling and then at Edgar, he sighed and said, "Always gets 'is plaster lumpy. Can't break 'im of it." He then resumed his nap.

From the speed at which the Mr. Frome's worked today, I judge that the dining room sofa will be my bed for many nights to come.

It had been my intention to surprise Maude by wearing my toupee to the musicale this evening. Therefore, this afternoon, after locking myself in my bedroom, I glued the hairpiece into position and, with the aid of my shaving mirror, examined my head from every available angle. The change it makes in my appearance seemed even more startling today that when I last wore it and so, after thirty minutes' careful scrutiny, I returned Harket's gift to its hiding place at the back of my collar drawer.

The journey to Miss Throbbitt's residence necessitates changing buses three times. In view of this and because I wished to arrive at the musicale punctually (the invitation said 7:30 P.M.), I called at THE NEST for Maude, with my Fono-Fiddle neatly wrapped in on old bicycle cape, at 5:45 P.M. On arrival, after first removing my pince-nez, we kissed and I was flattered to see that Maude was wearing pink coral ear-rings I gave her, in 1933, to commemorate the fifth year of our betrothal. She was also wearing her fawn lace evening gown, which, despite the avoirdupois she has gained since its purchase five years ago, gives her, in my estimation, and almost patrician air. The garment reveals her arms, which, although short, are smooth and very beautiful. I have often thought to what splendid advantage they would be seen were she to play the harp. However, as this is a somewhat cumbersome instrument and Maude is tone deaf, I have never mentioned it.

True to her sex, my betrothed kept me waiting. She had left, until the last moment, the repairs to the Red Indian headdress which we had agreed she should wear during her recitation. As I sat watching her replace the missing eagle feathers with some from a hen which had graced our festive board on Christmas Day, I marveled, as I have many times before, at the dexterity of her plump fingers.

Harrison, in chastened mood, was industriously studying his home lessons. His eyes are still blackened and his nose still swollen and, as he sat in profile to me, the light threw into sharp relief the furriness of his upper lip. This, together with the manner in which his voice had cracked when he said "Good evening, Uncle Edwin," made me realize the urgency of the "nice long talk" which Maude is so anxious for me to have with the boy. Mrs. Ottey was there also. I had arranged with her (for an added compensation) to take charge of my future step-son during our absence and, with her Ouija board on her lap, she sat, comfortably ensconced before the fire, munching nougat.

Maude's task took much longer than anticipated and it was 6:40 P.M. before we left THE NEST. In view of the tiresome trek before us I was slightly perturbed. Maude told me to "stop fussing" and said that, in the world of society, prompt arrival at any function is deemed most unfashionable. I replied, "In that case, we shall be the most fashionable people present." Maude, I fear, missed the cleverness of my remark, for she said, "Please don't try to be funny," and we walked to the bus-stop without further conversation.

To our surprise, we were prevented from boarding either of the first two buses that came along. The conductors, in each instance, said, "No livestock permitted," and signaled their vehicles to proceed. Maude became, quite justifiably, irate at this odd treatment and I was completely nonplused. The mystery was clarified with the arrival of the third bus. As it came to a halt before us, Maude, by grabbing the handrail and placing one foot on the mounting platform, dared the vehicle to proceed and when the conductor shouted, "Stand back. No livestock," her eyes flashed and she demanded, "What's all this rubbish about livestock?" The conductor pointed at me. "The turkey the gentleman's trying to hide under his coat," he replied. Bringing the feathered headdress into full view, I let the man examine it. He laughed uproariously and, after saying, "Where's the papoose?" allowed us to embark. Both Maude and I agreed that the situation was far from humourous and, as the hands of my watch showed it to be 7:10 P.M., we maintained a tense silence throughout the remainder of our journey.

It was 8:13 P.M. when, finally, we reached Miss Throbbitt's large, old-fashioned domicile. The greenhouse, which runs the entire length of the house on the north side, was illuminated and from it issued a male voice singing "Beloved, It Is Morn." Although I rang the bell three times, it was not until the song was almost ended that Miss Throbbitt, a silencing finger to her lips, opened the door. As we shed our outer garments the strains of a piano, introducing "The Lost Chord," fell upon our ears and Miss Throbbitt, while apologizing profusely, asked if we would mind postponing our entrance until Mr. Roach had finished singing. We agreed. Or, rather, I agreed. Maude did not speak and, on looking at her, I saw that her jaw was set.

The beautiful old ballad has several verses and the singer (a tenor with a marked tremolo in his upper register) sang them with great expression. As we waited in the hall, the gooseflesh on Maude's arms confirmed my suspicion that the house was inadequately heated. Mr. Roach finished, at least, and Miss Throbbitt, after drying her eyes (apparently "The Lost Chord" had been her twin sister's favourite song), ushered us into, what she called, "the conservatoire." Here the devotees of Orpheus, perhaps twenty in number, were applauding Mr. Roach. He was bowing gracefully as we entered. An upright piano, standing before a tastefully arranged bank of aspidistra and fern, occupied one end of the glass structure, around the walls of which the guests sat on benches. Chinese lanterns supplied the illumination and the temperature was, at least, fifteen degrees lower than in the hall.

I had not known that Miss Costaine would be present. I espied her, in a corner, talking earnestly to three taut-looking young women, who smoked, and two equally taut-looking young men, who did not. Miss Throbbitt informed me that they were members of the Folk Dancing Academy which Miss Costaine attended and added, excitedly, that, later in the evening, the entire group was going to entertain us with something "very modern." Maude introduced me to Mr. Roach, whom, I learned she had known during her girlhood when he was a boy soprano at St. Jude's. I was unimpressed by this gentleman. He was dressed entirely in brownish yellow (even his linen), and this, together with his shiny brown hair and quick, rustling gestures, made his resemblance to the nocturnal insect, whose name he bore, quite remarkable. After shaking my hand (his was hot and dry), he said it was a great shame that, by arriving late, I had missed his rendition of "Blow, Blow Thou Winter Wind," and, turning his back, gave his undivided attention to my betrothed. I coughed twice, but failed to catch Maude's eyes, which, I noticed, were sparkling with interest as she listened to Mr. Roach's pretentious chatter.

Looking round the room, I caught sight of the treasurers of our Society of Health through Sanitation, Mr. and Mrs. Claude Tisdale, and hurried over to greet them. They were looking extremely well and I said so. Whereupon Mrs. Tisdale informed me that she was but newly arisen from her sick-bed, where she had been confined, for three weeks, with shingles. As everyone knows, this complaint can be fatal if the inflamed area completely encircles the waist. Consequently, I was shocked to hear, from Mrs. Tisdale, that she had narrowly escaped extinction by a scant four inches. I was even more shocked when I heard Mr. Tisdale mutter to himself, "More's the pity." Having reminded them that our Society would be meeting on the 24th, I excused myself with the intention of rejoining Maude. As I crossed the room I was waylaid by Miss Costaine, who said warmly, "*Ave*, Mine host. *Quo vadis?*"

I have done my best to avoid our paying guest since the dreadful night of her somnambulation, but to have ignored her greeting this evening would have been both boorish and cowardly. She appeared to be in exceedingly high spirits and, although I could not bring myself to look her in the eye, I bowed. With a vivacity I had never before observed in her, Miss Costaine slipped her arm, intimately, through mine and said, "Don't you find these bohemian parties wonderfully stimulating?" I replied that I had attended few such affairs, whereupon she insisted that I meet her friends. As we neared them, she whispered in my ear that they were all artistic and highly sophisticated. Apparently last names are frowned upon in Bohemia, for the three young women were introduced to me as Tiny, Bunny, and Piggy and the two young men as Marius and Hilary. There was a disturbing intensity about them all and Miss Piggy enquired, rather imperiously, what I thought of "Poulenc." (She spelled it for me.) Fortunately I was saved the embarrassment of having to answer this question by Miss Throbbitt, who, after blowing a small whistle to attract everyone's attention, introduced the next performer, a Mrs. Lionel Gunn. The lady, a coloratura soprano, sang "Lo, Hear the Gentle Lark," and our hostess accompanied. During the song some extremely effective bird calls were judiciously interpolated by an invisible *siffleur*. It was not until Mrs. Gunn had finished singing that the whistler, Mr. Lionel Gun, emerged from behind the bank of fern and shared with his wife their well-earned applause. I enjoyed it immensely and applauded as long as I could, for I found that clapping my hands made me feel much warmer.

I saw Maude and Mr. Roach, sitting very close together, at the far end of the greenhouse and, although they applauded, they chatted and looked at each other almost continuously. I went and stood by them (there were no vacant chairs) and had great difficulty in participating in their conversation. Words gushed from Mr. Roach, like water from a broken hydrant, and it was not until I had repeated "Mrs. Gunn is a beautiful soprano" three times that this gentleman gave me a pitying look and replied, "Mrs. Gunn is a mezzo," and I said, "Oh."

Miss Throbbitt's whistle prevented any further argument and Maude told me to sit down. One chair had become available, some distance from my betrothed and, as I crossed the room, our hostess, who had begun to announce the next entertainer, stopped speaking and waited until I was seated before continuing. I found it very embarrassing. Miss Throbbitt finished her introduction of a Mr. Samuel Leeson and that gentleman proceeded to enthrall everyone present with "In a Persian Market," by A. Ketelby. Never have I heard a musical saw played with more skill.

My complete enjoyment of Mr. Leeson's performance was marred, however, by the load, rumbling noises which emanated from the interior of a clergyman seated on my left. Each time this embarrassment occurred, the poor fellow would lean toward me and whisper, "Forgive me." As we were applauding, he smiled blandly and said, "I trust you were not too disturbed by my *borborygmi*?" I said, "Not at all," and asked how it was spelled. He told me, but I have been unable to find the word in either my dictionary or the *Encyclopaedia Britannica*. (I could not find Poulenc either.)

As well as being chilled to the bone, I was becoming increasingly hungry, for the invitation had stated that refreshments would be served and I had refrained from eating since noon. They were not forthcoming, however, until after Mr. Tisdale had sung several comic songs. Which, incidentally, he did very well. The last one, a stuttering song entitled "Come and see what Charlie's d-d-d-doing," was a trifle risqué, but I laughed heartily and Mr. Tisdale received a splendid ovation from everyone except Miss Costaine and her group.

Sometimes I think that highly sophisticated people miss much of the fun in life.

When, at last, the refreshments did arrive they consisted of

Watercress Sandwiches
Sausage Rolls (small)
Blancmange
(choice of pink or white)
Lemonade
Or
Cocoa

This dismayed me somewhat.

Luckily, I managed to secure a plate of the foregoing and take it to Maude before Mr. Roach returned from a similar mission. I also took his chair and, when he rejoined us, I had the great pleasure of telling him that my fiancée's needs had been taken care of. In my haste, I had secured no sustenance for myself and, before I could tell Mr. Roach of my willingness to relieve him of his extra plate, he gave it to an elderly lady, in a wheel chair, who sat next to me. Consequently, the pangs of my hunger went unappeased, for I did not dare leave my place while Maude's odious friend hovered about us, which he did until just before Miss Throbbitt blew her whistle for the musicale to continue. By the time I reached the buffet, our hostess was announcing that she, herself, would entertain us and, there being but one watercress sandwich left, I wrapped it in my handkerchief to enjoy later.

Miss Throbbitt plays the pianoforte well, but this evening, both Maude and I agreed, she played far too much. Commencing with "Claire de Lune," she plunged into "The Wedding of the Painted Doll" and, without pause, continued with the entire "Ballet Egyptienne Suite." She is also a pianist who tends to embarrass her audience with exaggerated, writhing movements of both arms and body. I remarked on this to Maude (*sotto voce*), whereupon she squeezed my hand and said I was a dear. When, eventually, our hostess's recital terminated, there was vociferous applause and, in addition to hand-clapping, there was much stamping, which, I am convinced, the guests indulged in to warm their feet, rather than to show their musical appreciation.

I had unwrapped and was about to enjoy my sandwich, when Miss Throbbitt came over and informed us that we were next on the programme. After secreting the morsel in my handkerchief for the second time, I escorted Maude, as unobtrusively as possible, to behind the bank of ferns where my Fono-Fiddle and her headdress were cached. Maude donned the feathered relic and, with it in position, her appearance was most regal. I told her so and asked if she felt nervous. She replied, "No, frozen." Standing there, waiting for our hostess to begin our introduction, the dear creature looked so magnificent that I could not restrain myself from kissing her cheek. Unfortunately, the chain of my pince-nez became entangled with the beaded binding which held the plumes of her headgear in place. It took us some time to extricate ourselves from this dilemma and Miss Throbbitt's voice had long finished announcing "Hiawatha's Wedding Feast, recited by Mrs. Maude Phelps, aided by her fiancé, Mr. Edwin Carp," before I was able to take my position, on the chair in front of the ferns, preparatory to Maude's entrance. I had had no time to tune my instrument and, as I played the first not of "Little Redwing," I knew that it was sadly off key. Nothing could be done, however, for, at that moment, my betrothed made her appearance. Although her dear face looked pinched with cold (the temperature within the greenhouse was dropping rapidly), I felt inordinately proud when, as Maude took up her position before the piano, three of the guests applauded.

With great assurance Maude began to speak the immortal lines of H. W. Longfellow and, according to my private plan, I succeeded in drowning out her mispronunciation of the first tongue-twister—"Chibiabos"—most successfully. For this, I regret to say, I was rewarded with a very sharp look from my bride-to-be. Apart from this and the fact that, with each note, my Fono-Fiddle was becoming increasingly out of tune, all went well until Maude reached the description of the menu at the wedding feast:

> ... First they ate the sturgeon, Nahma,
> And the pike, the Maskenozha,
> Caught and cooked by old Nokomis:
> Then on Pemican they feasted
> Pemican and Buffalo marrow,
> Haunch of deer and hump of bison,
> Yellow cakes of the Mondamin,
> And the wild rice of the river. . . .

Due, perhaps, to my undernourished condition, this description of food (which Maude declaimed beautifully) made me feel quite faint and the sea of faces before me began to undulate in the most distressing fashion. I was saved from making a complete spectacle of myself, however, by the Fono-Fiddle which fell from my relaxed grasp and hit the cement floor with a loud clatter. The look Maude gave me also helped in my recovery and, after only the briefest pause, I managed to continue.

The audience had become restive and I was intensely annoyed by the sniggers which issued from Miss Piggy and her friends. Maude, by increasing her vocal volume, managed to make herself heard and, gradually, the fidgeting and chair-scraping died down.

The two lines of the poem with which Maude has always had great difficulty during our practice periods are:

> . . . Pugasaing, the Bowl and Counters,
> Kuntassoo, the Game of Plum Stone. . . .

Therefore, as she spoke them, I played fortissimo with all my might. I bore down with a great flourish of the bow and, to my dismay, the string of my instrument broke with so great a twanging reverberation that the elderly lady in the wheel chair cried out.

Maude handled the situation with her usual *savoir-faire*. With but a fleeting glance in my direction, she continued the recitation and I was forced to sit before the audience with my Fono-Fiddle, mute and useless, on my lap. The predicament, in which I found myself, quickly became a terrifying ordeal. Knowing that I had, at least, five minutes to sit there before the poem's termination and, not wanting to distract in any way from Maude's splendid performance, I focused my eyes on an imaginary spot in the middle distance and tried to preserve absolute immobility. The minutes, as they passed, seemed interminable, and quiet sniggers began to come from Miss Piggy and her group with increasing frequency. In spite of the fact that I could see my breath, beads of perspiration began to form on my brow and, eventually, one trickled down into my eye, causing a smarting sensation. With the least possible movement, I managed to take my handkerchief out of my pocket and, as I did so, the audience let out a great yelp of laughter. This disturbing sound grew in volume and I looked at Maude. She was regarding me with, I regret to say, great animosity. After a second her eyes moved from mine and looked at something on the floor by my chair. Fearfully, I let my gaze follow hers and saw, at my feet, my battered watercress sandwich.

After such a debacle, it would have been futile to continue with "Hiawatha's Wedding Feast" and Maude, I presume, realized this for, after bowing to the highly amused guest (the Misses Tiny, Bunny and Piggy were hysterical with laughter), she made as dignified an exit as was possible under such humiliating circumstances.

I exited too, but decided it was better for me not to bow. Unfortunately I forgot to pick up my sandwich and, when I returned to retrieve it, the audience applauded deafeningly. I bowed. This brought joyous cries of "Bravo," "Encore," and "Yoohoo," from the more uninhibited guest) and, when I finally rejoined Maude behind the ferns, her face was like thunder. Her breathing, as she removed her headdress, was most irregular and, finally, she said, "I suppose you think you're very funny?" From her inflection it was quite obvious that she would have resented an answer to her question.

Although the musicale was by no means over, Maude insisted on leaving immediately and, after the most perfunctory good night to our hostess, she went into the hall. I attempted to follow her, but was waylaid by Mr. Tisdale who informed me that never, during all the years he has been patronizing music-halls, had he seen an "act" as funny as mine. His praise seemed to be sincere, but I am never certain with people of his type and, as I did not feel like pointing out to him the stupidity of his compliment, I bade him good night. I found Miss Throbbitt and proceeded to take my leave of her, but was further annoyed by her pretense that she, too, had though that the mishaps which had occurred during Maude's performance were intentional. Miss Costaine and her sophisticated friends joined us and did likewise. Indeed, Mr. Hilary and Miss Piggy raved about "subtle comedy nuances" to such an extent that my irritation got the better of my good manners and I walked away.

Maude's mood, when I joined her in the hall, was unimproved by having been kept waiting and, while I donned my coat, hat and galoshes, she maintained a foot-tapping aloofness which I found difficult to bear. Indeed, she refused to speak to me at all during the ninety-minute journey to Gubbion Avenue. On our arrival at THE NEST, I made my final attempt at a reconciliation. As she inserted her latch key, I said, "My dear, dear Maude ..." but with a withering look she reduced me to silence and closed her front door firmly in my face.

I walked disconsolately to my front gate and, as I entered it, I saw that Mrs. Luby was entering hers. Although it was 12:47 A.M., she was accompanied by a stranger in naval uniform and, on catching sight of me, she shouted "Good night, saucy," and laughed as though her greeting had been very witty. The sailor then made an extremely coarse remark, at which Mrs. Luby giggled and they both disappeared inside DUN ROVIN.

I managed to collect some leftover scraps in the kitchen and, after partaking of them, I went to my bed on the dining room sofa, where I have been recording, in my journal, the events of this day.

Never, in my entire lifetime, have I felt as low in spirit as I do at this moment.

February 19th

I slept fitfully again last night and, during one of my cat-naps, dreamed that Maude and I were exchanging nuptial vows in an enormous church, constructed entirely of glass. There were hundreds of guests, all bus conductors and each one of them was Mr. Murke. They laughed unceasingly and the officiating cleric, Doctor Triggs, was exceedingly angry. He shouted at me, "Do you, Borborygmi, take this Red Indian to be your lawful, wedded wife?" For some reason, my vocal chords were paralysed. My silence further incensed the good Doctor and he asked the same question of Maude. Instead of responding, she lifted her wedding veil (she wore it over the feathered headdress) and adjusted her hearing aid. Again Doctor Triggs shouted, "Do you, Borborygmi, take this Red Indian to be your lawful, wedded wife?" One of the bus conductors, whose face suddenly became that of Mrs. Luby, said, "Of course he doesn't." This remark convulsed the already amused guests and Maude held up a silencing hand. Something on it flashed, blindingly. It was a wedding ring. At once everything was still. Maude removed the ring and, after rolling up her sleeves to prove there was no trickery, made several, magical passes over it. The crowd started chanting, weirdly, "Chibiabos . . . Maskenozha," and pressed forward inexorably. That we would be crushed seemed inevitable, but, all at once a sweet, treble voice began to sing, "The Lost Chord" and, from the triforium, there floated down a very large cockroach, dressed as a choir-boy. As it alighted before us, the wedding ring turned into a fiddle string and Maude, after screaming "Pau-Puk-Keewis," turned into my Mother. Draping the string, halter fashion, about my neck, Mother shouted, "Gee up" and, as I cantered out of the church, the bus conductors showered us with watercress sandwiches.

I think the nightmare must have been caused by the ill-assorted collation which I had devoured before retiring.

Mr. Frome, I learned from his grandson, Edgar, overtaxed his strength yesterday. Therefore, the boy worked alone on my bedroom ceiling until late this afternoon. Today's work is much lumpier that yesterday's but the lad is so obviously trying to prove his worth that I decided not to find fault. Also, were I to insist on the ceiling being re-plastered correctly, it would mean many more nights on the dining room sofa, which, quite honestly, I do not believe my constitution could stand.

I must remember to obtain from Doctor Triggs another bottle of his tonic.

I believe a sagacious Chinaman is credited with first having said, "One picture speaks louder than ten thousand words." Mr. Bovey repeated the adage this morning when, in answer to a telephone call, I went along to his Photographic Art Studio and he handed me my finished portrait. The amount of detail this brilliant man has concentrated into the artistic likeness of myself is quite remarkable.

I am shown before a canvas curtain, on which are painted (by hand) a palm tree, a pyramid and part of a camel. On either side of me are potted palms (real), which, together with the imitation grass upon which by bamboo chair stands, blend into the background most subtly. Mr. Bovey seemed immensely pleased with his work and called my attention, several time, to the feeling of tropical heat which he has managed to capture with his lens. I do look rather hot, I admit, but the umbrella I am holding in the portrait seemed, to me, to dissipate this effect somewhat. However, rather than detract from Mr. B.'s pride of achievement, I said nothing.

Although the crushed toecap of my left boot is quite noticeable, all doubts I had harboured regarding my facial expression were groundless. It is true that, in the proof copies, I appear to be in some pain (which of course I was), but, with a few, deft strokes of his re-touching brush, Mr. Bovey, that Cagliostro of the camera, has transformed my look of suffering into one of almost pleased assurance.

There were two poses from which to choose. One with hat and one without. The hatless pose would have been my preference (because of the pyramid), but unfortunately, through insufficient re-touching, I look more anxious than assured. Therefore, I have decided to give Maude, as a birthday gift, the portrait in which my pate is hidden. (I also feel that the hat makes me look younger.) Luckily, the frame, which Mr. Bovey had already made for me, fits the photograph perfectly. This saved added expenditure.

I have not seen my betrothed since last night's catastrophe, nor shall I make any attempt to do so until the celebration of her birthday tomorrow. In addition to my framed portrait, I have procured three other gifts. The first is one yard of Moroccan goatskin—for use in her art-work. The second, a two-ounce bottle of neat's-foot oil for dressing same. The third, a bowl of hyacinths which I have raised to blooming point on the bathroom shelf.

These offering will, I hope, prove to Maude that her good opinion of me is of paramount importance to my well-being.

February 20th
MAUDE'S BIRTHDAY

Every year, besides a visit to the theatre, another festivity which honours this event is a tea-party *chez moi*. Today, however, because of what had occurred on the night of the musicale, it was with something less than my usual enthusiasm that, at 4:30 P.M., I went along to THE NEST to collect my betrothed and her son. I knocked at the door and, there being no response, I knocked again more forcefully. To my surprise, the door opened of its own accord.

Slightly puzzled, I entered and stood in the dimness of the hallway. The house was unusually quiet. After a moment I called, "Maude?" There was no reply and I called again, this time with some urgency. Again I waited. All at once a faint, eerie moan broke the silence. Conquering my desire to leave the house immediately, I took a deep breath and, after depositing my gifts on the hall table, moved cautiously toward the drawing room, whence the sound had come. Reaching the doorway, I peered inside. The venetian blinds were down and the visibility poor. As I placed a tentative toe over the threshold a sudden, blood-curdling shriek made further movement on my part impossible. A second later, a white, shrouded form leapt from behind the piano and I became galvanized into action. As I turned to exit, Maude's laughing voice sounded by the window.

"That's enough, Harrison, dear," she said to the ghost and, after raising the blind, stood regarding me with great merriment. Her son removed his sheet and, thrusting and extremely dirty index finger in my face, squealed, delightedly, "Look, Mum, Uncle Edwin's gone all white." He then rolled over and over on the floor, hooting with glee.

"He's so excited about seeing the play tonight that I just had to humour him," said Maude, dotingly. "I'm glad you did," I said and, not wishing to spoil the success of this stupid and extremely dangerous practical joke, I added my hearty laugh to theirs. It took Maude some time to compose herself, but, eventually, her tears of amusement ceased to flow and she sent Harrison off to wash his hands.

As soon as we were alone, I waited to see whether Maude would refer to the musicale. Had she done so, I was fully prepared (with a memorised speech), to defend myself. Fortunately there was no reference to the subject and I "let sleeping dogs lie." I am happy to record that my birthday offerings were received with great delight: especially the bottle of neat's-foot oil, which is difficult to obtain locally. Maude's reaction to my photograph was, at first, disappointing, for she said, "Who's this supposed to be?" After careful examination, however, she recognized the handle of my umbrella and decided that it was an excellent likeness. She gave me a kiss for each gift (four in all) and I noticed that she was wearing a new perfume. When I commented on its fragrance, I learned that it was a present from Harrison and entitled *Nuid d'Amour*. Maude asked the meaning of the French words, but, in view of their connotation, I professed ignorance.

The sense of well-being, which is always mine when I hold my dear one in my arms, remained after she had gone upstairs to don her new hat and, filled with this pleasant glow, I wandered into the dining room. On the table was a bowl of dark red roses. Their scent was rich and I leaned over to enjoy it more fully. As I did so, a card, hidden in the foliage, caught my eye. I extracted it and read—

> It was indeed charming to see you again,
> Sincerely,
> Walter Roach.

Replacing the card, I returned to the drawing room and sat down.

I felt depressed.

Because of the unconscionable time Maude took with her hat, we did not get home for high tea until 5:37 P.M. and my Mother, who was wearing new batteries for the occasion, was in ill humour. The tension, generated by her mood, was in no way eased when, during the serving of the poached salmon (cooked whole, very life-like), Harrison squirted her with the water pistol which, of late, he is rarely without.

Maude's new hat has, as trimming, two dark red roses. Otherwise, it is most becoming.

I had little appetite for the numerous tasty viands and Maude remarked, three times, on my lack of interest in the prune whip.

Both my Mother and my betrothed are excellent cooks, but there exists between them a spirit of rivalry which is always to be found when two creative talents vie one with another. While Maude excels at tartlets, game pies and the more savoury dishes, her fruit cakes, I regret to say are invariably soggy. Although of trifling consequence, it is interesting to note that for the past eight years, my Mother's birthday gift to Maude has been a large, delectable fruit cake.

Today, the bringing in of this *piéce de résistance* was delayed by Harrison. As his appetite remained unappeased by three helpings of salmon, two bananas and a meat patty, I was force to wait while he consumed bread and jam, stewed gooseberries and several glasses of lemonade before signaling Mrs. Ottey that the moment had arrived. That my Mother had surpassed herself this year was obvious from the gasp of admiration which Maude could not restrain when after kicking open the door, Mrs. Ottey entered with the tribute ablaze with candles. She placed it before my betrothed and, with a familiarity which I deprecate, but of which I cannot break her, said, "Happy Returns, Maude, old girl. . . . Forty-three candles this year. . . .Getting a bit long in the tooth, aren't we?" Before leaving the room, she added that she wanted a "lump" to take home, but Maude was counting the candles and from her expression, I am certain, did not hear the request. Having assured herself that there were, indeed, forty-three candles, instead of the forty there should have been, Maude looked, accusingly, at my Mother, who, with rapt expression, was gazing through the window.

I prefer to think that absent-mindedness, rather than design, caused my parent to insert the three extra candles; but, after I had given Maude my whispered assurance that it was the former, I noticed my Mother smiling, secretly, to herself. She was also rolling, between her thumb and forefinger, a pill of breadcrumbs, which, after a complacent look at Maude, she squashed with a certain satisfaction. Maude's expression disturbed me.

During the foregoing clash of temperaments, Harrison had been repeating, with increasing volume, a clamorous demand that he be allowed to blow out the candles. Without moving her eyes from my Mother's face, Maude granted her son his wish and, after several attempts, he succeeded in extinguishing the blaze. The resultant smoke was unusually dense and necessitated my opening the window. This prompted my Mother to enquire what purpose was being served by placing her in a direct draught. I closed the window and opened the door, where upon Maude asked me, rather tersely, to get her coat. I did so and reseated myself. With great deliberation, Maude removed the waxen offenders from the cake and picked up the knife.

A moment I always dread on these festive occasions is the cutting of the cake. Being unable to bake such a confection herself, I have noticed in past years that, no matter how well Maude may be enjoying the proceedings, her interest flags and she becomes increasingly morose with the serving of each succulent slice. Today, because of my Mother's profligate use of fruit, candied peel and nuts, the cake looked more delicious than any I can remember and, as Maude passed us our portions, I found the mounting tension in the atmosphere almost more than I could endure.

Probably because he was already gorged, Harrison was not, as he usually is, the first to sample the culinary masterpiece. My Mother's smile, as she looked around the table, was serenely assured and, under her level gaze, Maude, reluctantly, took the first bite. She masticated sullenly for a few seconds and then over her countenance there flitted a series of completely contradictory emotions. Distaste, disbelief, and finally, after she had swallowed with some difficulty, triumphant pleasure.

My Mother and Harrison were next to taste the cake. My Mother gasped and gulped an entire cup of tea more rapidly that I would have deemed possible for a woman of her age. Harrison, his cheeks grotesquely distended with a gargantuan mouthful, looked stunned for a moment, then grimacing horribly, made a muffled request to his Mother that he be allowed to "spit it out." Maude smiled sweetly. "Certainly, dear," she said. "Go upstairs and do it." The boy fled before the sentence was completed.

Fearfully, I placed a morsel on my tongue. The instant it touched my taste buds, I knew the reason for Maude's look of transcendental joy.

The cake was made with salt instead of sugar.

From the hostile way she looked at Maude, I suspect that the "attack" which my Mother suffered following this incident was due to ill temper rather than ill health, and it was with some difficulty that I got her to her room. Mrs. Ottey agreed to remain in charge until we returned from the theatre (for and added compensation) and we left the house at 7:16 P.M.

I do not remember having seen Maude in such high spirits since out trip to the cemetery.

To visit Theatreland, with its gaudy thoroughfares, its lights, its laughter; to become part of a pleasure-bent throng, besieging some glittering Temple of Thespis; to sit in red plush twilight and hear voices stilled as the curtain rises on a limitless continent of make-believe—these are sights and sounds, which, on my annual visit to "The Play," I find most stimulating.

Consequently, this evening, on our arrival at The Arts Experimental Theatre (by taxi), I was chagrined to find it located several miles from the theatrical district, in the basement of a disused furniture repository. So dingy was this edifice that, when our machine halted before it, I accused the driver of mistaking our destination. His reply was offensive and, had it been addressed to one less self-controlled than I, fisticuffs would have ensued. We disembarked, but, because of his manner, Maude would not allow me to tip the man. Both she and Harrison were beyond earshot when the taxi drove off. This was fortunate, for I should have been distressed had either of them heard the two words which the driver addressed to me as he let in his clutch.

When I joined them, Harrison, his face aglow with excitement, was reading aloud to his mother from the playbill which flapped on the crumbling façade of the warehouse:

THE GAS LIGHT AND COKE COMPANY'S
AMATEUR DRAMATIC SOCIETY
Proudly presents
Ghosts
By
Henrik Ibsen

I noticed that the boy's voice cracked several times.

Maude's gaiety this evening was unquenchable and, when I attempted to apologize for having brought her to so depressing a place on her birthday, she squeezed my arm and said that it did not matter—that just the tree of us being together made her happier than anything she could think of. When, a moment later, Harrison smiled at me and took my other arm, my cup was full. We went inside.

There was a fair sprinkling of people in the dimly lit hall and a strong smell of Lysol. The three seats, to which Mr. Murke's tickets entitled us, were in the rear. Two of them commanded and unobstructed view of the stage. Mine had a post in front of it. I suggested that w all move down one, but, no sooner had we done so, than a large lady arrived and, as Maude was occupying her place, we were forced to move back again. After sundry, uncomfortable experiments, I discovered that, by putting all my weight on my right hip, the pillar in front of me hid only one third of the stage. When, a moment later, the occupant of the next seat (a fine-feathered old gentleman with a snuff-stained moustache) allowed me the use of his armrest, the vista was even better. I thanked my neighbour for his courtesy and he whispered, "A progressive thinker like yourself, sir, deserves to be comfortable." This statement puzzled me and I enquired, of my companion, its meaning. After looking at Maude and Harrison, he replied, "No one but a progressive thinker would bring his wife and a son of that age to see this play. Strong meat, my dear sir. Very strong meat." Although his reference to "strong meat" alarmed me, I feigned nonchalance and explained that I was not, as yet, married to Maude. Where-upon the old gentleman shook my hand warmly and said, "So you're a Free Thinker too, eh? Splendid."

From the experience, I have learned the wisdom of humouring the aged. Therefore, I let his mistake go uncorrected and, after smiling at him turned my attention to the programme. I read that the action of *Ghosts* takes place at a country house in western Norway. This struck me as being fairly innocuous and my fears, that the play we were about to witness was perhaps unsuitable for children, were allayed. My attention was diverted, at this point, by Harrison, who had crawled under my seat in search of some Liquorice Allsors, which, due to his excited condition, he had dropped. I assisted him with the collection of those within reach and had barely resumed my seat when the recording of Grieg's *Ich liebe dich* ceased; the light went out and, after a series of spasmodic jerks, the curtain rose.

The opening scene was between a bad-tempered housemaid and a man whom I could not see because of the post. From his accent, I deduced that he was a yokel. Acoustically, the hall left much to be desired and Harrison's loud, frequent repetition of "Where's the ghost?" caused so much unrest among the people seated nearby that I had some difficulty in following the dialogue. In spite of Mr. Murke's assurance that the plot would "make me sit up,' I found it exceedingly banal. It concerned a Mrs. Alving (the leading lady), who wasted a lot of time talking to a clergyman and who worried about her son Oswald. That she had cause for concern I do not doubt, for the young man suffered with headaches and appeared to be far too highly strung. Mrs. Alving also talked, with great depression, about her unhappy marriage, but, as her husband was dead, I could not help feeling that her low spirits were unnecessary.

Dramaturgy is a science of which I know little. Nevertheless, the playwright who gives his work a misleading title is, in my opinion, a complete fraud and as deserving of censure as a criminal who obtains money by false pretenses. Obviously, Mr. Henrik Ibsen is one such, for we did not see a ghost the entire evening. It is true that Mrs. Alving said she saw two in the dining room, but whether she did or not is a moot point, for immediately following her statement, the curtain descended.

Harrison's howl of disappointment was heartfelt and, when the lights came on, I noticed that he was unnaturally pale. I also noticed the box, which had held the Liquorice Allsorts, empty on his lap. Remembering his over-indulgence at the tea table, I watched him carefully and, when his complexion developed a greenish tint, I suggested that he accompany me outside. He refused, I asked Maude to persuade her son, but she was in heated discussion with a lady in front of her (who had hitherto refused to remove her hat) and did not hear me. Quite soon, moisture bedewed the boy's forehead and, not wishing to be present when disaster struck, I went outside to stretch my cramped limbs.

On reaching the foyer, I discovered that due to the awkward position in which I had been forced to sit, my right, lower back was completely numb. It was while massaging this area, as unobtrusively as possible, that I saw Maude hurrying her ashen-faced son into the ladies' cloakroom. They remained within throughout the intermission. When the curtain ascended on the second act, I watched the play from the back of the hall. Although Oswald's headache got steadily worse and Mrs. Alving forgot her lines several times, nothing of real interest transpired.

Thirty minutes elapsed before Maude, leading a sadly debilitated Harrison, rejoined me. Her new hat was askew, but on her dear face was a look of efficiency that told me a difficult task had been well accomplished. We stood watching the play for a while, but it grew increasingly inferior and, when Harrison began to whimper miserably, we left the building.

Heedless of expense, I chartered a taxi for the homeward journey.

Because of Harrison's condition, the ride was fraught with suspense. He managed, somehow, to contain himself until we pulled up in front of THE NEST, but it was only Maude's adroitness, in opening the taxi door and rushing him behind a privet hedge, that prevented a catastrophe taking place inside the vehicle. This was fortunate, for although I tipped the driver lavishly, I sensed that, characteristic of his kind, his personality was belligerent.

Knowing that Harrison's indisposition would keep my betrothed busily occupied, I took my leave of them on the doorstep. Maude sent the boy inside and, after thanking me for a lovely birthday, kissed me with such warmth that I responded with more ardour than was seemly. Maude broke away from me and said, "Why, Edwin!" I was momentarily embarrassed, but, from the smile of understanding she gave as she closed the door, I knew that no offence had been taken.

I walked to my house with a light heart.

It is odd how frequently of late my return home has coincided with the departure or arrival of gentlemen guests at DUN ROVIN. Tonight, on reaching my front gate, I was astonished to see Mrs. Luby making her giggling adieus to Mr. Murke. After a lengthy exchange of roguish badinage, Mrs. L. closed her door and my paying guest hailed me. His gait, as he approached, was steady, but his lusty greeting—redolent of *Sen Sen*—told me that he had been indulging. He was in jovial mood and took my arm as we walked up the path. "Good old Ed," he said. As we entered the house, he said, "Good old Dot," and tripped on the door mat. Only his hold on me prevented what might have been a nasty fall. As I bolted the front door, I said casually, "I was not aware that you were a friend of Mrs. Luby's." Murke chuckled to himself. "I'm not," he replied. "I'm a customer." He then wished me "sweet dreams" and, after more chuckling, began a careful ascent of the stairs. A repeated mumbling of "Good old Dot . . .Good old Ed," accompanied his climb and it was not until he had disappeared from view and the phrase was silenced by the closing of his bedroom door that I moved.

I sat down.

The inference I had drawn from Murke's remark, regarding the tenant of DUN ROVEN, had shaken me badly.

Recently, whenever I have considered the problem of Mrs. Luby, there has obtruded on my sensibilities a suspicion so shocking that my mind has balked at exploring further such noxious avenues of thought and I have turned my attention to things less sordid. Such self-deception is no longer possible. No matter how disturbing they may be, the facts must be faced.

DUN ROVEN, 31 Gubbion Avenue, that proud example of my poor Father's artistry, has become a . . .

I cannot defile these pages with such a word.

My mind is made up. Mrs. Luby must vacate immediately. I shall call on her first thing tomorrow. The fact that her rent is several months in arrears will make my demand legitimate and, no matter what blandishments she may attempt, I shall remain adamant.

February 21st

The formulation of my speech to Mrs. Luby and the practicing of its delivery before the bathroom mirror took longer than I anticipated and it was not until 5:20 P.M. that I strode along to DUN ROVIN to beard my tenant. There was no response to my first four knocks, but, being convinced that Mrs. Luby was within, I knocked a fifth time. As I did so, my eye fell upon an empty milk bottle, from the neck of which protruded a note. I extracted it and read:

> Back later. 1 pint please,
> Love,
> Dot.

Before I could replace the missive, an all too familiar giggle sounded in the distance and, on turning, I beheld Mrs. Luby, on the arm of the fat sergeant with whom I had seen her once previously approaching the house. As they entered the front gate she said, cheerily:

"Hullo, old sport. How's tricks?" I replied that I was in splendid health.

"I want you to meet my . . . cousin, Bill," said Mrs. Luby. "Bill, this is Ed Carp, the kindest landlord poor old Dot's ever had."

The sergeant blushed (he was young) and avoided my eye. My tenant unlocked the front door.

"Go inside, Bill, there's a dear," she said. "Won't be a minute, just want to have a word with dear old Ed." The sergeant shuffled, sheepishly, past me and entered the house.

"Mrs. Luby," I said, sternly.

"Now, Ed, you don't have to use that tone to poor old Dot," laughed Mrs. Luby. "I know what you're thinking and I don't blame you. But old Dot always pays her debts." She took a bulky envelope from her handbag and thrust it into my hand.

"I was going to shove it in your letter box. . . . It's all there. . . . Things are looking up lately. . . . I wrote a note with it. . . . Got to fly now ducks, Bill's due back at the barracks at seven."

She patted my cheek, brushed past me and, before I could utter a word, I found myself, alone, in front of the closed door. It was some minutes before I collected myself sufficiently to open the envelope. It contained a bundle of currency, on the wrapping paper of which was scrawled:

Dear old Ed:

  Here's the back rent I owe you, plus three months in advance, also what you left under the butter dish that day. Thanks for everything,

Yours,

Dot.

I reached home feeling most unwell. Against my wishes, my Mother sent for Doctor Triggs. He has prescribed a bottle of tonic and, although it was impossible for me to explain to him the cause of my ill health, I shall follow his advice and remain in bed for at least another twenty-four hours.

February 22nd

The unevenness of my bedroom ceiling is proving to be something of a boon. Lying here, in my bed, I find that, whenever the insoluble problem of DUN ROVIN and its occupant proves too distressing, I am able to divert my harassed mind by contemplation of the fantastic designs which my fertile imagination weaves out of Edgar Frome's lumpy work.

I have not seen Maude. When she called this morning, I pretended to be sleeping. So keen is her intuition that I feared she might guess that my indisposition is mental, rather than physical.

Whether I feel better tomorrow or not, I shall get up and busy myself with the daily tasks. Coddling never cures.

February 23rd

As daily women go, our Mrs. Ottey is, I suppose, no more garrulous that the rest of her ilk. This, augmented by her intense preoccupation with the lives and doings of others, makes her, on occasion, oracular. In my dictionary, the following definitions are given for this word.

> ORACULAR: 1. Giving forth utterances as if inspired
> Or infallible
> 2. Ambiguous or obscure
> 3. Portentous

This morning—though still weak—I forced myself to arise and when I went into the kitchen to polish my footwear, Mrs. O. was saying to my Mother;

"Just imagine, Mrs. Carp, getting' your hair cut off in a bus. The window cleaner said his Elsie was ever so upset when she found she'd been 'bobbed.' She told her Dad the man just sat down next to her on the bus—ever so nice lookin' she said he was—offered to pay her fare. 'Course she wouldn't let him and he didn't say any more. She says she sort of remembers him puttin' his arm on the back of her seat, but she swears she didn't feel a thing 'till after the man got off. Then she felt a draught and screamed. Fine sort of hobby, I must say, goin' around cuttin' off people's hair in buses—don't you think so, Mrs. Carp?"

My Mother, who was cleaning the spoons, did not answer and I saw that the indicator on her hearing aid pointed to "Off."

"Mrs. Carp," repeated Mrs. Ottey. "I asked you what you thought about cuttin' people's hair off in buses?"

There was, of course, silence from my Mother and Mrs. Ottey looked at me with an injured expression.

"Has she switched herself off?" she asked.

I pretended to examine my Mother's hearing apparatus. "I'm afraid she has," I said and added, quickly, "it saves the batteries, you know."

With a look of disgust, Mrs. Ottey turned back to the sink and I busied myself with the saddle soap. Suddenly, she said:

"There's a new cat next door at MON REPOS—it's called Sylvia."

As I am not on speaking terms with my tenant, Mr. Dimmock, his acquisition of a feline was of little interest to me and I made no reply.

Mrs. Ottey threw me a quizzical glance and after a moment, said:

"Your Maude isn't looking at all well, is she?"

"Mrs. Phelps was in perfect health when last I saw her,' I replied, with dignity.

"When was that?" she asked.

"Why do you ask?" I countered.

She looked at me for a moment and then pursed her lips.

"Oh, nothing," she said. "I just thought she looked rather peaked last night when I saw them." She stressed the word "them" significantly.

Mrs. Ottey has an uncanny facility for involving me in discussions against my will. It happens frequently and, although I can sometimes avoid her conversational traps by remaining mum, this morning was not one of those occasions.

Quite casually I said, "By 'them,' you of course refer to Mrs. Phelps and her son Harrison." Mrs. Ottey stopped singing "Tea for Two."

"What makes you think so?" she said, airily. With some effort I controlled my irritation.

"Was it Master Harrison, or was it not?" I asked, quietly. Mrs. Ottey peered deep into the sink.

"Who's been pouring bacon fat down this drain?" she said and started to sing "Lover come back to me."

"Mrs. Ottey," I said, firmly. She stopped singing and looked at me with some surprise.

"What?" she said.

"I demand to know where and with whom you saw my fiancée last evening." I spite of my authoritative tone, I did not quite succeed in keeping an emotional quaver from my voice. Mrs. Ottey smiled playfully.

"Well, in that case, I'd better tell you, hadn't I?" She looked at my Mother.

"Is she still switched off?" she asked.

"She is," I said.

"That's good." Mrs. Ottey's tone was conspiratorial. "Last night on my way home, I dropped in at St. Jude's....I always do when the choir's practicing. Nothing like resting you feet to music, I always say....Well, there wasn't many people there and, after the practice was over, the gent who sings the high bits comes down from that stall thing, next to the organ, and joins a woman sitting up in front. Well ... after a minute, she turns round and when I sees it's your Maude—why, you could have knocked me down with a feather."

Mrs. Ottey watched me as I poured and drank two glasses of water.

"You say Mrs. Phelps looked ill?" I said.

She gave a jolly chuckle.

"Oh, I just said that to make it more interesting," she said and, drawing a pack of greasy playing cards from her apron pocket, she added, brightly, "like me to tell your fortune?"

I went out into the garden.

As I walked round and round the rockery, emotions of which I had always believed myself incapable seethed in my breast. In the distance I could hear Mrs. Ottey singing happily. Her voice is shrill and tuneless, but the words she sang seemed, to my bemused brain, terrifyingly apt:

> And, while I'm waiting here,
> My lonely heart is singing
> Lover come back to me.

February 24ᵗʰ

Although I possess great emotional stability, recent events have left my nerves somewhat frayed. Last night, in spite of the two cups of hot Ovaltine which I sipped slowly before retiring, I remained awake, battling with the green-eyed monster until the hooter on the gas works sounded at 6 A.M. Thereafter I dozed sporadically until 7:30 A.M. when, still unrefreshed, I arose and commenced shaving. As I plied my razor the blemishes in the bathroom mirror (caused by dampness) seemed, to my jaundiced eye, to form the repugnant face of Walter Roach and I cut myself three times. Never before have I nicked an earlobe so severely. While attempting to staunch the flow of blood with my styptic pencil, a great truth was borne in upon me. I realized that, unless my reason was to me completely engulfed by the maelstrom of doubt in which it spun, expunction of the morbid speculations with which I was torturing myself was essential. I gripped the sides of the washbasin, closed my eyes and, by exercising great will power, managed, after several attempts, to void my consciousness of these noisome images. Unfortunately they were immediately replaced by the smirking face of Mrs. Luby and a wave of despair swept through my being.

At this juncture, the styptic pencil slipped from my trembling fingers and fell down the drain. This trivial mishap proved to be my salvation, for the recovery of this article (a birthday gift from my friend Harket) called for great concentration and occupied my attention for the following fifty minutes. The waste trap beneath the fitment is ingeniously assembled and the dismantling of it (a challenge in itself) demanded skilful use of the pipe-wrench. Because of the inaccessibility of the lock-nut, the position I was forced to assume induced slight vertigo and made it impossible for me to acknowledge Mr. Murke's greeting when he arrived to perform his ablutions. I dislike inconveniencing our guests, but, because of my constricted position, was unable to say so. After standing about and whistling for, perhaps, twenty minutes, Mr. M. went downstairs to the kitchen, where, I subsequently learned, he annoyed my Mother by washing in the sink and getting toothpaste on her kipper.

I persevered with my task and, just as the crick in my neck became unendurable, the waste trap gave way under the pressure of my wrench. With a thrill of triumph I retrieved my styptic pencil, together with the terminal from a hearing-aid battery, four hairpins and a penny. Oddly enough, the latter was minted during the year of my birth—1894—I am keeping it as a souvenir. By the time I has massaged my neck with liniment and completed my toilet, I felt immeasurably relaxed.

I telephoned the Ace Plumbing Company (a competitor of Rolfe's) to come and reassemble the drain.

In order to keep my thoughts strictly impersonal, the morning was spent committing to memory the excerpts from *The Activated Sludge Process* with which I intended to regale our Committee members at this afternoon's meeting of The Society of Health through Sanitation. By noon I was word perfect and, after a brisk walk round the reservoir, returned home with my appetite keener than it has been for days. In spite of the fact that ham rissoles are by no means my favourite dish, the relish with which I disposed of three of them surprised me and seemed to restore, to some extent, my Mother's good humour.

I had called the Committee Meeting for 3:30 P.M. Miss Throbbitt arrived at 3:15 P.M., bringing with her a message from our Vice-President—V. Rolfe—that pressure of work prevented his attendance. I saw through this feeble pretext immediately. The truth is, of course, that, after my trenchant remarks to him on the day of the "crushed toe" episode, he is afraid to face me.

Miss Throbbitt was in kittenish mood and, while assisting me with the arrangement of the chairs and the placing of the water carafe, made three oblique references to the new blouse she was wearing. Obviously, this feminine wile was intended to extract a compliment from me, but, not wishing to excite her, I refrained from comment. We discussed the weather and I learned that last night's frost had had a deleterious effect upon her fig tree. From then on we sat in silence awaiting the arrival of our joint Treasurers—Mr. and Mrs. Tisdale. At 4:32 I invited Miss T. to join me in a glass of water. She accepted. As we drank, we agreed that the City's recently installed chlorination plant has vastly improved the flavour of the local Adam's Ale. At 4:50 P.M. I telephoned the Tisdale residence but there was no reply and I decided that further delay on their account was useless. Returning to the drawing room, I called the meeting to order with my gavel (hand-carved by my late Father) and instructed Miss Throbbitt to read the minutes. She informed me that there were none and we each drank another glass of water. I then commenced the dissertation I had memorized from Mr. A. J. Martin's book. Miss T. is an excellent listener (a rare thing in a woman) and I was gratified to note the rapt attention with which she received the educational facts I imparted regarding Horizontal Agitator Type Sludge Channels and Fill and Draw Sedimentation Tanks with Continuous Filters.

At the completion of my lecture I enquired if there were any questions. Miss Throbbitt had none and I wound up the meeting by opening our family album and showing her a snapshot of my Mother taken by myself last summer during our annual vacation at Leigh-on-Sea. The background is of great interest for it shows, in splendid detail, a Rotary Type Percolating Sewage Filter in action. Miss T. studied it intently and asked what the blur was in the foreground. I was about to explain to her that it was my Mother, who had unfortunately moved at the time of exposure, when through the window, I espied Maude entering the front gate.

It is strange how certain circumstances will evoke, even in the most well-adjusted of us, an upsurge of atavistic emotion. Though it be to my discredit, honesty forces me to confess that the sight of my beloved added fuel to the fires of resentment which had been consuming me for the past forty-eight hours. A demonic scheme began to formulate in my mind. I ignored Maude's knock at the door and, seating myself on the settee quite close to Miss Throbbitt, I turned the pages of the album to a rather intimate (partially draped) portrait of myself at the age of six months. After colouring slightly, Miss T. went into a rhapsody of praise, during which Mrs. Ottey's footsteps could be heard clomping along the hall to the front door. I was determined that Maude should taste the bitter cup of jealousy and, while making a pretense of discussing with Miss T. the merits of my portrait, I waited for my betrothed to enter the room.

The door-knob turned and I heard Mrs. Ottey say, "His Lordship's in here, Maude, talking about drains." My next move was a masterpiece of timing. As Maude came into the room I concentrated my gaze on Miss Throbbitt, leant toward her and, as though oblivious of a third party, said, very distinctly, "Dear lady, I think the blouse you are wearing is quite the most attractive I have ever seen." Then, pretending to become aware of Maude's presence, I simulated a slight start and, turning to her, said casually, "Forgive me, my dear, I did not hear you enter."

That the arrow of my revenge had found its mark was obvious from the way Maude's jaw changed its position.

"Are you getting deaf or something?" she asked. "I knocked at the front door till I was almost blue in the face."

"Really,' I replied. "I am afraid we were engrossed in our discussion." I turned to Miss T., "Were we not, dear lady?" Miss Throbbitt rose, jerkily, from the settee.

"Yes ... I mean ... er no. We ..." An attack of snorting prevented her from completing her speech and, after knocking over the bowl of artificial sweet peas with her handbag, she gathered up her coat, muttered an almost inaudible "Good afternoon," and hurried from the room.

As the door closed, my betrothed turned to me, her eyes flashing.

"Edwin," she said, ominously. "I demand an explanation." I gave a puzzled smile.

"Of what, my dear?" I said and, in order to sustain my air of nonchalance, carefully righted the sweet peas.

"Stop fiddling with those things. Take that silly look off your face and sit down," commanded Maude.

"Your solicitude for my comfort is appreciated, my dear, but I am by no means weary," I replied.

Maude took a deep breath. "Edwin!" she said, exhaling stertorously. I sat down.

"Now, if you please," she continued, "I would like to hear what you think you're up to with that silly woman?" Her eyes searched mine and I returned her look unflinchingly.

"Sauce for the goose is sauce for the gander," I replied.

"and what might that remark mean, pray?" she asked.

Still holding her eyes with mine, I said, "Considering the circumstances, my use of the time-worn proverb is surely explanation enough."

Maude clicked her tongue. "Stop talking so 'la-di-da' and tell me what you're getting at," she said, irritably.

"What I am getting at, my dear Maude," I replied, spacing my words carefully, "is that you have no right to criticize whatever I may be 'up to' with Miss Throbbitt, until I take exception to what you are 'up to' with Mr. Walter Roach." The look of guilt I had expected to see on my betrothed's face did not appear. Instead, I was surprised to see furrows of apparently genuine bewilderment crease her brow. After a moment her expression changed to one of deep concern and, crossing to me, she laid a cool hand on my forehead.

"You don't feel as though you'd got a temperature," she said.

I shook her hand away and rose. "Do not change the subject," I said, sternly. Maude looked at me uncertainly.

"You're trying to be funny, aren't you, Edwin?" she said.

I was never more serious in my life," I replied, my voice shaking.

Maude stared at me in amazement. "Walter Roach and me!" she said and, as if to make her show of incredulity more convincing, she sat down heavily on the settee.

"You mean, 'Walter Roach and *I*,'" I corrected.

"Never mind what *I* mean, Edwin Carp," she snapped. "What do *you* mean?"

Slowly, I seated myself, facing her. "On the occasion of your last birthday, did you, or did you not, receive, from the gentleman in question, a bouquet of dark red roses?" I said.

The look of puzzled ill-temper left my betrothed's face and she lowered her eyes. "Yes. But they weren't for my birthday. They were for ..."

"Please do not quibble," I said, cutting her h=off. There was a moment's silence.

Then, without raising her eyes, Maude said, quietly, "Please go on."

"On the occasion of my recent indisposition, were you, or were you not, in the company of the same gentleman during choir practice as St. Jude's?" Unfortunately, emotional tension gave my question a plaintive, rather than an accusatory, ring, but I did not take my eyes from Maude's face. There was another pause.

"I was," she said, finally. "What else?" She raised her eyes to mine. To my astonishment, I saw that they were twinkling with merriment. That Maude could derive amusement from this agonizing situation left me stunned.

"What else! ..." I repeated, incredulously. "Isn't that enough? If you knew what these last three days have been like you'd ... you'd ..." A stinging sensation in the eyes and a constriction of the throat made it impossible for me to continue. Turning my head away, I stood up and, with intentionally casual gait, sauntered to the window and looked out. It was raining heavily. I could not trust myself to speak and in order to gain time, blew my nose and polished my pince-nez. The room was very still. The only sound was the splash of rainwater from the cracked downspout outside. Maude, at last broke the silence.

"Edwin," she said, gently. I stood, implacable, watching the down-spout.

"I know you're all upset," continued Maude.

"No I'm not," I said quickly.

"Then stop sniffling," said Maude. "Wally sent me those roses because ..."

"So you call him 'Wally,'" I interrupted. There was a sneer in my voice.

"Well, I've known him for twenty-nine years, haven't I?" said Maude, testily.

"I neither know, nor care, how long you've ..." I began.

Maude rattled her umbrella impatiently against the table leg. "If you interrupt me once more, Edwin Carp, I won't explain anything. I'll go straight out of this house and leave you to stew in your own juice." From the sharpness of her inflection, an eavesdropper would have assumed that she was the injured party. I let this pass.

"Wally sent those roses because he was grateful to me," said Maude. There was silence. "Well?" she continued. "Don't you want to know what he was grateful for?"

"You just told me not to interrupt," I said shortly. I was not looking at my betrothed, but the noisy inhalation which greeted my remark seemed to imply that her patience was being tried. With a great rustling of skirts, she rose and joined me at the window. I continued to look at the spout.

"Oh! I'd like to ... to shake you," she said. "Wally's in love with ..." I waited, breathlessly, for her to complete her confession. The silence continued and I turned to her. To my surprise her back was to me. Her attention was focused on something down the street, beyond my line of vision. Peering over her shoulder I saw what held her interest. Walter Roach was approaching the house. On his arm was a lady. Although her features were obscured by a dripping umbrella, I recognized the waterproof cape which flapped about her ankles. The lady was my paying guest, Miss Miriam Costaine.

I watched them, my mind spinning with confusion. As they neared the front gate, Maude, with a quick gesture, adjusted the lace curtains so that we could observe them undetected. Having opened the gate, Walter Roach stepped gallantly aside and allowed Miss Costaine to precede him. Her face glowed with happiness and she looked much younger than usual. Her escort's eyes never left her as he followed her up the path. They reached the portico and disappeared from view. Some time elapsed before the latch key sounded in the front door. Although their conversation was, for the most part, drowned by the noise from the cracked down-spout, Miss Costaine's musical laugh and her joyous "Until tomorrow then," were clearly audible. The door opened and closed and we heard her mount the stairs. As she ascended she sang, softly, to herself the famous words of Christina Rosetti:

> My heart is like a singing bird,
> Whose nest is in a watered shoot,
> My heart is like an apple tree
> Whose boughs are bent with thick-set fruit, etc. . . .

Walter Roach dallied for a while in the front garden, gazing up at the window of her room. When at last he strode off down the street, it was obvious that he was in a state of elation.

Maude turned to me triumphantly. "There, you old silly. . . . Now do understand?"

I stumbled across the room, seated myself in the nearest available chair (my poor Father's, I later discovered) and hid my face in my hands. Maude went on talking.

"Wally sent me the roses because I introduced him to Miriam at that horrid musicale. He's very lonely, you know. I think that's why he talks all the time. Then I had them both to tea the next day and when he invited her to go to the choir practice, she asked me to go along as chaperone. Why she wanted a chaperone in church I don't know, especially at her age. But there you are . . . she's not used to men and you have to make allowances."

The misery I felt cannot be described. That my dear one should see me in such a hapless condition filled me with shame and I kept my face hidden.

"Oh, Maude," I mumbled at last. "What must you think of me." There was a long pause. I felt her move close to me.

"Look at me, Edwin," she said, softly. I did so. Gently she took my face between her hands. They smelled fragrant.

"Take a good look at me, Edwin," she said. "I'm fat, I'm middle-aged, my hair's going grey and yet . . . and yet you were jealous of me. I think you must love me very much and I think I'm very lucky." Her eyes brimmed with tears and she kissed me. We held each other very close.

When, at last, I released her, she said that what we both needed was a nice hot cup of tea and, wiping her eyes, she hurried from the room to make it. I sat quite still trying to regain my composure. Through the window, I saw that the rain had ceased and in the southern sky a patch of blue increased in size as I watched it. The relief I felt that my fears had been groundless was accompanied by that enervation which is always the aftermath of an emotional storm and, as I sat pondering on my stupidity, I recalled the following lines:

> O! beware, my Lord, of jealousy;
> It is the green-eyed monster
> Which doth mock the meat it feeds on.
> I must have the down-spout repaired.

February 25th

I am amazed at my recuperative powers. Last night's sleep was serene and dreamless and, at 6:47 A.M., I arose in the pink of condition. Raising the blind and window, I inhaled deeply. Although cold, the air was invigorating and, on leaning out and looking down the alley in a northerly direction, I saw that hoar-frost had coated the flora in my back garden with a glittering patina. Next door, at MON REPOS, Mr. Dimmock's hen-house was transformed, by an incrustation of the same sparkling rime, into a thing of beauty and, for the first time, I regretted the argument my Mother had had with its owner regarding the unsightliness of the structure. (Mr. Dimmock pays his rent regularly, but we have not spoken for eighteen months.)

Roofs and telegraph poles glistened in the crisp sunshine and only consideration for the other members of my household, who, I realized, were probably sleeping, prevented me from bursting into song. I am certain that such a superb sense of well-being is experienced by few men of my age. Such vigour, however, demands a vent and so I unearthed, from my sock-drawer, the chest expander which Dr. Triggs had prescribed some years ago during my convalescence from an attack of bronchi-ectasis. My blood was soon racing, but the exercise was of short duration. I discovered that Time has perished the elastic strands on the apparatus and after, perhaps twenty strokes, an over-flaccidity rendered it useless. Having returned the expander to the sock-drawer, I stood erect. Then by bending over I attempted to make my fingertips touch the linoleum without bending my knees. An acute pain in both Achilles tendons informed me that I had overestimated my suppleness and, while applying tincture of arnica to my calf muscles, I noticed that the nail on my injured great toe had loosened. In order to prevent its premature detachment, I bound the digit with adhesive tape. It was this precautionary measure which caused me to reach the bathroom later than is my wont and I was forced to relinquish my use of it to Mr. Murke. His arrival had coincided with mine and, as he is a paying guest, I try to treat him preferentially. While waiting for him to vacate, I have been making the foregoing entry.

It is written in pencil, the cold weather having caused the ink in my fountain pen to congeal.

I have heard Miss Costaine leave her room. . . .

I have just looked through the keyhole of my bedroom door. . . .

She is waiting outside the bathroom for Mr. M. to complete his ablutions. This is unusual for it if not her custom (in her waking moments) to stand about in, what she calls, her "peignoir." She sounds in high spirits for she is singing to herself:

> My heart is like a rainbow shell,
> That paddles in a halcyon sea,
> My heart is gladder than all these
> Because my love is . . .

Mr. Murke has just come out and Miss Costaine has gone in. I am afraid I shall be late for breakfast.

When, finally, I reached the dining room, my Mother was concentrating on a kipper and *The Soul of Lilith* by Marie Corelli; Mr. Murke had departed for his day's toil and Miss Costaine was helping herself to the last of the kedgeree. I noticed, for the first time, that she has cut her hair and tinted it a mahogany shade. It is most becoming. In response to my cherry "Good morning," she smiled, radiantly, and said, "God's in His Heaven, all's right with the world." "Browning!" I replied, immediately. "Correct, mine host," she said and I held her chair until she was seated.

It is said that a hearty appetite needs no sauce. This morning I proved the veracity of this old adage by disposing of two helpings of cold porridge while waiting for Mrs. Ottey to bring my egg. When, at last, she arrived with it, she caused me some embarrassment by staring at Miss Costaine's hair and saying to me, "That henna rinse has knocked twenty years off of her, hasn't it?" I ignored the remark and was surprised to hear Miss Costaine say, un-self-consciously, "Thank you, Grace." Mrs. Ottey then asked her if "Wally" had seen it. Miss Costaine laughed, happily, and replied that he had and that he approved. Mrs. Ottey chuckled. "That's the stuff, dear. . . . Keep up the good work and you'll have him hooked in no time." As she left the room, she looked at me and added, "Talking of hair, yours needs cutting."

I was about to apologize for Mrs. Ottey's rudeness when Miss Costaine asked me if I thought room could be made in the lounge (she meant drawing room) for a clavichord. I replied that this could probably be arranged, whereupon she informed me that she was about to receive one as a gift. She did not mention the donor's name, but I think I know. During the remainder of the meal she entertained me with some highly instructive facts about these old-world instruments. Apparently, there are two kinds: (a) the fretted or *gebunden* and (b) the fret free or *bundfrei*. I learned that Miss Costaine's will be toe *gebunden* type.

As I was folding my serviette, my Mother switched on her hearing aid and told me that she had read *The Soul of Lilith* before. Actually, she has read it four time, but, until today, had had no recollection of so doing. I telephoned Dr. Triggs at once. He said that her memory must be improving. This delighted me.

Mrs. Ottey's remark regarding my need of tonsorial attention, although ill-timed, was well-founded. I pride myself on being well-groomed and my trim has been overdue since the 14th inst. The reason I have procrastinated about paying Harket a visit is because of the toupee. Were I to enter his establishment without it, I am certain his feeling would be hurt. All creative artists are sensitive, and to offend so good a man would distress me. The difficulty has been to get out of my house, unobserved by my Mother, while wearing Harket's gift. This morning I determined to essay this.

Having completed my telephone conversation with Dr. Triggs, I took my hat and coat from the hall-stand and ascended to my room. After sticking the toupee in position, I donned my hat and coat and cautiously opened the door. Luckily, the coast was clear and, after a nimble descent of the stairs, I escaped, unseen, into the street. Unfortunately, Mrs. Luby was in her front garden chatting with a naval gentleman and, in order to avoid raising my hat to her, I was forced to turn east, instead of west, and make my way to the bus-stop by a circuitous route.

Upon my arrival at Harket et Cie, I had some difficulty removing my hat and Joseph warned me never again to wear it until the adhesive on the toupee is dry. He asked me if I had any objection to sitting in the chair by the window. This placed me in full view of the passers-by and, although I would have preferred a less exposed position, I had not the heart to refuse his request for he said I was a splendid advertisement for him. As he worked skillfully on the sides and back of my head, I learned that his eldest daughter, Doreen, had become engaged to our milkman, Terence Blythe. I recalled, with some misgivings, the note I had seen in Mrs. Luby's milk bottle addressed to this young man, but in spite of this I congratulated Joseph. Apropos of milk, my good friend then recounted an extremely amusing anecdote about an inexperienced farmhand and a cow. While I was laughing at its surprising denouement, I became aware of being watched. Glancing through the window I saw, to my dismay, Walter Roach staring in at me. From his puzzled expression I realized that, because of my toupee, he was finding it difficult to place me. Casually, I raised the copy of Dalton's Weekly which lay on my lip, thereby obstructing his view. When I lowered it a moment later, he was gone. He is older than I thought and much better-looking.

On leaving Harket's, I purchased, at Woolworth's a small bottle of toilet water. Thence I made my way to the Public Library, where, in the privacy of the gentlemen's convenience and with the aid of the aforementioned spirit, I removed the toupee. The toilet water had a heady fragrance (Shem-El-Nessim), and, not wishing to return home until this had evaporated, I decided to while away an hour in the Reading Room. All the newspapers and most of the magazines were in use. Although I have no particular interest in fish, I finally settled myself in a secluded corner with The Aquarium Keepers' Annual. One article caught my eye which I found so remarkable that I transcribed the first paragraph of it into my pocket memorandum. I reproduce it herewith:

THE CASE OF BONELLIA

The marine worm, *Bonellia Viridis*, displays a remarkable degree of
Sex-dimorphism. The female has a body about the size of a plum.
The male is a microscopic pygmy whose internal organs save those
Concerned with reproduction, are degenerate and who lives as a
Parasite within the body of the female. The fertilized eggs hatch out
as free-swimming larvae. If a larva settles down upon the sea bottom,
it becomes, with few exceptions and after a short neuter period, a
female: but if it settles upon the proboscis of a female it becomes a male.

I read the article twice and, while musing on the miracle of procreation in general, remembered that, as yet, I had not fulfilled my promise to Maude anent a "nice long talk" with Harrison. Leaving the Reading Room, I proceeded to the main hall. The attendant in charge was the one I had been forced to reprimand last January. In view of the letter I had written the Borough Council regarding this fellow's uncouth behaviour, I was surprised to see him still employed and looked about me for some other, more capable official.

Next to a large bronze bust of William Caxton (inventor of the printing press) a desk marked "Head Librarian" caught my eye. The chair behind it was unoccupied and I pressed a bell-push beneath which the legend read "Please Ring." After a few moments, the door on my left opened and there emerged a middle-aged, heavily built lady who held a handkerchief to her nose and spelled strongly of eucalyptus.

"May I help you?" she asked, indistinctly. I would have preferred making the request I had in mind to a man, but, having gone so far, I decided to continue.

"Do you know of any books on sex instruction for adolescents?" I whispered.

"You'll have to talk louder than that," she said and blew her nose vigorously. I repeated my question with slightly more volume.

"I still can't hear you," she replied. "This cold's got me all stuffed up."

Again I tried using almost normal pitch.

"Sex for *what?*" she said, in startled tones, and three young ladies who were inspecting William Caxton laughed.

"It is of no consequence," I muttered and backed away. The Head Librarian watched me suspiciously and then, fortunately, was overcome by a paroxysm of sneezing. As I passed the young ladies on my way to the exit, one of them said to her companions, "Smells nice, don't he?"

On my return journey, I debarked from the bus at the brewery and walked to the reservoir. It was frozen and I circled it, hat in hand, allowing the breeze to blow the lingering redolence of Shem-El-Nessim from my brow. A group of young men were indulging in raucous horseplay on the ice. As I passed them, one yelled, "Come an' 'ave a slide, Dad." I ignored the remark and quickened my pace. This brought forth other well-meant, but vulgarly phrased, sallies and I could not help thinking what a deplorable amount of unemployment there is among today's working class. I then recalled, with regret, that, during my boyhood, my Mother had forbidden—besides roller-skating—all winter sports.

Sometimes I wonder if, perhaps, my up-bringing was not over-cautious.

The crisp sunshine soon dispelled these sober thoughts, however, and, on rounding the bend by the pump-house, I came upon a deserted corner of the reservoir where the ice shone irresistibly. After removing my galoshes, I walked out on the frozen expanse. Having assured myself that it was solid and that I was unobserved, I took a short preparatory run and glided quite a creditable distance. My sense of balance has always been good (probably a compensation for myopia) and I was soon sliding back and forth with an agility that surprised me. It was most exhilarating. Time lost all meaning and when eventually, I looked at my watch, I discovered that I was already eleven minutes late for luncheon with my betrothed.

I reached THE NEST at 1:07 P.M. and upon explaining to Maude, before a cosy fire, the reason for my tardiness and ruddy cheeks, she laughed merrily, kissed me for a second time and said that "all men are boys at heart."

The meal was delectable, especially the rabbit pie, and, as I assisted with the washing-up, I felt closer (spiritually) to Maude than I have for several weeks. I believe there is a deeper understanding between us since my jealous outburst yesterday.

My hands are badly chapped since my escapade this morning. As I write, I see that the knuckles are swollen and there is some irritation. I fear I have contracted Erythema pernio (chilblains).

February 26th

Incapacitated by chilblains. Painful swelling of feet, nose-tip, fingers.

Difficult to hold pen.

Confined to house.

March 5th

A week since my last entry.

> Other's follies teach us not
> Nor much their wisdom teaches;

And most, of sterling worth, is what
Our own Experience preaches.
                    Alfred, Lord Tennyson

I have learned my lesson and, in future, shall forego all winter sports. Thanks to an unguent concocted by my Mother—glycerin, lemon-juice and lamb-fat—the affected areas are healing nicely. There is still a small lesion on the knuckle of my right index finger, but I am able to get into my out-door boots by removing the arch-supports.

For one as active as myself, the recent incarceration has been something of an ordeal. But time has not been wasted. I am an avid reader, and, in view of the imminent man-to-man talk with Harrison (I am taking him on an outing next Saturday) I have culled a hose of useful knowledge from *What to Do until the Doctor Arrives*, by Nurse Cooper and *The Origin of Species*, by Charles Darwin. The latter volume was left with us by our first paying guest—Mr. Luther Bostwick (deceased).

Maude's frequent visits have been rays of sunshine during these past, dark days (a pea-soup fog followed the frost), and she has presented me with two pairs of heavy woolen gloves which she knitted, years ago, for Fred Phelps.

Miss Costaine's clavichord arrived on Tuesday. Its accommodation in the drawing room necessitated moving my poor Father's pet pigeon—Tinker—(now stuffed and in a glass case) to a new location in the hall. This disturbed my Mother considerably and she refused to eat. Her memory of present events is so short-lived, however, that, within twenty-four hours, she was back on normal diet.

Walter Roach has visited Miss Costaine twice. I allowed them the privacy of the drawing room, and, on both occasions, Roach gallantly paid the extra fee for a coal fire, which, in view of the high cost of living, I am forced to charge during the winter months. They are an admirably suited couple—both being musical—and, from the kitchen, I have enjoyed to the full their rendition of "The Holy City" and "Tit Willow," for both of which Miss Costaine has arranged settings for the clavichord. The tone of this instrument is sweet and delicate and is characterized by a tremulous hesitancy which I find charming but which Maude considers tinny.

Closer acquaintance with Roach proves him to be a most like-able fellow. I admire his singing voice (he has an enormous range) and, as both of us are non-smokers, we have much in common. Last night I noticed him scrutinizing my thinning hair, but he said nothing and I am convinced that he has decided it was not I whom he saw in Harket's window.

He is a widower, Mrs. Roach having passed away in 1931 after a meal of tainted scallops.

March 8th

Today I received a visit from Mr. Coggins. He has been pro-moted from Police Constable to Inspector and, because of his plain clothes, my recognition of him was not immediate. A big, usually cheerful man, he seemed ill at ease, and I was surprised at the brusqueness with which he refused a chair upon being ushered into the drawing room. After clearing his throat, he said that the matter he wished to discuss was of a private nature and I instructed Mrs. Ottey, who was cleaning the leaves of the aspidistra with milk, to leave the room. When we were alone, Coggins cleared his throat again and said, solemnly, "Bein' an Inspector's not all beer and skit-tles, sir." I replied that one would hardly expect it to be. Coggins looked at his boots.

"There's lots of things we 'ave to do, that we wish we didn't 'ave to do," he said. I remained silent. Coggins walked slowly to the window and looked out.

"This is a nice respectable street, wouldn't you say, sir?" he asked. Although puzzled, I agreed that the street was as he described it. Scratching his head, Coggins moved to the fireplace and stood with his back to it.

"Unfortunately, sir, you can't tell a book by its cover," he said cryptically and, after scratching his head again, took a sheaf of dog-eared papers from his breast pocket. He leafed through them with a moistened thumb.

"P'raps it'll be easier if I read the notes what I've got wrote down, sir," he said.

A certain apprehension began to seep through me, but I nodded affirmatively. Coggins wiped his moustache with the back of his hand, donned a pair of steel-rimmed spectacles and, in an expressionless voice, began to read:

> Certain reports from Naval and Military Authorities, lead us to believe that at DUN ROVEN, 31 Gubbion Avenue, property of E. Carp, certain goin's on are takin' place. Said goin's on are in violation of the Vagrancy Act passed in 1898. Police Constable Parkhurst reports 'avin' observed soldiers and sailors enterin' and leavin' the aforementioned premises at all hours of the day and night and, in his opinion, the occupant of said premises is practicing prostit . . .

There was a loud crash.

An involuntary twitch of my right arm had knocked Aunt Ruth's photograph from the small table at my elbow. Startled, Coggins looked up from his report. As his slightly bloodshot eyes scanned my face, his expression changed to one of compassion.

"Now, now, sir, don't get yourself all upset," he said. I did not move. Kneeling down, Coggins began gathering up the shard of broken glass and what remained of the photo-frame.

"I know what a shock this must be to you, Mr. Carp," he continued. "You bein' such a quiet sort of gent. It's a nasty business I know, but, as you own the 'ouse, I thought it might save a bit of unpleasantness if I gave you the chance to tell the old . . . er . . . the lady to get out, instead of me doin' it official like."

He deposited the debris carefully in the fireplace and stood up.

"'Course, if she tries any 'anky-panky I'll 'ave to arrest 'er, but, for your sake, let's 'ope she leaves without any fuss."

I opened my mouth to speak, but could emit no sound. Coggins must have sensed my speech difficulty, for he patted my shoulder, comfortingly.

"I'd be obliged if you could 'ave a talk with 'er as soon as possible, sir," he said.

I attempted to rise, but he pressed me gently back into the chair. "You just sit quiet, sir, you'll soon feel better. . . .I'll let myself out." Placing Aunt Ruth's frameless portrait on my lap, he quietly left the room.

In times of crisis, I have noticed that one's attention is invariably arrested by some quite irrelevant detail. Today, as the door closed on

Coggins, I remember looking down at Aunt Ruth and thinking how cleverly the photographer had camouflaged the acute strabismus from which she had suffered.

I went to bed at 6:30 P.M.

As I complete this entry, it is 3:41 A.M.

March 9ᵗʰ

Severe indigestion all day. Because of it, I forwent breakfast and luncheon and arrived at THE NEST for tea, somewhat debilitated. Maude's concern for my health is always gratifying, but, when we are in company, it can be oppressive. This afternoon, therefore, Miss Costaine having joined us for "the cup that cheers," I did not inform my betrothed of my indisposition and, being ravenously hungry, foolishly partook of sardines and seed-cake. Within a short time I was paying for this idiocy with gastric pains so acute that Maude stopped her animated conversation with Miss C. to ask it he cat had got my tongue. In spite of my discomfort, I managed a smile and said, "What cat?" Both ladies laughed heartily, but the effort of making the joke caused me to perspire round the waist.

At the conclusion of the meal, Maude asked, very sweetly, if I would mind taking a stroll in the garden as she wished to speak, privately, with Miss Costaine. My curiosity was, of course, piqued, but pyloric spasms were tearing at my vitals and so, on the pretext of having letters to write, I returned home.

As I inserted my latch-key, I was startled by a hissing noise in the laurel bush adjacent to the front door. I turned. The leaves parted and Police Constable Parkhurst emerged. His manner was furtive. "Sst . . .sir. I 'ope it's orlright with you, me 'idin' 'ere?" he whispered dramatically. "My orders are to watch DUN ROVIN and I don't want 'er to spot me." A knot of pain centered in the region of my duodenum. "The Army's put this street out of bounds," continued Parkhurst, leering suggestively. "Wish the Navy'd do the same thing . . . she's 'ad a sailor in there since four pip emma. . . .Navy don't seem to care what their boys get up to, do they, sir?"

Before I could think of a suitable reply, he gave a slow, salacious wink and disappeared once again into the laurel bush. As I gazed numbly at the trembling leaves, a hand, holding an empty cup, was thrust through them. It seemed to hang from the shrub like some bizarre fruit. "Thank Mrs. Ottey for the tea," said a disembodied voice. Picking the cup, I went inside.

When I entered the kitchen, Mrs. Ottey was laying out her playing cards on the draining board. She ignored me and I mixed myself a dose of bicarbonate of soda. As I drained the glass she gave a depressing sigh.

"From the looks of these cards, you're goin' to need a lot of that stuff," she said. "See that eight of clubs? That means unpleasantness between a heart man and a spade woman. Dot Luby's a spade woman, if ever I saw one and you're a heart man—or you would be if you'd got more hair. Have you told her yet?" Her inquisitive look and the ill-mannered directness of her question filled me with irritation.

"Mrs. Ottey . . ." I began, frigidly.

"It's no good you lookin' as though you don't know what I'm talkin' about," she interrupted. "I listened at the drawing room door yesterday and heard every word Coggins said. Now . . . Have you told her to get out—or haven't you?"

"I would prefer not to discuss the subject," I said, with dignity. Mrs. Ottey ignored this.

"You haven't told her yet; I can tell by your face," she said and turned up the two of spades.

"There! See that? Worst card in the pack. It means a disaster comin' to the house, or, if you're out in a boat, it means shipwreck." She looked at me, appraisingly. "You look like death warmed over," she said.

I turned to leave. As I reached the door, she spoke again.

"Why can't they leave the old girl alone? Fancy makin' Mr. Parkhurst hide in a bush to watch her. Live and let live, I say. She's never done anyone any harm. She helps to keep the boys out of the pubs and I've never heard her say a mean thing about anyone. She's a real good sort. Why, when I told her this morning that Coggins was on to her . . ."

"You told her, Mrs. Ottey?" I said in amazement.

"Of course I did," she replied, defiantly. "And d'you know what she said? She laughed and said that you were a real gent and that no matter what the police tried to do you wouldn't never let 'em throw her out. And she believes it with all her heart."

I closed the door and went up to my room.

March 10th

When a man who is capable of clear thinking and decisive action is forced, by cruel circumstance, to wallow in a slough of vacillation, he is humiliated. He is also enraged.

This morning, therefore—after a heartburn-haunted night—I arose at 6 A.M. in an extremely ill temper. Having performed a hurried toilet, I broke my fast with a stale bismuth tablet (it was in my stud-box) and went downstairs. When in this mood, four walls are intolerable to me and, even though dawn had not broken, I dressed warmly for the street and slammed the front door on the sleeping household as Terence Blythe was delivering the milk.

For the Majority, solitude is essential to the solving of knotty problems. I differ. Although not gregarious by nature, I have found that, whenever Life calls upon me to make a decision of vital importance, lucidity is facilitated if I am among a crowd of my fellow men. I cannot explain this interesting temperamental quirk, but for some reason the babel and bustle of a seething through stimulates my thinking, rendering it even more keen.

To cite an instance.

I have attended but on football match in my life. It was in 1928, when, after a year's acquaintance with my dear Maude, doubt still lingered in my mind as to the prudence of sacrificing my bachelor freedom—at thing no man relinquishes lightly—by asking her for her hand. My knowledge of football has always been scant, but the excitement in the grandstand that day was intense (the home team lost, I remember) and, although I did not join with my neighbors in booing the referee, the exhilaration I experienced cleared my brain. I returned home with my perspicacity fully restored. The tendrils of dubiety, which had choked my intellect for weeks, vanished, and, within twenty-four hours, I was able to decide that my future would be meaningless unless I made Maude mine. Even after nine years, although connubial bliss is not yet in sight for me, I have never once regretted my decision.

This morning, as I trudged the dark streets, the problem of Mrs. Luby—while it in no way parallels the above—was equally clamourous in its demand for solution. My entry, dated February 21st, records how abortive had been my first attempt to evict the tenant of DUN ROVEN. Mrs. Ottey's account of her chat with the lady yesterday (though worthy of small credence) implied that, because of Mrs. Luby's faith in me as a gentleman, a second attempt on my part would also meet with failure. But, if I could not bring about the evacuation of my property, Coggins would arrest the poor creature and a plethora of unsavoury publicity would inevitably ensue. The complexities of my dilemma caused my esophagus to churn painfully. I quickened my pace, for I needed a suitable setting in which to cogitate.

It is no simple feat to find a multitude of mankind at 6:45 A.M. in windy March. To the unresourceful it would, I imagine, pose quite a riddle. By the time I had reached the fish-market, my destination was clearly in mind. I headed for the one place, where, in any great city, cacophonous activity is unceasing—the Railway Station.

My arrival at The Great Western Terminus coincided with the appearance of a watery sun which tried, in vain, to pierce the pall of smoke hanging over the huge, soot-stained structure. I entered and was immediately engulfed by the eddying streams of humanity which gushed, in full spate, from every platform. From past visits I remembered a splendid vantage point by Gate 11, adjacent to a chocolate vending machine, and I attempted to make my way thence. Although my objective was less than thirty yards from me, I was an unconscionable time reaching it, for, as I battled the horde, my umbrella handle became caught in a young woman's snood, and, before disentanglement could be effected, the tide of travelers bore us both out into the street. While attempting to release her hair-covering from the hand-carved whippet head which tops my umbrella, the young woman gave me her baby and a large hamper to hold. The child, though small, was very active. It (I could not determine its sex) had unusually large blue eyes, a jam-covered face and a fierce determination to possess my pince-nez. By throwing back my head I managed to thwart its desire, but, in so doing, my hat fell off and was trampled underfoot. Luckily, a porter rescued it. As he replaced it on my head, he laughed and said, "Looks like Granpa's got 'is 'ands full." I did not thank him.

When the young woman handed my umbrella, the snood was still attached and I was shocked to hear her say, "You seem to want the blank thing, mister. You keep it. . . . It ain't no blank use to me with a blank 'ole in it." Then, grabbing her hamper and child, she walked angrily away. As I re-entered the station I noticed that my left glove and sleeve were slightly damp.

Some ten minutes later, disheveled but victorious, I took my stance by the chocolate machine. Homo sapiens, en masse, is a fascinating sight. As I surveyed the swirling exodus before me and breathed the acrid smell of smoke and metal, my ill temper gradually gave way to blandness. The babel of many sounds stimulated me. The impatience of whistles—the vehemence of voices—the hiss of steam: all these struck my fanciful ear in brilliant counterpoint, like treble instruments in some frenetic orchestra, whose bass notes were supplied by the clangour of milk-cans and the gasping grunt of locomotives coming to rest.

Eight A.M. saw a marked change in the quality of the arriving throngs. The noisy labourers, artisans, etc., who had formed the milling crowds hitherto, were replaced by a quieter, more prosperously dressed type. From the hunted look many of them gave the station clock as they hurried to the exits, I identified them as office workers. Although more sedate in mien that the earlier arrivals, they looked far less healthy.

At the cessation of the rush-hour, the pangs of hunger made themselves felt and, after inserting a coin in the chocolate machine, I withdrew a bar of Nut-milk. Upon unwrapping the confection, I noticed that it was riddled with tiny perforations, a closer inspection of which revealed weevils. I made my way to the Station Master's Office.

Two clerks were in attendance, the younger o whom—an alert, sandy-haired stripling—listened to my complaint with some surprise. After exchanging a look with his colleague, his mouth began to twitch, oddly. He covered it immediately with his handkerchief, took the infested bar of Nut-milk which I proffered as evidence and both men went into an inner office. A moment later, guffaws of boisterous laughter could be heard. When eventually they returned, both wore expressions of poorly simulated gravity. The younger clerk placed a coin on the counter before me and, with an unctuous smile, said, "Sir, the President of The Great Western Railway asks if you will accept this money as reimbursement for your disastrous investment. At the same time he wished to tender his deepest apologies for the inconvenience to which you have been put." His mouth began to twitch again and I looked him levelly in the eye.

"Young man," I said. "When you grow up, I trust you will learn that a true gentleman never finds delight in the misfortunes of others." I picked up the coin. "I shall take this as a matter of principle," I added and walked out. In spite of the ribald laughter which accompanied my exit, I knew that I had won my point.

Realizing the concern my non-appearance at breakfast would cause my Mother, I telephoned Mrs. Ottey and informed her that I should return, probably, by 4 P.M. I was beginning to enjoy the rare treat of a day away from home, and, to celebrate, I went to the Refreshment Room where, at a secluded table, I disposed of half a pork pie, two cups of tea and a slice of particularly delicious apricot flan. While waiting for digestion to take place, I have been making this portion of today's entry in my journal.

I shall now go down to the docks and watch the ships.

My two-hour walk took me through the busiest thoroughfares of the city. I enjoyed it immensely. The stimulus afforded by my visit to the station made calm, disciplined reasoning once again possible and, before I had reached the waterfront, I had decided upon a satisfactory solution to the problem of Mrs. Luby.

I scanned the river and saw that shipping was virtually at a standstill. The only boat around which there was any activity was small and rusty-hulled. Picking my way to it, along the litter-strewn wharf, I found myself hoping that it was a banana boat, for, although I have never felt an urge to travel, I enjoy watching the unloading of exotic fruits. It titillates my imagination, enabling me to conjure up visions of far-off, steaming jungles and fearsome, marine hazards which the gallant merchant ships must face in order to bring these delicacies to our tables.

Barely discernible on the ship's prow were the words KRISTIN BJORNSON SVELVIK and in her shadow, sweating stevedores toiled and shouted. Their tongue was unintelligible, but I noticed a repetitive use of the uvular *r*. As I drew nearer, one of their number dropped the barrel he was hoisting and pointed me out to two of his friends. All three laughed. Sensing no hostility, I waved my umbrella by way of greeting. For some reason they found this gesture highly amusing and, while one mimicked it, the other two gave way to uncontrollable mirth; hitting each other playfully, but with great violence. Their capering was curtailed by a stridently reprimanding voice from the ship's deck and, throwing reproachful looks in my direction, the men resumed the unloading of the cargo. It was not bananas. From its pungency, I surmised it to be fish oil (probably, whale), but, as it had obviously traveled the seas without refrigeration, I did not loiter long.

Dockland, in spite of its dirt, is rich in sea-faring tradition and I spent a pleasant hour exploring its narrow streets, warehouses and curio shops. In one of the latter, while purchasing a nose-ring from Borneo, which I intended to have made in a brooch for Maude, I saw a strange sight—a flaxen-haired Chinaman. While my purchase was being wrapped, he left the shop, and, in order to make conversation, I remarked affably to the proprietor (a true cockney) that such colouring was unusual in an Oriental. Fixing me with his one eye, the proprietor expectorated into a brass incense burner without moving his head. "Are you trying to be funny, mister?" he said, belligerently. "That's my brother-in-law, Charlie Clark. . . .'Ad jaundice since Christmas. . . .The doctor says 'e's never seen such a liver." I apologized and left hurriedly. It was while eating luncheon at The Capstan Café & Restaurant that I realized I had left the nose-ring in the shop. Because of the proprietor's personality and in spite of the financial loss incurred, I decided not to return for it.

The homeward journey was uneventful. On the bus I made a mental résumé of the salient points in the speech I was about to deliver to Mrs. Luby. Their well-phrased succinctness gratified me. It was 3:28 P.M. when I approached DUN ROVEN and, for the first time, I felt none of the perturbation which the prospect of an interview with my wayward tenant had hitherto engendered. The front garden looked depressingly unkempt, and, after pushing two beer bottles and mildewed puttee out of sight beneath some ivy, I knocked at the door authoritatively. I waited. I knocked again, using great force. Again I waited. For twenty minutes I knocked and waited. My efforts caused Mr. Dimmock to peer at me twice through the window of MON REPOS but, otherwise, nothing stirred. At 3:50 P.M. I returned home with my mission unaccomplished. As I opened my front door, I realized I was extremely tired.

Having shed my outer garments, I felt the dire need of tea. But, being in no mood for Mrs. Ottey's loquacity, instead of going to the kitchen, I went upstairs, quaffed a glass of citrate of magnesia in the bathroom and proceeded to m room. While removing my galoshes, I was struck by the stillness of the house. My room adjoins my Mother's. During her postprandial nap, her deep breathing and the resultant vibration of her brass bedstead cause a reverberation which is quite noticeable in my quarters. Today this was absent. I put my head to the wall, but could hear nothing. Remembering that I had once read another method of sound detection in *The Woodcraftsman's Handbook* (left with us by the late Mr. Luther Bostwick—Scoutmaster), I knelt down and pressed an ear against the linoleum. I was in this position when, without knocking, Mrs. Ottey burst into the room. "Expectin' some Indians?" she asked flippantly. I was badly startled, but, before I could compose a reply, she said, "You're wanted downstairs at once. . . . It's urgent," and, after throwing a letter on the bed, she left the room.

I dusted my knees and hurried to my Mother's room. The fact that her bed had not been slept in did nothing to ease my mounting concern for her well-being. Indeed, when I reached the foot of the stairs and once again became aware of the oppressive silence about me, it increased. The kitchen was empty, as was the dining room. With my hand on the drawing room door-knob, I paused. From within came an unintelligible, rustling whisper. Panic seized me. It sounded in the one word "Mother!" which I cried as I flung open the door. My senses reeled beneath the explosion of sound which greeted my gesture. The room was crowded. Loud voices sang, "For He's a Jolly Good Fellow." I could not believe my eyes—My Mother, the Harkets, Walter Roach, Mrs. Ottey, Murke, Miss Throbbitt, Harrison, Miss Costaine (at the clavichord) and Maude—all singing at the top of their voices. I stood in the doorway, stupefied. Then Maude took me in her arms. "Why, you old silly," she whispered.

"You look as white as a sheet . . .what's the matter with you? It's your birthday."

"For He's a Jolly Good Fellow," sang the others. Maude joined in with them and, guiding me to a chair, stood, with my hand in hers, smiling down at me. I looked round the room at the happy singing faces. All my friends . . . singing and smiling for me. All my good friends.

They sang it twice and when, as they commenced a third time Harrison's voice cracked, everyone laughed with great good humour and descended upon me. I was deluged with handshakes, back slaps, vociferous good wishes and, from my Mother and Maude, embraces. To my consternation, I felt my throat tighten, but, as the stinging began in my eyes, Maude quickly bent over me and, while kissing me again, unobtrusively passed me her handkerchief. I blew my nose twice, in rapid succession, and the danger passed.

Memory of any emotionally disturbing event is often faulty. For this reason I shall not attempt to describe in detail the joyous birthday party that ensued. I remember only two incidents clearly—both of them with regret.

(1) My stupidity when in response to my guests' noisy demands for a speech, I was unable to say more than a barely intelligible "Thank you, one and all."

(2) My untruthfulness to Harket when, as the guests were departing at 6:45 P.M., he looked at my head and whispered, "Why aren't you wearing it?" and I replied that I had run out of adhesive.

That I should have forgotten today was my natal day can only be accounted for by my recent preoccupation with other problems. My dearest Maude confessed to me this evening as I took her home that it was in order to plan the surprise party, she spoke privately with Miss Costaine yesterday. I am amazed at my density.

On my bed before me, as I write these words, is the pile of gifts with which my dear friends showered me. I list them below, preceded by the name of each donor:

> Mother—Set of ankle-length, winter-weight undergarments
> Maude—Umbrella with hand-tooled, leather-covered handle
> (her own work)
> Harket—Packet of four razor blades (double edged)

Miss Costaine—One Handkerchief
Mrs. Ottey—One Handkerchief
Miss Throbbitt—Two Handkerchiefs
Mr. Murke—One Birthday Card (risqué)

I am indeed blessed and have, just now, composed the following:

Though rich in pelf and worldly good,
Still pauperish are they
Who go through Life and never feel
The warmth of Friendship's ray.

It is unfortunate that inspiration came so tardily. The foregoing would have made a perfect response to the demand for a speech which I met so inadequately this afternoon. On the other hand, the sentiment contained therein will perhaps be more enduring if I send each of my friends a copy. . . . I shall do this.

The advent of my forty-third year has been an unforgettable experience. However, of all the beautiful things I received today, that which affords me the greatest joy is none of the above. It is the letter which Mrs. Ottey threw on my bed this afternoon and which I opened barely an hour ago. It reads:

Dear old Ed:

Dear old Ottey tells me that it's your Birthday so I'll start with wishing Many Happy Returns.

I expect you know that things have been bad with poor old Dot lately and dear old Ottey says that according to the cards they'll get worse if I stay here. She turned up 2 of Spades three times this morning. So I'm going down to the seaside and stay with my friend Ruby what used to be in business with me before she got married to that Ernie Dowsett whose had to go off on a submarine she says but I think he's left her. Anyway I'm off to stay with her and I'll send for my belongings before the rent what I've paid you runs out in a month or two. I'd ask you to return the rent that I've paid but seeing that I'm skipping off without notice that wouldn't be fair because you've got to live too.

Lots of luck, dear old Ed. Be a good boy and thanks for everything.
Yours,
Dot.
X X

I have just realized that, since opening the dining room door this afternoon, I have not had one twinge of intestinal distress.

March 11ᵗʰ

"Heavy precipitation in south-easterly area" was the Clerk of the Weather's prediction for today. Fortunately, during the night, a capricious north wind gave him the lie by putting to rout the lowering clouds and, at 10:02 A.M., when Harrison and I embarked on our "outing," Gubbion Avenue was bathed in winter sunshine. The boy wore his best suit, some new shoes and a freshly blackened left eye. The latter, Maude had explained while packing our luncheon (hard-boiled eggs and bloater paste sandwiches), was the result of a strenuous game of "Mothers and Fathers" played, last night, with Ursula Monks. Our departure had been delayed by Harrison's two visits to the bathroom and, during his second absence, Maude had revealed a certain apprehension regarding the purpose of my forthcoming junket with the lad, viz., "a nice long talk." Her references to his tender years and his innocence, together with sundry other remarks, implied that the revelation of Life's facts, to one so hypersensitive, might induce shock unless divulged with the utmost delicacy. I did my best to reassure her, but, when we kissed good-bye, she clung to me and, with tears in her eyes, begged me to "be gentle with him."

As we walked to the bus-stop, I reminded Harrison that his new shoes would last longer if he picked up his feet. He seemed not to hear this and I made a covert inspection of my stepson-to-be. The sullen angle of his down-covered jaw (he is slightly undershot) made his sensitivity difficult to discern, and I wondered if Mother Love might possibly have had a warping effect on Maude's judgment of her offspring's character. While we waited for the bus, I attempted to break through the boy's reserve by patting his shoulder with an air of camaraderie. There being no reaction to my gesture, I said, cheerfully, "Well old chap, where would you like to go this fine day?" Harrison's reply was immediate. "Home," he said.

My question having been purely rhetorical—I had decided on our destination a week ago—I ignored his churlishness and fell silent. Harrison then began a careful scrutiny of my feet which I found most disconcerting. Suddenly, he said, "Why do you wear those old galoshes when the sun's shining?" My benign reply that "Prevention is better than Cure" was rewarded with a snort of disgust and he said, "Ursy Monks says you wear 'em in bed." I decided to treat this as childish humour and laughed with appropriate heartiness. Harrison regarded me pityingly. "Ursy Monks doesn't think it's funny—she thinks it's insanitary," he said. At this juncture the bus arrived and we embarked.

Choosing the ideal locale for our excursion had been no easy task. The atmosphere of immediate surroundings colours the moods of men (and children) far more than is generally suspected, and, during my chilblain incarceration, I had given the matter deep thought. A setting conducive to Harrison's ready understanding of certain basic laws was essential—but where to find it? Inspiration had come to me while conning the immortal works of William Wordsworth; two lines in the first stanza of "The Tables Turned" supplying me with the answer:

Come for the into the light of things,
Let Nature be your Teacher.

This morning, therefore, when the bus-conductor demanded our fares, I said, "Two to the Zoo."

I had hoped that Harrison, upon learning our destination would evince pleasure. Instead, he said loudly, "The Zoo smells." For some reason his remark amused several of the other passengers and one of them, a gentle old lady, told him that all boys should love animals. Harrison's expression changed immediately from disgruntlement to piety, and, turning to her, he gave a wan smile. The lady gasped and said, "Why you poor child, where did you get that terrible eye?" Harrison thought for a moment. Then, leaning toward her, he whispered something. The nature of his communication can only be conjectured, but I found the balefully accusing stare with which the old lady transfixed me for the remainder of the journey most embarrassing. The incident had a cheering effect upon Harrison however, and, by the time we reached the zoo, he was in comparatively tractable mood.

Upon entering the beautifully appointed gardens, my charge insisted on an immediate inspection of the wart-hog. As we stood before its cage, I enquired the reason for his interest in so repulsive a beast. Harrison filled his mouth with peanuts I had purchased for squirrels and said "Ursy Monks says her Aunty Win looks just like a wart-hog."

"Poor lady," I murmured, sympathetically.

"She's not poor," replied Harrison. "Ursy Monks says she's had five husbands . . . all millionaires." There was a pause, during which we studied the wart-hog.

"Your little friend's aunt probably has a beautiful nature," I said at last.

"Ursy Monks says she's a horrible ole cow," the boy replied casually, and, after hitting the wart-hog on the snout with a peanut shell, he strolled over to another exhibit.

Words cannot describe the shock I received upon hearing those young lips utter so vulgar a phrase. At any other time I should have reprimanded the boy immediately. To have done so today, however, would have jeopardized the *rapprochement* which I had sensed burgeoning between us during our discussion of Miss Monks' Aunt Winifred. Harmonious comradeship was essential to the success of my project. Therefore, when Harrison called me over to look at the *Choiropotamus porcus*—or Cameroon Painted Pig—I controlled myself and made no reference to his deplorable smile.

The call of Nature necessitated Harrison's leaving the Wild Swine Enclosure, and, while I waited before the cage of a White Lipped Peccary for him to return, I planned the next maneuver in my campaign for his enlightenment. It required inveigling him into the Bird House. Once there, I fondly hoped that the dainty, but peculiar, habits of some of our feathered friends would excite his interest sufficiently enough to warrant my introducing weightier discourse.

Twenty minutes elapsed before Harrison rejoined me, during which—with the aid of a bloater-paste sandwich—I became friendly with several sparrows. The boy's return and his petulant wail of "You're giving my dinner away" scared a small hen-bird from my left forefinger and caused a wave of anger to surge through me. My self-control was immediately engulfed and I do not think Maude, herself, could have stopped the scathing homily on Greed and Selfishness with which I upbraided her son. When, finally, lack of breath brought my harangue to a hale, the boy raised his downcast eyes to mine. Instead of the sullen resentment which I had expected to see in them, there was a look so closely akin to respect that I had great difficulty concealing my amazement. In a meek voice, he said, "I'm sorry, Uncle Ed. I didn't mean it." There was a pause and I patted his shoulder. We smiled at each other and I sensed the birth of a new and better understanding.

I wonder if, at last, I have discovered the correct method of handling my stepson-to-be?

The one small detail which prevents me from being entirely convinced is that, directly after this episode, Harrison insisted on taking charge of our luncheon bag.

We headed for the Aviaries, but, en route, the Reptile House proved an irresistible lure to my charge and I spent an unpleasant forty-five minutes in its foetid atmosphere while he watched a Boa Constrictor crush and engorge a small rabbit. My attempts to pry him away from this gruesome spectacle were fruitless and not until the mammoth snake, distended and surfeited, collapsed into a coma would he consent to leave. Never have I seen him merrier.

At Penguin Pool, the quaint, flightless sea-birds were entertaining a large crowd with their almost human antics. One pair of Adelie Penguins (*Pygosceles adeliae*) were indulging in the strange dance of courtship and I directed Harrison's attention thereto. The male, after executing various odd figures, would pick up a pebble with his bill and present it to his prospective mate with great ceremony. It was a charming sight. The clumsy courtliness of the bird's behaviour—enhanced by the formal black and white of his plumage—evoked much laughter, but the little creature gave no heed to his human audience and continued his cavortings.

Apparently penguins are unlike dogs, who hate being laughed at.

We continued to watch and, after the birds had performed a particularly intimate *pas-de-deux*, Harrison tugged at my sleeve.

I turned to him, bracing myself for the leading question which I felt certain he was about to ask. Instead, he said, "I'll be back in a minute, Uncle Ed."

"Where are you going?" I asked.

"You know,' he answered.

"But you just went," I said, impatiently.

"No I didn't—I couldn't find it," the boy replied and walked rapidly away.

As I watched Harrison disappear, I pondered the prudence of having Doctor Triggs give him a thorough examination and, in my pocket memorandum, made a note to discuss the matter with Maude.

After inspecting the Grebes, two Crested Screamers—who resented my new umbrella—and a repulsive African Shoebill which bore a striking resemblance to V. Rolfe, I came to rest before a solitary Argus Pheasant. From a friendly Zoo attendant, I learned that the male of this handsome species will only court the female if she remains absolutely stationary. Should she be restive, he will display before some other, motionless object. The man explained that this particular bird had lost his wife last spring (she had become egg-bound) and, since her demise, the bird had been displaying before his water-trough. I found the story touching and stood in contemplation of the lonely creature for quite a while. Suddenly, the Argus Pheasant strutted as close to me a searching look, proceeded to display his spectacular plumage in the most flattering manner. The attendant laughed and asked if I was a good "egg-layer." In order to hide my embarrassment, I looked at my watch and was disturbed to discover that an hour had elapsed since Harrison's departure. After wishing the man "good-day," I hurried off to find the boy.

For thirty minutes I searched, with mounting alarm, in the Lion House, Small Mammal House, Beaver Pond, Bear Pit and four structures marked "Gentlemen." There was no trace of my errant charge and, somewhat distraught, I made my way to the Lost and Found Department. The elderly gentleman in attendance, on seeing my breathless condition, offered me a chair and listened to my description of Harrison with a look of kindly wisdom. When I had finished he said, with an Irish accent, "How old's the lad?" I told him. He thought for a moment and then smiled.

"Did you try Monkey Hill?" he asked. I confessed that I had not.

"That's the first place to look for a boy of his age. If the young rapscallion isn't there, let me know," he said and winked, knowingly. The implication in his look disconcerted me, but I dissembled and, after thanking him, sped on my way.

The first intimation that I was on Harrison's track came in the form of a fragment of hard-boiled egg which struck my cheek as I passed the cage of a Chimpanzee named "Mildred." My suspicion that it was part of our luncheon was confirmed when, in the adjoining cage, I espied on Orangutan waving several bloater-paste sandwiches and eating a mutilated paper bat. A few moments later— true to the Irish gentleman's prediction—I saw Harrison lolling over the railing which surrounded Monkey Hill. He was watching, with open-mouthed fascination, the indecorous behaviour of a horde of Rhesus Monkeys (*Macaca mulatta*). From a distance I watched the boy. After, perhaps, three minutes, the uninhibited antics of a small, male Rhesus made the distraction of my charge's attention imperative and I called his name.

Upon seeing me, Harrison grabbed my arm and said, joyfully, "Uncle Ed, you should have been here. These are the best. You should see the things they do." I was relieved to see that his delight was completely unself-conscious and decided that to scold him for his disappearance, at this time, would be inadvisable. Instead, I said, "Where is our luncheon?"

The boy hung his head and, after a lengthy pause said, "I . . .I gave it to some monkeys."

"Look at me, Harrison,' I said, quietly. Reluctantly, he did so and I continued, "Are you sure you *gave* it to the monkeys?"

His eyes searched mine, shifted uneasily and then looked down at his new shoes. I waited. After swallowing twice, he blurted out, "No, Uncle Ed, I didn't give it to them. . . ." He pointed to the Primate House. "That ugly old red one in there grabbed it out of my hand." His voice broke during the confession, and, as I looked down at the dejected figure, I experienced a sudden, inexplicable and quite surprising feeling of pride and affection for my future step-son. Tentatively, I placed my arm about his shoulders and, sensing no resistance, drew him close to my side. He looked up at me and we smiled at each other. It was a repetition of the moment we had had in the Wild Swine Enclosure, but I sensed a deeper sincerity in the boy which gave me great pleasure.

His eyes are the same colour as Maude's.

"Never mind the sandwiches, son," I said. "We'll have something to eat in the Restaurant."

As we turned to leave, Harrison drew my attention to a female Rhesus who was suckling a minute baby. "Look, Uncle Ed, it's like a real mother."

"But she is a real mother," I said.

"I mean a grown-up woman mother," the boy replied. In order to avoid the frankness of his gaze, I looked at my watch. It was 1:33 P.M.

On our way to the Restaurant, we paused to look at the Indian Elephants. Harrison seemed greatly impressed by the size of the giant pachyderms. Suddenly, he said, "Uncle Ed, d'you know how long it takes an elephant to have a baby?" Before I could phrase a fitting reply, he said, "Eighteen months. Twice as long as a woman. Ursy Monks says so."

Keeping my eyes straight ahead, I said, "Really," and we recommenced walking. Harrison's expansive mood continued and we had gone but a short distance when he said, "Ursy Monks says she's going to have twelve babies by the time she's twenty-six."

Moisture began to bedew my brow, but in spite of it and the sudden tightness of my collar, I succeeded in keeping the tome of my reply purely conversational.

"What makes her think she can have so many children in so short a time?" I asked.

"She's got it all worked out. She told me how it's done," replied Harrison.

"Indeed," I said, noncommittally.

"Yes. We're going to get married when she's seventeen and then one baby every nine months. That'll take nine years. She'll be twenty-six by the time she's finished."

"It sounds very simple," I murmured and stopped to look at a Bactrian Camel.

"It's not true about them living without water," said Harrison. "Ursy Monks' Aunty Win proved it."

"How?" I asked.

"She didn't give hers any water and it died of thirst in four days," the boy replied.

We were fortunate enough to get a table on the terrace outside the Restaurant and, although I had no appetite, Harrison won the approval of the waitress by ordering grapefruit, sausage and mashed potatoes, a double banana split and lemonade. While we awaited the food's arrival, I noticed him looking at me curiously. All at once he said, "Have you ever been married, Uncle Ed?"

"Not so far," I answered cautiously.

"Nor has Mr. Murke, has he?"

"Not to my knowledge," I said.

Harrison gave a sigh of depression. "Then why do *I* have to?" he asked.

"If you are going to have twelve children, it might be advisable," I said, gently.

Harrison sighed again. "That's what Ursy Monks says," he said and lapsed into a frowning silence. For a moment I watched the troubled young face. "Do you think she will make you a good wife?" I asked.

To my surprise, Harrison said, fiercely, "That old Ursy Monks . . . I hate her!" He then kicked the table leg twice, with great force.

"Then why are you going to marry her?" I asked.

He looked at me with tragic eyes. "I've got to."

My umbrella fell to the ground with a great clatter and, as I bent to retrieve it, I wiped my fore head surreptitiously with my serviette. When, at last, I spoke, my voice sounded very far away.

"Why have you . . . *got to?*" I said.

"She says she'll hit me if I don't," the boy replied and picking up a highly polished tablespoon, he began an examination of his blackened eye.

By the time Harrison's food arrived, I discovered that my appetite had returned. I ordered a portion of pork pie and a pot of tea. The pie, although tasty, was by no means as succulent as that which I had enjoyed at The Great Western Railway Station, but in spite of this I left but a few crumbs.

While we were waiting to board the bus for home, Harrison made on more reference to the marital problems which he seems convinced he will have to face in a few years. As we watched the traffic flash by, he said, cheerfully, "Uncle Ed, p'raps Ursy Monks'll get run over before she's seventeen."

During tea at THE NEST, Maude avoided my eyes while Harrison was present. This, and her over-vivacious reaction to the boy's description of the various animals, was, I sensed, due to her anxiety to know the result of our excursion. Harrison, I was relieved to note, made no reference to the Rhesus Monkeys and, after a hearty meal—which included four portions of his mother's latest fruit cake (another soggy failure)—he departed to play in the garden. Maude and I sat in silence for several minutes. Then, placing her hand gently in mine, she looked into my eyes and said, tremulously, "Well?"

I pressed her hand and smiled reassuringly. "He knows," I said.

Maude looked down at a raisin on her plate and her fingers tightened in mine. "How much?" she asked, softly.

I cleared my throat. "Enough," I answered.

Maude emitted a relieved sigh. "I had a feeling you hadn't told him,' she said.

"Why?" I asked.

"He ate so much for tea," replied Maude, quietly. Then brightening, she added, "He's just like his father. . . .Nothing spoils his appetite. Poor Fred . . . the day he died—even with all that pain—he had three helpings of bread pudding." Her eyes softened and, not wishing to disturb her reverie, I refrained from replying.

Later, when Harrison had retired, Maude entertained me in the drawing room with a spirited rendition of "Anitra's Dance' by Grieg and a piece she has recently learned by Sidney Smith. It is entitled "*Le Jet d'eau*" (The Jet of Water) and calls for brilliant fingering in the treble clef. I was greatly impressed by Maude's faultless execution of the innumerable runs and arpeggios which are supposed to represent water squirting from a fountain. However, we both agreed that it will sound even better when Walter Roach has tuned the piano (he is a professional) and replaced the two missing strings (middle C and B flat) which Ursula Monks removed recently while playing "Hospital" with Harrison.

It was a wonderful evening and, after cocoa, as I held Maude in my arms, she whispered, "Thank you, my dear, for what you have done today for my . . . our boy."

I was deeply moved by her speech. I think she was too, for our good night kiss was of longer duration than usual and the looks we exchanged when I took my leave made words unnecessary.

As I walked home, I marveled at the feeling of strength which I derived from my dear one's faith in me.

It has just occurred to me that I omitted to discuss Harrison's kidneys.

March 12th

This morning, while in the bathroom reading *The Master Christian* by Marie Corelli, my Mother suffered an attack. Her hysterical cries were pitiful to hear and, by the time Mr. Murke had helped me remove the door from its hinges (it took thirty minutes), I was completely unnerved. Access to the bathroom having been gained, Mrs. Ottey took charge and, while I waited below, she transferred my Mother to the bedroom. The application of hot-water bottles to the feet and vinegar to the temples did little to reduce the paroxysms which convulsed my hapless parent and Mrs. Ottey left the room. A moment later she returned with a purposeful look and an egg-cupfull of water which she dashed into my Mother's face. The effect was immediate. The twitchings ceased; my Mother's eyes opened and, having examined her saturated jabot, she sat bolt upright on the bed and gave Mrs. Ottey a look of great hostility. Arms akimbo, Mrs. Ottey eyed her dispassionately. Then, with surprising gentleness, she began to dry my Mother's face with her apron. While so doing she looked at me and said:

"Of course the best thing is to hit 'em across the face with a raw beef heart. . . . It brings 'em out of it like lightning. But, if you haven't got one handy, a cold dousing'll usually do the trick." She patted my Mother's hand, comfortingly. "There you are, old dear. . . . How d'you feel now?"

Snatching her hand away, my Mother turned to me "Edwin," she said, crossly, "I saw a mouse on the wash basin. Go and catch it at once." As I hurried off to do her bidding, she shouted after me, "It was eating the soap."

An inspection of the nearly new bar of Fels Naphtha revealed to incisor marks and, although I spent twenty minutes on hands and knees examining the bathroom wainscoting, I could discover no orifice through which a rodent marauder might have entered. During my gropings beneath the bath-tub, my fingers encountered a loose floor-board. I dislodged it with difficulty and, from beneath, extracted a dust-encrusted, half-full bottle of Teachers Highland Cream Whiskey.

This is the second of my poor Father's caches I have discovered since his demise. The first one came to light after the violent electric storm of 1931. Forked lightning cracked the urn which my Mother kept (for sentimental reasons) on top of the rockery in our modest garden. The receptacle was found to contain—together with Grandfather Gubbion's ashes—a bottle of port.

This morning, remembering the distress the earlier discovery had caused my Mother, I replaced both whiskey and floor-board and, having washed my hands, returned to her room. She seemed more normal and was listening, with interest, while Mrs. Ottey read aloud to her from *The Sunday Chronicle*. I did not speak until Mrs. O. had finished an account of a baby farmer's arrest at Walton on the Naze. Then I said, gently:

"I could not find the mouse, Mother"

My parent looked at me, irritably. "What mouse?" she said, abruptly. Then turning to Mrs. Ottey, she continued, "What's he talking about, Grace? . . . Who said anything about mice? . . . I hate mice."

"Never mind him, old dear . . . he's barmy," Mrs. Ottey replied quickly and switched off my Mother's hearing aid. The conspiratorial wink she gave me as she spoke lessened the sting of her insulting remark and, sensing that my presence in the sickroom was extraneous, I withdrew.

Having unearthed two traps from the tool-shed I placed them in strategic positions on the bathroom floor. One is a humane box-trap; the other a cruel "break-back." I would not have used the latter were I not convinced that the mouse exists only in the hallucinatory recesses of my Mother's weary mind.

I ate a solitary luncheon, for Mr. Murke had returned to bed (he was out until 4 A.M.) and Miss Costaine had accompanied Walter Roach to Wootton Bassett where he was to sing at his late wife's nephew's wedding. My mood brightened considerably, however, when, while serving the treacle tart, Mrs. Ottey reminded me that Doctor Triggs and his alienist friend Mr. Hume were expected for tea.

My Sunday afternoon nap is a minor indulgence which I enjoy and which today—it being imperative to restore privacy to the bathroom—I was forced to forgo. I commenced re-hanging the door at 2:01 P.M. Because of the infuriating perversity of inanimate objects, I found the task trickier than might be supposed and by 3 P.M. had achieved nothing but four deep gouges in the wall and one in the thumb. After anointing my wound with what remained of the chilblain unguent, I went to enlist the aid of Mr. Murke. He sleeps with his window open and, as I have long since abandoned my attempts to dissuade him from this foolhardy practice, I took the precaution of donning my overcoat before entering his room. It was icy. Mr. M. was snoring loudly—his face covered with a highly coloured periodical entitled *Bathing Beauties*. In response to my vigorous proddings he rolled over and, without opening his eyes, said thickly:

"Leave me alone, Millie. . . . Go to sleep."

The poor fellow appeared to be so completely exhausted that I decided not to disturb his dreams. After glancing through the magazine (a bold publication), I returned to my work.

As I have said to my dear Maude many times, "Pertinacity pays." That I practice what I preach is proven by the fact that, at four o'clock, I had the bathroom door back in position and a neatly printed notice tacked to its inner surface. It reads:

DURING OCCUPANCY KINDLY
PLACE CHAIR UNDER DOOR-
KNOB WHILE REPAIRS TO
LOCK ARE BEING EFFECTED.
THANK YOU.

There is a chance that the lock is beyond repair. During a ruffled moment, I imprudently tried to force the door into place by kicking it. This resulted in the key breaking and the fulcrum-stump being forced into a position where it will no longer engage with the feather-spring. However, if necessary, a new lock can be installed and, once Edgar Frome has repaired the holes in the ceiling and refilled the gouges in the walls, there will be no evidence that anything untoward has occurred.

I had barely changed my collar, redressed my thumb and lanced two blood blisters, when Doctor Triggs arrived with his friend. The latter's full title is Professor Thaddeus Hume and I judged him to be the good Doctor's senior by some years. The Professor's head is large, ping and highly polished. No vestige of hair is discernible on either scalp, brows or eyelids, and his Adam's apple is never still. While conversing with him it is difficult to focus one's eyes on anything but this restless thyroid cartilage. When he speaks, it darts frantically up and down and when he is silent, it flutters from side to side with the rapidity of a moth's wing. He has great personal charm and is amazingly erudite, but, as all his teeth have recently been removed, his diction is somewhat muddy (especially the consonants). In spite of this I could detect no trace of an accent and, when I went upstairs to ascertain whether my Mother was well enough to receive guests, I checked the word "alienist" in my dictionary. To my surprise, I discovered that it does not mean "a foreigner" as I had supposed, but—"a psychiatrist who specializes in giving legal advice."

I am always willing to learn.

Upon entering my Mother's room, I found her sitting by the window holding my poor Father's photograph. She did not hear me and when I touched her shoulder she said, without looking up, "When Edwin comes home from school, don't let him go out on his skates."

Realizing that her mind was in the past, I returned to the drawing room. Both Doctor Triggs and the Professor nodded sagely as I described my parent's condition and the imaginary mouse which had been its cause. My story was interrupted by Mrs. Ottey, who, having brought in the tea, insisted on Doctor Triggs examining a whitlow which has recently erupted on her right forefinger.

Her habit of obtaining gratuitous medical advice from the good Doctor whenever he calls is both embarrassing and annoying. I must speak to her again.

After the meal Doctor Triggs invited his friend to go upstairs with him and visit my Mother. The Professor declined gracefully, explaining that he is rather self-conscious about meeting ladies until his new dentures are installed, which, I understand, will not be until Easter. Subsequent chatting revealed that this learned man is the author of a book entitled *Sidelights on Senility* and the proprietor of The Journey's End Rest Home. Before leaving he gave me his card and assured me that his rates are reasonable and that he "can always make room for one more," should I ever decide to place my Mother in his care. I was surprised to hear Doctor Triggs concur with his friend's suggestion that "it might be a good idea." My reply was polite but noncommittal, for this is a step I shall never take. I feel most strongly that my Mother's welfare is my responsibility and, no matter what personal happiness I must sacrifice, my duty to her is something I will never shirk.

It has been a trying day and I am retiring early.

I have just discovered, while disrobing, that the nail on my injured great toe has detached itself. Doubtless the result of kicking the bathroom door.

March 14th

Because of my Mother's failing health I have trained myself in recent years to slumber lightly. Last night, therefore, awakening suddenly with every faculty on the *qui vive*, I knew that something unusual must have rent the veil of sleep. The echo of a strange sound welled up from my subconscious but, in spite of concentrated effort, I could not recall whether it had been human or feline. I stared into the inky blackness. My eyelids soon became heavy and I decided that, in all probability, it had been Mr. Dimmock's cat, Sylvia, in assignation beneath my window. Having pushed the chilled hot-water bottle to a far corner f the bed, I loosened my pyjama cord and reclosed my eyes. No sooner had I done so than a whimpering cry (human) brought me to a sting position and I switched on the light. It was 4:52 A.M. Hastily donning my dressing gown, I sped to my Mother's room—disentangling the chain of my pince-nez with sleep-numbed fingers en route.

I found my Mother sleeping peacefully, her bedstead vibrating rhythmically with her respiration. Relieved but mystified I returned to my room. I had all but closed the door when a noise came from the bathroom. Hidden from view, I peered into the shadows and saw the figure of Miss Costaine emerge. She was not wearing her "peignoir" and from the slapping noise her feet made upon the linoleum, I knew she was without slippers. Slowly, with a strange hopping movement, she approached her room and, with a small moan of pain, entered. A moment later something was ejected, quite forcibly, from within and the door closed. The object landed with a slight clatter some three feet from me. Waiting until silence once again reigned, I cautiously retrieved it.

It proved to be the "break-back" mousetrap. Although sprung, I noticed that the cheese was still intact.

Because of my concern for Miss C., I had great difficulty returning to sleep. From her state of *déshabillé* I deduced that she had entered the bathroom while taking a somnambulistic stroll. To be rudely awakened from such a condition by treading on a mousetrap must have been a painful experience. It is a miracle that the shock to her delicate nervous system did not kill her.

When I descended to breakfast this morning, Miss Costaine was toying with her finnan haddie and returned my greeting without raising her eyes. She looked pale. Mr. Murke winked at me and, with a shrug of his shoulders, implied that Miss C.'s mood mystified him. While eating my porridge I waited to see if she would voice a quite justifiable complaint. She did not broach the subject of the trap (or any other), and when Mrs. Ottey brought in the marmalade and said to her, "We're lookin' a bit washed out this mornin'. What happened . . . have a tiff with Wally?" the poor lady rose hurriedly and hobbled from the room.

Mrs. Ottey regarded this exit with amazement and turning to me, said, "My goodness, we're touch this mornin', aren't we? What's she limping for?" I ignored her and she picked up Miss Costaine's plate.

"Oh, well. It's no good letting this lovely hunk of haddock go to waste, is it? . . . I'll have it for me tea." She took it into the kitchen.

Mr. Murke helped himself to the last of the bacon. "You don't think Roach kicked her, do you?" he asked with a leer.

I assured him that I did not think such was the case and, knowing how warped his sense of humour can be on occasion, I decided to withhold from him the secret of Miss Costaine's distress.

I have placed the mousetrap over the back fence where It can do no further harm.

March 15ᵗʰ

Doctor Triggs became acquainted with my parents in 1891 after my poor Father had fallen from a mansard roof while carrying a hoe. So satisfactory was the truss which the good Doctor prescribed that, three years later, he was invited to attend the occasion of my birth. Since that time he has been our family's sole medical adviser. As a minister to the ills of the flesh there is no finer practitioner and I hold his skill in high regard, but his approach to certain problems of human behaviour leaves much to be desired.

I am thinking, in particular, of this kindly man's reaction to the length of my engagement to Maude. Two years after that event was celebrated he began urging me to plunge into wedlock without further delay. Although cognizant of the fact that such procedure would be in direct opposition to my Mother's wishes, he pooh-poohed the idea that it would endanger her health and, since that time, has subjected me to yearly lectures. The theme is always the same—"Marry and stop wasting your life." Last year, after the Hot Cross Bun episode,* he lost some of his habitual calm and said, "Edwin, my boy, you're a damn fool to let your life be ruined by that selfish old woman." (He meant my Mother.) Where another would have taken offense at so insulting a remark, I reacted as I have to all his previous diatribes—with tolerance. I realize that his motives—although misguided—are altruistic.

Today, I was afforded a further example of the good Doctor's complete lack of understanding of this delicate situation. Having spent some thirty minutes at my Mother's bedside, he invited me into the drawing room and began a lengthy dissertation anent the advisability of placing my parent in the care of Professor Thaddeus Hume. He bolstered his argument by pointing out that, by so removing the incubus (he meant my Mother), there would be nothing to hinder my immediate marriage to Maude. I listened politely. Fortunately I was saved the embarrassment of voicing my opinion by the intrusion of Mrs. Ottey. She entered the room (without knocking), waved her sore finger under the good man's nose and said, with pride:

"Look at the size of it since Sunday, Doctor, and it's throbbin' like one o'clock."

While Doctor Triggs examined the swollen digit, I crept unobtrusively from the room and ascended to the bathroom, where I remained until I heard him leave the house.

I suppose it is the clinical nature of the good Doctor's work which accounts for his being unable to comprehend that there exists a thing called "Filial Obligation." His suggestion regarding my Mother is, of course, not only impossible but ridiculous.

*See entry dated January 29th. R.H.

March 17th

For the past two days our household has been disrupted by Mrs. Ottey's whitlow. In spite of Doctor Trigg's assurance that the inflammation is of minor consequence, she has bandaged her right hand heavily and carries it, dramatically suspended, in a sling made from some purple drapery recently cast off by Miss Costaine. My suggestions that she absent herself from work until recovered from her disability have been met with good-humoured scorn, and the amount of damage concomitant with the one-handed performance of her duties becomes more alarming daily. Although I have insisted on washing the china after meals, I have been unable to dissuade the good woman from "drying." To date, our dinner service has been depleted by approximately one half. While the broken pieces can be replaced (at some expense) from open stock, it is her illogical reaction to each disaster which tries my patience almost beyond endurance. As she drops and shatters some article, she rocks with laughter and says, "Oops ... There goes another piece of Woolworth's best." How any reasonable adult can derive humour from such calamities is beyond my comprehension.

Mealtimes are fast becoming tension-fraught ordeals because of the overloaded trays which Mrs. Ottey balances on her left hand in defiance of gravitational laws. This morning, at breakfast, Mr. Murke received a poached egg on the shoulder and at luncheon she dropped into my Mother's lap an entire rice pudding. Luckily it was only lukewarm.

During this domestic crisis my dear Maude's assistance has been inestimable. Each day she has devoted several hours to bed-making, linoleum-waxing and other tasks which the smooth running of our household necessitates. The happy willingness with which she performs her self-imposed duties is a joy to behold. Indeed, yesterday, when I entered the kitchen and discovered her ironing our paying guests' personal laundry, I was so affected by her flushed, smiling face that I could not refrain from taking her in my arms and kissing her. My impulsiveness caused her to scorch Mr. Murke's dickey. Fortunately it is reversible.

This afternoon my betrothed decided that our drawing room needed spring cleaning and, in order to be near her, I ensconced myself by the window and set to work polishing my poor Father's sterling silver egg-warmer.* We talked very little but it did not matter, for of all my friends—and I am blessed with many—Maude is the only one with whom I can be alone and at ease without conversation. Among my most treasured memories are evenings spent silently, before a cosy fire at THE NEST, watching her gentle fingers ply crochet hook or knitting needle. Those are the truly peaceful hours: hours when propinquity and wordless communion are all-satisfying: hours which are unknown to those who do not love.

Today, from time to time, we would pause in our industry in order to smile at each other and, whenever Maude passed by me, she would allow her hand to rest momentarily upon my shoulder. The atmosphere was soothing and, because of it, I eschewed the idea of discussing Harrison's kidneys as had been my intention.

*See entry dated February 5th R.H.

Having swept the drugget, my dear one commenced dusting the various *objets d'art* with which our drawing room abounds. In one corner, surmounting the what-not, is a majolica epergne. It contains pampas grass of a delicate ochroid tint which matches the garlands of convolvuli festooning our wallpaper. (The feathery, almost everlasting fronds were given me by Maude in 1932 in order to brighten my convalescence from a deep chest cold.)

Maude dusted these decorative flora with great care and, while so doing, I saw her extract from the epergne a small white object. I could not identify it as my vision was somewhat impaired by the film of jeweller's rouge (used in the polishing of silver), which coated the lenses of my pince-nez. Maude inspected her find and, as she did so, her tuneless humming ceased. Suddenly she rushed across the room, flung her arms about my neck and kissed me with disconcerting fervour. Although surprised by her ebullience, I enjoyed the demonstration of affection to the full. Some seconds later, still clinging to me and with her face hidden in my shirt-front, Maude said, excitedly:

"Oh! Edwin ... Edwin. Are you really going to do it?"

Puzzled, I released her. Her expression was radiant. "Do what, my dear?" I asked quietly.

Maude thrust a small, white pasteboard into my hand. It was Professor Hume's card bearing the name and address of The Journey's End Rest Home. I looked at Maude. Her eyes shone with joy.

"Take that silly look off your face, Edwin Carp," she said, teasingly. "You don't have to pretend, dear. I know you ... and I know what you're up to. You've decided to put your Mother in the Professor's care and you weren't going to tell me until it was all arranged, so that it would be a wonderful surprise."

That Maude could have jumped to so erroneous a conclusion left me speechless. Suddenly her eyes filled with tears and she buried her face in my shoulder. As I held her close to me I could feel her body trembling.

"I'm not really crying, dear," she said, her voice muffled by my coat. "I'm such an old silly. .... Doctor Triggs told me, weeks ago, that he was going to try to persuade you. He says the Professor's a fine man and the old lady will be well taken care of. He told me how you didn't say much when he suggested sending her to the Home ... but he said he felt sure you'd do it because you know it's for the best."

My brain seemed numb and I could think of no way to phrase the facts and not hurt her. I pressed her cheek to mine, whereupon she began to sob. She spoke and it was as though the words were torn from her.

"Oh! My dear . . . After all these years . . . We're going to be together . . . really together. . . . It's been so long . . . so long to wait . . . so lonely."

I held her to me. I felt that I must never let her go for I knew that she was wrong. The years of waiting were not over. There were others ahead for both of us. I wondered how many—how many years were waiting for us to live through them—before we could be together.

And so I stood holding Maude in my arms and did not speak. For I had no words to say.

Gradually Maude's sobs subsided. Releasing herself, she took my handkerchief from my breast pocket.

"We're a fine pair, aren't we?" she said, smiling at me through her tears. "Making fools of ourselves just because we're happy."

With great tenderness she removed my pince-nez and began to dry my eyes. Her ministrations were more that I could bear and, brushing her hand roughly aside, I went to the window and stood looking out. There was silence. An interminable silence which was eventually broken by Maude saying my name. I did not move Maude said it again.

"Edwin . . . Edwin, look at me." Her voice was no longer happy. She sounded afraid. I felt her move toward me and then her hand was on my arm. Slowly she turned me until we faced each other. Her eyes searched mine and, after a moment, her hand fell limply to her side. I opened my mouth, but before I could speak, she said:

"No. Don't say anything, You don't have to say anything, I can see it in your face. Your Mother's not going to the Home . . . you're going to keep her here, aren't you?" Her voice sounded lost and hopeless. I raised my arms but she stepped back, avoiding them and went on talking.

"It's all right, dear. . . . It's my fault. . . . I . . . I made a mistake." She tried to give a little laugh. "Everyone makes mistakes sometimes. Especially when they want . . . when they . . ."

Again the tears welled up in her eyes and, in order to hide them from me, she turned away and commenced polishing my pince-nez. When they were finished to her satisfaction she handed them to me.

"You'd better put these on before you get a headache," she said. To anyone but myself her voice would have sounded normal. She looked round the room.

"I've wasted all this time when I should have been working. I haven't even finished the dusting yet." She looked at me and then quickly away.

"Maude ..." I said, pleadingly. Before I could continue, she said:

"I think, if you don't mind, dear, I'll finish the room tomorrow. . . . I should be getting home now. Harrison'll be back from school and wondering where I am." She took off her apron and walked to the door.

"Maude," I said again. She stopped by the settee with her back to me.

"Maude, please, you must try to understand why I can't send Mother to that place. . . . She's old and ill . . .she needs me."

Maude moved to the door and opened it. She turned and, after looking at me for a long time, she said, very quietly:

"I need you too, Edwin." Then she was gone.

I stood still until the front door opened and closed. Then going to the window, I watched her walking slowly down the garden path, away from me. She disappeared from view and, even when a crash of china and Mrs. Ottey's laugh sounded from the kitchen, I did not move. I continued to look at the long shadows which the afternoon sunlight cast upon the empty street.

March 18th

This afternoon, when I called at THE NEST, Harrison informed me that his mother was suffering from one of her headaches and was resting. I gave him the bunch of anemones which I had purchased for Maude in the High Street. They are the first of the season.

March 19th

Again, today, Maude was resting when I called. I enquired of Harrison if she had left any message for me. She had not. I also enquired if she had liked the flowers. Harrison said he did not know.

March 20th

Mrs. Ottey has broken our best teapot (late Aunt Hester Gubbion's wedding gift to my Mother). I was justifiably annoyed by this disaster and reprimanded Mrs. O. with great severity. I pointed out to her—among other things—that Wedgwood did not grow on trees and the destruction of so valuable a piece was no laughing matter. Although she had the grace to cease her chortling during my harangue, the look she gave me upon its completion was not contrite. It was patronizingly omniscient.

"Something wrong between you and your Maude?" she asked, quizzically.

"The subject is Wedgwood teapots, Mrs. Ottey." I countered, my voice shaking with irritation. She sat down on the stairs and began fingering the tealeaf-moistened fragments of china.

"Have it your own way . . . all I know is that for the last two days you've been like a bear with a sore head," she said and started to sing "Rio Rita." Not daring to trust myself further, I made for the kitchen. As I entered, Mrs. Ottey shouted after me:

"If this was Wedgwood, why did it have 'made in Japan' written on its bottom?"

Miss Costaine is no longer limping.

March 21st

Spring, with that nameless pathos in the air
Which dwells with all things fair,
Spring, with her golden suns and silver rain,
Is with us once again.

Henry Timrod

I am in splendid fettle.

This morning, on his way to school, Harrison brought me a note from my dear Maude. In it she thanked me for the anemones and explained that she had deemed it prudent to remain in retirement for the past few days as certain of her symptoms indicated Spanish Influenza. Her fears were groundless however and luckily she has suffered no more than headache, ear-ache, and clogging of the antrum. She concluded by inviting me to tea.

The missive so delighted me that I gave Harrison pocket money with which to buy Liquorice Allsorts. Although the boy thanked me politely, he seemed troubled and I enquired if anything were amiss. He seemed to gain confidence from my sympathetic tone and, thrusting his face very close to mine, he said:

"Look, Uncle Ed, isn't it awful?"

I inspected the angry pimple on his nose-tip. "That's nothing to worry about old chap," I said, solicitously. "All lads of your age have spots."

"I don't mean my old boil," Harrison said, impatiently. "I mean all this stuff." He brushed his hand angrily through the heavy down which now completely enshrouds his jaw and upper lip.

"Uncle Ed, please talk to Mum, will you? She says I can't shave for a whole year. I'll go mad if I have to wait a whole year." His voice began to mount emotionally. "I've told her I'll kill myself if she doesn't let me shave. But she won't listen. . . . She just laughs." Tears of frustration appeared in the boy's eyes. "She doesn't know what it's like at school. All the boys call me 'Fuzzface'. . . and that old Ursy Monks keeps trying to set it alight with matches. . . . Make Mum let me shave, Uncle Ed. Please . . . please make her."

Harrison was fast becoming hysterical and I placed a calming hand upon his shoulder. Having given him my handkerchief, I waited until he had blown his nose several times before I spoke.

"I'll talk to your mother this afternoon, son. We'll see what can be done."

Relief transformed Harrison's face. "Thanks, Uncle Ed . . . she'll listen to you . . . she's potty about you."

He raced down the garden path. At the gate he turned and shouted:

"Don't tell her about the Liquorice Allsorts, she says they're bad for my pimples." He smiled at me through the rain. The boy has excellent teeth.

As I closed the front door, I caught sight of the hall calendar and realized the cause of my sudden sense of zestful well-being. It was the 21st March—the first day of Spring.

In the verse by Henry Timrod (1829-1867) which prefaces this
entry, there is reference to Spring's "silver rain." Today's downpour—
which began at dawn—has been literally silver, for it contains a high
percentage of sleet. However, I am happy to report that, in spite of
the weather's inclemency, my spirits have remained undampened.

After Harrison's departure, I re-read Maude's note and bounded
up the stairs (two at a time) to compose a poem about the most
invigorating of all four seasons. The first two lines delight me:

> At last the murkey, mournful, months of Winter's
> > moribundity
> Make way before soft Springtime's dancing days of
> > Sweet fecundity. . . .

Unfortunately my over-stimulated condition and the dearth
of words ending with ". . . undity" forced be to abandon my creative effort and, noticing a hiatus in the precipitation, I donned
my galoshes and went out to inspect the back garden. Three green
shoots are to be observed on our laburnum tree, and I am convinced that Mr. Dimmock's White Minorca hen is broody. Her
strident cackle has changed to a low, comforting cluck. When I
reentered the kitchen, Mrs. Ottey was humming Mendelssohn's
"Spring Song" and I remarked, pleasantly:

"Today, marking as it does the advent of the vernal season, your
song is peculiarly apt, Mrs. Ottey."

"Say that again in English," she said.

My mood was impervious to her rudeness and I began explaining
that today was the first day of Spring. As usual, she interrupted me.

"I knew there was somethin' goin' on when your Ma had two
kippers for her breakfast," she said.

As I left the room I was surprised to note that Mrs. O. made
no reference to the muddy tracks I had left on the linoleum. Her
right hand is no longer bandaged.

This afternoon, my departure for THE NEST was delayed by the
arrival of Edgar Frome. He had come to repair the bathroom. With
him was a friend whom he introduced as Mr. Valentine Thrale. Mr.
Thrale's speech is impeded by a stammer so acute that conversation
with him in well nigh impossible, but young Frome assured me that

the gentleman is an expert locksmith. They set to work immediately and I noticed that Mr. Thrale accompanied his labours with an unmusical whistle of high and penetrating frequency. So piercing was this sound that my Mother—for whom I had just installed new batteries—came out of her bedroom twice to ascertain who was playing the ocarina. Her mood was fractious and not until Mrs. Ottey had pacified her by promising kippers for tea was I able to steal away for my assignation with Maude.

Having envisioned a *tête-á-tête* tea with my betrothed, I was somewhat chagrined, on arriving at THE NEST, to find Miss Costaine present. Maude showed no signs of recent indisposition but, from the way she avoided my eye and her over-animated loquacity, it crossed my mind that perhaps because of circumstances of our last meeting, she felt uneasy in my presence. However, imagination plays tricks with the best of us and it could have been Miss Costaine's exciting news which accounted for my dear one's odd manner.

Walter Roach has proposed and my paying guest has accepted. The engagement ring is a chrysoberyl surrounded by diamond splinters and is exceedingly becoming to Miss C.'s patrician hand. She explained, with great verve, that as soon as Mr. Hotchkiss, the jeweler, returns from his holiday at Stonehenge, the inscription will be changed from "Walter & Judith" (Roach's late wife's name was Judith) to "Walter & Miriam." Happiness has done much for Miss Costaine. As I watched her vivaciously expounding on her plans for the future, she looked very little older than Maude. Marriage means fulfillment to every woman. I incorporated this thought in my congratulatory remarks to Miss Costaine. It caused Maude to look directly at me for the first time since I had entered the house. Miss C. eyed us both for a moment and then said:

"Mine host, why don't you and dearest Maude take your vows when Walter and I do—in June?"

There was an awkward pause. Then Maude rose and left the room, saying, "I think I hear the kettle boiling."

As soon as we were alone, Miss Costaine leant toward me and whispered, "Forgive me. I did not realize that dearest Maude was against double weddings. Some people are, you know ... personally, I think they are delicious."

She smiled archly and I noticed that the roots of her hair no longer match the rest of her mahogany coiffeur. Excusing myself, I harried to the kitchen in order to assist Maude with the tea tray. She was arranging hot buttered scones on a dish. I approached her and said:

"My dear, you are a sight for sore eyes."

"Am I? Your eyes don't look very sore to me," she replied coolly and, before I could kiss her as had been my intention, she whisked up the loaded tray and bore it into the drawing room.

During the meal, the ladies kept the ball of conversation in active play. They discussed: Hairnets, High-heeled shoes, Ginger marmalade, and a newly-marketed medicament which prevents chafing. All topics which hold no interest for a mere male. It was not until I had said, "Today is the first day of Spring," for the third time that I was given a hearing. Maude turned to me and said, "What are you chattering about?" I repeated my statement, whereupon Miss Costaine rose and, after striking a graceful pose by the harmonium, recited in cultured accents:

> In the Spring a livelier iris changes on the burnished dove;
> In the Spring a young man's fancy lightly turns to thoughts of Love.

Both Maude and I applauded and I said, "Alfred, Lord Tennyson?"

"Correct, mine host," replied Miss C. and, reseating herself, partook of another buttered scone.

Upon Harrison's return from school, Miss Costaine took her leave and, while Maude was speeding the parting guest in the hall, my stepson-to-be besieged me with feverish questions.

"What did Mum say, Uncle Ed? Can I shave? Did she say she'd let me shave? Is Mum going to let me cut it off . . . is she, Uncle Ed?"

My reply was forestalled by Maude's reappearance. She entered the room saying, "Am I going to let you cut what off Harrison dear?"

Harrison's eyes went from me to his mother and back again. "Haven't you told her yet, Uncle Ed? But you promised . . . you promised you'd make her let me shave."

For the second time today Maude looked directly at me. Her expression was implacable. She spoke and although her words were addressed to her son, her eyes never left mine.

"Harrison. I am telling you for the last time. I will allow you to shave when you are fifteen years old and not one minute sooner. Nothing you—or anyone else—may say will alter my decision. That is final."

Sobbing with temper, Harrison fled from the room, slamming the door with such violence that his father's picture was dislodged from the wall. In spite of its clattering impact with the floor, Maude and I remained facing each other—our gazes locked. We stood thus until Harrison's bedroom door closed noisily above us and his bed creaked as he flung himself upon it.

I considered Maude's edict unreasonable and I found myself infuriated by her stubborn expression. Somehow I kept my emotions in check, for instinct warned me that much depended on the outcome of this clash of wills.

With great deliberation I withdrew from my pockets shaving soap, shaving brush, a Gillette razor and one of the double-edged blades which Harket had presented to me on my birthday. I arranged them carefully on the tea table next to the quince preserve. As Maude watched my actions the pink of her neck deepened to crimson and, with menacing incredulity, she said:

"Are you defying me, Edwin Carp?"

"Of course not, my dear," I replied quietly. "These are merely the instruments with which Harrison will shave—Not when he is fifteen, *but before I leave this house today.*"

Maude drew a gasping breath of amazement and, having sat down heavily, burst into tears.

"How dare you try to make a fool of me before my own son," she wailed. The handkerchief I proffered was snatched from my hand. When the first flood of her lachrymose rage abated, I said:

"No mother is a fool to her son, my dear, you know that perfectly well. But has it occurred to you that by making him the laughing stock of his playmates you are risking the loss of his regard for you?" Still sniffling, Maude raised reddened eyes to mine. With well-modulated firmness I continued: "Harrison will shave *today;*

but if he knows it is with your permission he will realize that you
understand his problem and want him to be happy."

Maude dabbed at her eyes for a moment. Then in more flexible
tone, she said:

"But he's such a baby to start shaving."

"Babies grow up, my dear," I said. "Remember, too, the boy
comes of hirsute stock."

"What kind of stock?" asked Maude, sniffling.

"Hairy," I replied. "I seem to recall you telling me that his father
had quite a noticeable moustache at the age of twelve."

Breathing with the shuddering gasps which always follow a
bout of weeping, Maude crossed the room and picked up Fred
Phelps's picture from the floor (the glass was unbroken". She looked
down at it and sighed. "Poor Fred . . . he never wore an undervest.
He used to say that God had given him one." Having re-hung the
picture, she turned and gave me a wan smile. "All right, Edwin, you
win. Harrison can shave . . . but you tell him. I couldn't bear to face
him after all I've said about it."

"No, Maude, you must tell him. And please, dear, don't say that
I have won. Nobody has won. You must not think of it in that way.
We have both agreed to let Harrison have his wish—that is all."

Maude came close to me. "Edwin Carp, when you make up your
mind about something, you can be as stubborn as a mule," she said
and in her voice was something very close to admiration

"I don't mean to be stubborn, my dear. It's just that I want my
son to be happy," I replied.

Maude looked down at the tear-stained handkerchief. "He's not
your son—yet," she said in a low voice.

"But he will be one day, won't he?" I said. Maude was silent.
"Won't he?" I reiterated and to my dismay I heard a note of plead-
ing in my voice. Instead of answering, Maude kissed me gently on
the mouth.

Apart from splashing shaving soap in the boy's left eye, my bar-
bering of Harrison was highly successful and his gratitude warmed
my heart. As a final touch I massaged a few drops of Maude's *Nuit
d'Amour* into his gleaming chin. When I had finished, Harrison
proceeded to gather together the lather-sodden fuzz I had removed
from his face and place it in a paper bag. I enquired his reason for

doing this. "I'm going to take it to school tomorrow and stuff it down that old Ursy Monks' neck," he replied with relish. I refrained from comment.

When Maude returned from her walk in the sleet (she had been too nervous to remain in the house during the operation), Harrison did as I had bidden and thanked her for allowing him to shave. I am certain that his sincerity was genuine and there followed a moment between mother and son which I found most touching.

My understanding of the boy is gradually increasing and I am convinced that, it time, we shall become true friends.

During the remainder of my visit Maude was very dear and feminine and, when Harrison had departed to study his lessons, she graciously admitted that I had been right in over-ruling her. She also claimed that my handiwork made her son look younger. Had she said that he looked cleaner I could have agree, but I let her comment pass and, in order to change the subject, enfolded her in my arms.

Later, as I walked happily homeward pondering on my feelings for Maude, I recalled the poem which Miss Costaine had recited so effectively during tea. Loathe as I am to quibble with a Poet Laureate, I cannot help feeling that if Alfred, Lord Tennyson had understood the mentality of "Middle Age" as fully as he did that of "Youth," he would have thought twice before handing down to Posterity a line such as:

In the Spring a *young* man's fancy lightly turns to thoughts of Love.

The smoothness with which Edgar Frome has refilled the gouges in the bathroom walls and ceiling shows marked improvement in his technique, and were the colour to match (unfortunately the lad is colour-blind), the repairs would be imperceptible. His locksmith friend, Mr. Thrale, found it necessary to install a new lock on the door. To circumvent future bathroom disasters, I have ordered an extra key to be cut. I shall secrete It behind the reproduction of Sir Edwin Landseer's famous painting "Fighting Dogs Getting Wind" which hangs above the staircase.

March 22nd

A beautifully printed card from my good friend Joseph Harket, requesting the presence of Maude and myself at a party on the 26th inst., to celebrate the official proclamation of his daughter's engagement to our milkman—Terence Blythe.

Accompanying the invitation was a tube of adhesive for my toupee.

March 24th

Providentially, I was first in the bathroom this morning, for, as I performed my ablutions, a pitiful squeaking drew my attention to the box-trap. It was occupied by a small and very perturbed rodent. The blunt snout, short tail and inconspicuous ears enabled me to identify it—tentatively—as a Field Vole or Dormouse (*Microtus agreatis*). Its state of terror disturbed me and I decided to test the theory that certain of our dumb friends are responsive to music. My singing of "Less Than the Dust" had little effect. In fact, when I reached the line, "Less than the rust that never stained thy sword," the little creature's distress appeared to increase. I tried whistling softly. This produced a much more gratifying reaction and, by the time I had finished one verse of "Onaway, Awake Beloved!" the vole was completely calm (almost comatose). It revived slightly while I was trimming my moustache and I was amazed at the bright interest with which its tiny eyes watched my every movement. I continued my toilet, pondering on the most humane method of disposal. My first thought was to release it in the garden, but I eschewed this plan because of the mousing propensity of Mr. Dimmock's cat, Sylvia. It was a ticklish problem and not until I had cleaned my teeth and was gargling did a solution present itself.

Because of an altercation with Mrs. Ottey—resulting from my refusal to tell her what purpose I needed a morsel of cheese-rind—it was 9:32 A.M. before I left the house and, with the trap and its occupant in a paper bag, headed for the reservoir—on the banks of which I intended to give my rodent captive its small freedom. The day was crystal clear and although a blustering March wind necessitated my keeping a firm grip on both hat and pince-nez (no easy task when burdened with umbrella and paper bag), the exercise was invigorating. My route led through Rottingdean Crescent and, as I came abreast of Doctor Triggs' residence (number fifty-seven. Consulting Hours 9-11 A.M.), two thoughts came to mind: both of them so inspirational that I leant against the front gate, amazed at my perspicacity.

I realized (a) that what my Mother had seen in the bathroom was no hallucination, but a real live dormouse (or vole); (b) that exhibition of the captive to the good Doctor would prove, irrefutably, how faulty was his diagnosis of my parent's mental condition.

I entered the waiting room. Save for a neatly dressed little girl of perhaps six or seven years, it was unoccupied. I seated myself, whereupon the child slid off her chair and, having clambered upon another on the opposite side of the room, regarded me with unblinking and disconcerting intensity. Not wishing to be out-stared by one so young, I returned her gaze. Some forty-five seconds later, dryness of the optic vesicle forced me to blink and the little girl said:

"I won."

I decided to ignore the incident and, picking up a copy of The Lancet, began to peruse an article on "The Structural Changes in Nerve Endings Caused by Beri-Beri." I had barely read the first line when a piping voice said:

"Is your mother as fat as my mother?"

Feigning deafness I concentrated on the magazine. I heard the child slither from her seat and, after a moment, a small hand was placed on my knee. I looked up into white-lashed, pale blue eyes. The face was heavily freckled and, from the mouth, two upper central incisors were missing.

"I'm going to have a baby brother. Are you going to have a baby brother?" the child said. Because of the missing teeth, her speech was accompanied by a fine spray. Leaning back in order to avoid this, I replied, "Not to my knowledge."

"Where's your mother?" she asked.

"At home," I answered.

Pointing at the consulting room door, through which the rumble of Doctor Triggs' voice could be heard, the child said, "Mine's in there." She then grabbed the paper bag from my lap, held it to her ear and shook it vigorously. "What's in here?" she enquired.

"A present for the Doctor," I said and, after a slight tussle, managed to retrieve my property.

"What sort of present?"

I smiled indulgently and said, "You're full of questions, aren't you little girl?"

"What's the bag full of?" my young inquisitor demanded.

The cross-examination was fast becoming wearisome and, in order to halt it, I looked at her sternly. To my relief she returned to her chair and I resumed my perusal of The lancet. I had just finished reading that Beri-Beri can be induced by a diet of rice from which the entire pericarp and germ have been removed, when my attention was distracted by a raling intake of breath. I looked at the little girl. Her face was bright vermilion and strangely contorted.

"if you don't tell me what's in the bag I'll hold my breath until I suffocate," she said and inhaled with determination.

"A field vole," I replied instantly.

After a noisy exhalation, the child's expression changed to one of complacent triumph.

"I won again," she said. "Is the present in a bottle?"

"No, little girl, it is not," I replied patiently.

"Then the Doctor won't like it," she said with great finality and pulling her right leg up on to the seat, she commenced licking her knee. "Do your knees taste salty?" she enquired.

The onus of replying to such a question was removed by the emergence from the consulting room of Doctor Triggs and a lady. From the latter's white eyelashes, I knew that she was the child's mother and from her *embonpoint* it was evident that the stork was fast approaching journey's end.

"Stop sucking your knees, Portia, they're chapped enough already," the lady said to the little girl.

Doctor Triggs greeted me with a cheery "Good morning, my boy," and gestured toward the consulting room. I went in. Through the open door I heard the lady say:

"I'll rest a moment, if I may, Doctor. What you've just told me's rather a shock."

"Of course, Mrs. Small. Take your time," replied Doctor T.

"You couldn't have made a mistake . . . could you?" asked the lady.

Although the good Doctor lowered his voice, his answer was clearly audible. "There are two distinct heartbeats, Mrs. Small. . . . That means only one thing."

"Blimey! When Bert hears this he'll have a blue fit," said the lady.

Some muffled dialogue ensued which I could not catch and, a moment later, Doctor Triggs joined me and closed the door. While he washed his hands I explained that my visit was social rather than professional. He expressed his delight and, seating himself on the opposite side of the desk, enquired as to my Mother's health.

I cleared my throat. "Please do not think, Doctor, that what I am about to show you is in any way a criticism of your diagnosis, but Mother is in far better health than you have led me to believe," I said. The Doctor's look of affability gave way to one of puzzlement. Placing the paper bag before him, I continued, "In front of you is proof positive that what Mother saw in the bathroom was no hallucination." The good Doctor looked down at the paper bag. Without shifting my gaze from his countenance, I deftly tilted the bag and allowed the box-trap to slide out. There was another pause; then Doctor T. looked up at me and said, quietly, "I'm afraid I don't understand."

"but surely, Doctor, it is quite obvious that . . ." My sentence was never completed, for I looked at the trap and saw, to my consternation, that it was empty. A hasty examination of the paper bag failed to reveal any trace of the vole and I looked at the good Doctor, aghast.

"But it was there . . . I caught it," I said.

Doctor Triggs rose, rounded the desk, and patted my shoulder comfortingly. "Now . . . now, my boy, don't upset yourself. You've had a lot on your mind lately." But it was in the trap, Doctor. . . . A Field Vole . . . A Dormouse," I expostulated.

Doctor T. began to pat my shoulder more rapidly. "I'm sure it was, my boy. Now be calm. . . try to be calm," he said, with the same soothing inflection he employed when coaxing my Mother out of an "attack." The situation was ludicrous and I attempted a nonchalant laugh. The result was unsatisfactory. Doctor Triggs looked at me long and searchingly.

"How have you been sleeping lately?" he asked and in his eyes was a look of deep concern.

Indignation seized me and, shrugging his hand brusquely from my shoulder, I rose. "Are you suggesting, Doctor, that I imagined the Field Vole?" I said with dignity and far more volume than I had intended. Doctor Triggs backed nervously away. Not until the desk was between us and he had mopped his brow did he speak.

"Everything will be all right, Edwin," he said hurriedly and without conviction. "It's . . . it's your nerves. You're run down, my boy—that's all." He wiped his forehead again and began rummaging feverishly in his desk drawer. "I have a little bromide prescription somewhere here that'll do the trick. . . . If you take it regularly and keep away from highly seasoned food, you'll be as good as new in . . ."

A piercing shriek from the waiting room halted his words and gestures. For a second the good Doctor seemed as incapable of movement as I. Then, leaping from his chair, he rushed across the room, muttering, "Mrs. Small . . . But it's not possible. They're not due for a week."

As he entered the waiting room the street door crashed shut. Following cautiously, I looked over his shoulder. The room was empty. Doctor T. seemed dazed.

"Now what do you suppose made that silly woman scream like that?" he said, addressing no one in particular. I looked about me. On the north wall my eye lit upon the explanation of the hubbub. I directed Doctor Triggs' attention to his diploma which hangs above the fireplace. For atop its frame, my dormouse peered down at us with bright eyes an quivering whiskers.

"it must have escaped when the little girl shook the bag," I said.

Only a rudimentary knowledge of etiquette is necessary to realize that—in view of having doubted my word regarding the existence of the dormouse (or vole)—Doctor Triggs owed me an apology. From the way he spluttered, I assumed that he was having difficulty expressing himself. I waited patiently, for it was my intention to accept his words of penitence calmly and benignantly—as a gentleman should. To my surprise none was vouchsafed. Instead he strode to the doorway of his consulting room and, standing framed therein, turned upon me a face of rage. Explosive sounds issued from him and, from the phrases which interspersed them, I learned that he considered me an even greater fool than he had hitherto, that no one but an imbecile would bring vermin into a doctor's waiting room and that should Mrs. Small suffer a miscarriage because of my Field Vole, he would derive great pleasure from having me hung, drawn and quartered. Then the box-trap was flung at my feet and, having commanded me to catch the "germ-laden pest" and leave the building, Doctor Triggs slammed the door in my face.

To one as ripe in years as the good Doctor (he is seventy-one, but looks older), unbridled passion can be deleterious to health. As I stood before the closed door, the thought that my life-long mentor's outburst had, in all probability, jeopardized his longevity, filled me with sadness and several minutes passed before I turned my attention to recapturing the tiny creature which, unwittingly, had been its cause.

The rodent had abandoned its perch on the diploma and not until I had looked up the chimney and moved all the chairs did I sight it. It was entering a greatly enlarged and highly coloured plaster model of a human ear which graces the mantelpiece. A swift, agile leap carried me across the room but, unfortunately, the rattle of my umbrella entangling with the hat-stand scared my prey. By the time I had picked myself up and inspected my right elbow (quite a nasty graze), the vole had scampered inside the model and was peering at me from the inaccessible depths of the Eustachian Tube. Placing the box-trap flush with the only means of egress—viz., the External Auditory Meatus (or outer orifice), I tilted the model slowly. The vole seemed loathe to leave its sanctuary and only by jiggling the plaster ear with great force was I able to persuade it to enter the trap.

Success came not a moment too soon. Hardly was my captive secured that the street door was flung open an a Bath chair containing a white-haired, choleric-looking gentleman was wheeled awkwardly into the waiting room by a young woman in tweeds.

"Stop bumping me about, girl. You'll shake me to bits," shouted the old man, irascibly.

"I'm sorry, Father. I couldn't help it. That's such a high step," answered the young woman, meekly. Anxious as I was to depart, the Bath chair athwart the doorway blocked my path.

"Where did you put my kidney stone?" shouted the old man.

His daughter threw a glance in my direction and blushed. Then, whispering, she said:

"It's where you told me to put it, Father. In your waistcoat pocket, wrapped in tissue paper."

The old gentleman fumbled with his apparel and withdrew something which he examined with a gloating satisfaction.

"What time did I pass it?" he shouted.

"Father . . . Please! Not so loud," implored his daughter and, having maneuvered the chair away from the door, she added—*sotto voce*—"Three-fifteen this morning."

Avoiding her eye, I exited. As the door closed behind me the old man shouted:

"Wait till that damned old fool, Triggs, sees this. I've been telling him for months it wasn't my gall-bladder."

As I walked to the reservoir, I ruminated on the foregoing conversation and was further saddened, for it implied that the good Doctor had made another diagnostic blunder. While reconciling myself to the fact that my old friend's brilliant brain was beginning to show signs of Time's tarnish, I recalled the lines composed by Francis Turner Palgrave, between 1825 and 1897:

> Time's corrosive dewdrop eats
> The giant warrior to a crust
> Of earth in earth and rust in rust.

A dank drizzle was falling when I reached the reservoir. Placing the trap gently on the greensward, I opened it. The sight of so large a body of water appeared to intimidate the vole and almost a minute elapsed before it ventured forth. Freedom bewildered the little creature, for its first darting scamper caused I to bump into a rusty tin can which had once contained Bartlett Pears. Orientation soon took place however and, scurrying between the clumps of Bird's-foot Trefoil and Bog Asphodel, my erstwhile captive disappeared from view beneath a discarded inner tube. It did not look back once.

March 25ᵗʰ

Because of my interest in the constellation of Orion, I am suffering from an inflammation of the left tonsil which, I fear, presages quinsy. I am also intensely perturbed: not by my indisposition (I have an iron constitution), but by the circumstance which occasioned it.

Last evening, while reading to my Mother from *Old More's Almanack* (kindly loaned by Mrs. Ottey), I learned that, at midnight, the aforementioned star group would be only eleven hundred and eighty-two light years away from Earth, instead of its customary twelve hundred. The thought of getting a good look at Betelgeuse, Bellatrix, Rigel and Orionis filled me with joyous anticipation and, having taken the liberty of borrowing Miss Costaine's opera glasses (she was at Folk Dancing Class with W.R.), I set my alarm and retired at 8:30 P.M.

My hearty supper of boiled beef, carrots, and suet pudding caused me to sleep heavily and, when my trusty timepiece aroused me at 11:45 P.M., I had some difficulty in avoiding a return to the arms of Morpheus. Yeas of self-discipline stood me in good stead however and, at 11:51 P.M., I crawled from my couch.

So bemused was my brain and so dark the night that, having flung open the window, I wasted precious moments peering skyward before remembering that my room commands only a view of Mr. Dimmock's chimney stack. With the return of lucidity, I realized that the one room in the house from which the eastern firmament can be seen to advantage is Mr. Murke's. I crossed the landing noiselessly, but, even as I did so, a loud hiccough from behind my paying guest's door informed me that he had retired. I stood in the darkness, cogitating. The idea of going into the garden presented itself, but prudence warned that lengthy dalliance in the night air would be foolhardy. I was nonplused—but only momentarily, for I am not an easy man to thwart. Returning to my bedroom, I dressed hastily—suit over pyjamas and galoshes over bedsocks. Then, taking a latchkey from my stud-box, I crept down the stairs—into my hat and coat—and out of the house. A few brisk steps carried me to DUN ROVIN and as I turned the key, the distant chimes of St. Jude's struck twelve. The door swung back slowly and there ran through me that shiver of excitement which the venturesome always feel when standing upon the threshold of an unoccupied house at the witching hour.

More than two weeks have elapsed since Mrs. Luby's departure. Consequently, the air which assailed my nostrils when I entered DUN ROVIN was stale. In spite of its mustiness, my acute olfaction detected the lingering scent of my erstwhile tenant's face-powder and I wondered how the poor creature was faring at the seaside with her friend, Ruby.

Deeming it wiser not to use the electric light, I struck a wax vesta (although a non-smoker, experience has taught me never to be without several) and commenced a groping ascent of the stairs. Halfway up, the tiny flame expired. Simultaneously, something dank and furry enveloped my face. The sensation was eerie and not until I had rushed downstairs and out into the front garden did I discover that its cause had been a huge, but harmless, cobweb. Chiding myself for being so imaginative, I reentered DUN ROVIN and re-mounted the stairs whistling "The Kashmiri Song." The second ascent was without incident and entering the spare bedroom, I felt my way to the window which, I knew, commanded an uninterrupted vista of Heaven's vault. Disuse and congealed paint made the sash immovable. Having cleaned a portion of the window-pane with breath and the end of my muffler, I felt in my overcoat pocket. It was empty and I realized that Miss Costaine's opera glasses were still on the mantelpiece in my bedroom, next to the photograph of Maude dressed as Britannia. Risking optical strain, I peered through the window until my eye-balls became quite warm. But in vain. The constellation of Orion was indistinguishable, as was the warehouse wall opposite, which, in twenty-foot letters, advertises Carter's Little Liver Pills.

Myopia is a curse indeed.

Nothing remained but for me to return home and, acutely disappointed, I left the window. The darkness was stygian. My supply of vestas being exhausted, the descent to the lower floor was fraught with frequent and painful shin-barking and when, finally, I bumped into the hat-rack in the hall, I was chilled to the bone and somewhat tense. While groping for the front door, I heard the distant chug-chug of an automobile. Because of my attire, I decided to wait until it had passed before emerging. It drew nearer and, to my consternation, halted outside the house. Car doors opened and slammed shut. The front gate squeaked. Someone giggled and a voice I had hoped never to hear again said, "You're the spitting image of John Boles, you really are. . . . I can't think why you have to drive a taxi." There was a masculine grunt and the sound of a match striking. Flickering light illumined the frosted panes in the front door and two silhouettes appeared. As a key was fumblingly inserted in the lock, I fled toward the kitchen. Knowing that my only means of escape was via the garden and back alley, I flung myself through the door and managed to close it just as footsteps sounded in the hall. A line of brightness fell upon my galoshes. Mrs. Luby had switched on the light. With my back to the door, I cautiously stretched my arms before me. My fingers touched a wall, I groped to my left and right . . . more walls . . . and a faint odour of gas. As Mrs. Luby's voice said, "Just put dear old Dot's suitcase in the front room, there's a duck," I realized that I was not in the kitchen, but in the large cupboard beneath the stairs which houses both gas and electricity meters.

Although I bit the back of my hand quite severely, I did not give way to panic as most men in my predicament would have done. In an attempt to stop the violent trembling that shook me, I inhaled deeply—the gas fumes seemed stronger—and sat down on the meter. Its metal protuberances did not make for comfort and, after a moment, I sat on the floor. As I tried to relax, Logic whispered that Mrs. Luby would surely retire soon and that if escape was to be effected, Self Control and Patience on my part were essential. Also, that if my hiding place was discovered, such disaster must be met with Fortitude and nerves of steel.

The voices in the hall grew louder. An argument regarding the amount of the fare was in progress. Following the taxi-driver's refusal to accept my tenant's cheque, she said, "Now, now, Handsome, don't be unkind to poor old Dot . . . money's not everything, y'know." There was a long silence; then a grunt and a giggle. Then the sound of a slap and my tenant said, "Don't be rough, Handsome . . . I bruise easy." Then as the faraway chimes of St Jude's struck one a male voice said, "D'you rally think I look like John Boles?"

My pen balks at describing in detail what ensued. Suffice to say that Mrs. Luby entertained her guest until 3:30 A.M. After his departure, I allowed thirty minutes to elapse before emerging from the cupboard, but, although I made good my escape, my cramp-tortured limbs retarded my return home and I did not enter my bedroom until 4:33 A.M. Sleep was, of course, impossible. As well as being nauseated by gas and memories of my experience, my throat ached and I was stricken with paroxysms of sneezing. Foreboding plagued me when I conjectured what might happen now that Mrs. Luby was once again in residence. What steps would Inspector Coggins take? What should I do?

The hours until dawn dragged slowly by. Finally, I ceased pacing and attempted to quiet my mental turbulence with the *Encyclopaedia Britannica* (usually a sure soporific). It was futile. Perusal of Volume 14 (LIBI to MARY) did nothing but prove to me how foredoomed had been my hope of examining Orion. I discovered that:

One Light Year is equivalent to six million million miles.

The constellation is, approximately, twelve hundred Light Years distant from Earth.

$$6,000,000,000,000 \times 1,200 = 7,200,000,000,000,000 \text{ MILES}$$

Ergo: Even with normal eyesight and a clean window, I would have seen very little.

March 27th

High fever prevented me from recording yesterday's happenings, the first of which was a vigorous pounding on my door at 9:32 A.M. It was followed by Mrs. Ottey's voice peremptorily informing me that my egg was on the table and that unless I wanted it stone cold, I had better get a move on. The condition of my tonsil precluded reply and I think I must have moaned for, thrusting her head into the room, Mrs. O. scrutinized me for a moment and said, "You look like a dying duck in a thunderstorm. What's the matter . . . go the pip?" Sensing flippancy in her solicitude (Pip is a contagious disease of birds—especially poultry), I turned my face to the wall. When next I awakened the hall clock was striking eleven and, opening my eyes, I beheld my Mother weeping at the foot of the bed. Despite my throbbing throat, I enquired what was amiss. As I did so, Mrs. Ottey entered bearing hot milk. She switched off my Mother's hearing aid and said, cheerfully, "It's your face. She says you look like your Dad used to on the morning after the night before." My Mother left the room and, proffering the milk, Mrs. O. continued, "Come on now. Get this down you and stop feeling sorry for yourself." Unfortunately she released the glass a split second before I grasped it.

My Mother's time-worn remedy for burns is castor oil with white of egg. By the time I returned from the bathroom, having applied this mixture to my abdomen (hot milk scalds badly), Mrs. Ottey was changing the sheets singing, "I've Got You Under My Skin." She made no haste at her work and, as I waited on the chill linoleum hugging about me my dressing gown and pyjamas (the cords of both untied for obvious reasons), I marveled at the insensitivity which caused her to delay an invalid's return to the sick-bed. The fatuous words of her song irked me and when, during its third rendering, she reached the passage—

> Don't you know, little fool, you never can win.
> Use your Mentality.
> Wake up to Reality.

my nerves were a jangle. Only the fact that she exited saved her from a homily on dilatoriness.

At noon, Maude came to see me. My ill health caused her great concern (I did not mention my burn) and she asked if I would mind her examining my throat. Although I demurred, she had her way. She made me say "Aaaah" and peered into my mouth for quite a while. When I asked what she thought, she evaded the issue by saying that I should make an appointment with Mr. Merrihew as one of my wisdom teeth "looked funny."

Luckily, I have a clinical thermometer (won by Mr. Murke at a Masonic Whist Drive for being booby) and with the aid of this useful device, Maude took my temperature. It was 99.9 degrees. After putting Eau de Cologne on my temples, she sat stroking my forehead with cool hands. The proximity of my dear one never fails to bring me peace and, slowly, the horrors of DUN ROVIN faded from mind.

I was awakened two hours later by sharp prodding. Mrs. Ottey stood by the bed, holding a laden tray and rocking with laughter. "You look real gruesome, without your glasses," she chortled. "Come on now. Upsadaisy and have a nice snack." Sitting up was quite an effort and I was surprised to see with what care Mrs. O. arranged extra pillows at my back. Placing the tray before me, she said, "You'll be as right as rain when you get some of this lovely stewed tripe inside you. . . . I made it 'specially watery so's it'd slip down easy." Having told me that Maude would be returning later for tea, the good woman departed. I gazed down at the steaming bowl.

Even when I am in rude health, tripe has a viscosity which I find unappetizing. That it is nutritious I will not deny and, for this reason, I consumes a certain quantity. As I placed the tray aside, Doctor Triggs entered. Remembering our last encounter, I was surprised at the affability of his greeting. He diagnosed my swollen tonsil as laryngitic edema and painted it with glycerin and tannin. Because of his age, the good Doctor's hand is not as steady as could be wished and, during the operation, my uvula, soft palate, tongue—et al.— became coated with the ill tasting concoction. So astringent was its action that my entire mouth puckered. This temporarily affected my speech and when I bared my scalded abdomen to Doctor T., my explanation of the accident afforded him great amusement. The humour of the situation escaped me. My old friend proceeded to paint the epidermis in question with picric acid, thereby changing its hue from angry rose to saffron yellow. Then, with eyes a twinkle, he asked if anything else needed painting. Ill health makes one's reactions difficult to disguise and, seeing my look of reproach, the good Doctor sat down on the bed.

"You mustn't mind an old man's jokes, my boy. I was only trying to cheer you up," he said, kindly. I did not reply and he continued, "Edwin, I hope you have forgiven me for my outburst the other day." I assured him that I bore no rancour and enquired as to Mrs. Small's welfare. Doctor T.'s shoulders sagged slightly and, avoiding my eyes, he said, casually, "Mrs. Small is no longer in my care. Doctor White is attending her."

A feeling of guilt swept through me and I began apologizing for having lost him a patient. He interrupted me. "It wasn't your fault, my boy," he said.

Greatly disturbed, I replied, "But it was, Doctor, and you know it." Once again I attempted to express my regret. Unfortunately, my debilitated state gave my voice an over-emotional ring. A firm hand on my shoulder halted my spate of words and Doctor Triggs said:

"Edwin, you must not upset yourself. You must believe me when I say that you are not to blame."

More calmly, I said, "Doctor, you know that is not true. I insist on seeing Mrs. Small and telling her exactly what happened."

The good man rose and repacked his bag in silence. Then he sighed and said:

"Edwin, I have been a doctor for forty-seven years. I am a good doctor. And yet, in the last six months, nine other patients besides Mrs. Small have left me and gone to Doctor White. Do you know why?"

I shook my head. Doctor Triggs walked slowly to the window and stood looking at the overcast sky. Then, with his back to me, he said, "Doctor White is thirty-five years old. Next month I shall be seventy-three." There was a long pause. Returning to the bed, he picked up his bag, squared his shoulders and went to the door. He turned and smiled at me affectionately.

"Keep yourself warm, my boy. . . . I'll drop in tomorrow."

Before I could speak, he left the room.

The second post brought a letter from the Treasurer of our Society of Health through Sanitation. It read:

Dear Carp,

As you know, I own two houses on the river at Gravesend. Through Certain sources I hear that they are to be condemned. Through other sources I have discovered that the Sewage Commission intends to erect a Horizontal Agitator Type Activated Sludge Channel on this site of these desirable residences.

What good is The Rivers Pollution Act if I am to me made the victim of political corruption? You are the President of our Society and, if you are worth your salt, you will take immediate steps to

prevent the confiscation of my property. Let me know when you
have done so.

Yours truly,
Claud Tisdale

The imperious tone of the letter displeased me. Also, Tisdale
seems to have overlooked two important facts:

(1) Gravesend is served by a different Borough Council and is,
therefore, outside of our Society.
(2) Even though our Society has existed for thirty-four years,
Civic Authority's lack of recognition robs it of all power.

I shall of course commiserate with Tisdale at our next Committee
Meeting, but other than requesting Miss Throbbitt to make a tran-
scription of his letter in our Minute Book, there is little I can do.

The hour before tea-time was interminable. As I lay sneezing
in bed, the rapidity with which my pores opened and closed filled
me with alarm. Baths of perspiration alternated with ague-like paroxysms and when Maude entered—bearing a pound of grapes, two
oranges, and the tea-tray—I was too enfeebled to do more than
smile bravely. She took my temperature. Mr. Murke's thermometer
is, obviously, worn out, for it registered a mere 99.8 degrees. When
I told Maude that if I recovered I would invest in a new one, her
expression puzzled me. A comforting word would have meant much
to me at that moment, but my betrothed seemed averse to conversation and began to pour tea. As I watched her plump, capable fingers
flit from cup to pot to strainer, my depression deepened and my
fever rose. Moisture bedewed my brow. I started to pant. Maude
looked at me, put down the teapot, and examined the bed-clothes.
   "One—two—three blankets," she counted, "and an eiderdown.
Who wouldn't be hot? It's a wonder you're not parboiled—and why
have you got your muffler on?" Whipping the latter from my neck,
she removed the eiderdown and handed me my tea.
   In order to conserve my fast-ebbing strength, I forced myself to
dispose of the steaming brew, together with a salmon paste sandwich, two portions of Swiss Roll, and an orange. A bout of shivering

seized me as I held out my moustache-cup to be refilled, causing it to rattle violently in the saucer. Maude looked up from her bath-bun and eyed me dispassionately for some seconds before relieving me of the chinaware. I huddled down between the sheets.

"Maude," I said. Because of emotional and tonsillitic strain, my voice rasped dissonantly. "Maude—if anything should happen—I just want you to know that these past nine years—"

To my amazement, Maude interrupted by handing me my tea and saying, brusquely, "See if it's sweet enough."

Ignoring the cup, I closed my eyes and said, weakly, "Maude—before it's too late, I want you to know that—"

Again Maude interrupted. "Edwin," she said, sharply, and rose to her feet. The movement was accompanied by an ominous rustling of skirts which I knew, from past experience, denoted exasperation. I did not open my eyes and my betrothed continued.

"Now look here, Edwin. I've talked to Doctor Triggs. He says there's nothing the matter with you but a sore throat and a bit of a cold—that's all—nothing else. But if you think I'm going to stay here and be made a fool of while you do all this death-bed rubbish, you're very much mistaken.—It's no use you lying there with your eyes shut trying to look like a corpse. You men are all alike—you're a lot of babies. The moment you get a toe-ache, you start inviting people to the funeral."

Maude's nature is basically tender. Therefore, convinced that my parlous condition would ultimately evoke sympathy in her, I lay motionless with eyes closed. I waited—yearning for the gentle touch and compassionate voice which heal more surely than all the nostrums known to man. Gradually, the skirt-rustling subsided and I heard Maude begin to breathe with the tremulousness which, invariably, preludes weeping. When at last she spoke, her words—although tearful—were disappointing.

"And you're selfish, Edwin Carp—you're selfish to the core. Not once today have you asked me why I've got my thumb bandaged, or how I squashed it." Her sobs receded and were silenced by the door closing.

I opened my eyes and saw that I was alone.

At supper time, Mrs. Ottey's attempts to foist further tripe upon me were futile. My adamance was rewarded with a bowl of nourishing ox-tail soup and dumplings. I dislike being watched while eating, but Mrs. O. ignored my hints and, having placed the tray on my lap, stood by the bed caroling "Clap Hands, Here Comes Charlie." From her gaiety I sensed that she had tidings of a cataclysmic nature to impart. Mrs. Ottey is not one to miss an opportunity for dramatic effect and while bidding her time—awaiting the moment when divulgence of her news would wreak the greatest havoc—she consumed several clusters of my grapes. I could feel her watching my every gesture and, as I proceeded with the meal, apprehension grew.

I had just inserted a large piece of hot dumpling in my mouth, when suddenly she said:

"Dot Luby's back."

Serenely, I continued to munch my dumpling with no break in masticatory rhythm. That my aplomb galled Mrs. O. was obvious from the testy inflection of her next remark.

"I said Dot Luby's back. Have you been struck deaf?"

I regarded her coolly, savouring my dumpling and her chagrin to the full. Having assimilated the former, I said, "I appreciate your solicitude, Mrs. Ottey, but my hearing is in no way impaired."

Mrs. Ottey regarded me with amazement. "But aren't you surprised about old Dot's turning up again?"

I put down my soup-spoon and, after a leisurely sip of cocoa, said, "Mrs. Ottey, when one has seen as much of Life as I have—it holds few surprises."

Mrs. O. studied me speculatively and helped herself to more grapes. "Oh well—in that case you won't be surprised when it strikes, will you?" she said casually and put two grapes in her mouth at once. The wily gleam in her eye disturbed me.

"When what strikes?" I asked.

"Disaster," she replied, complacently. "I turned up the three of clubs six times today. That means Disaster will strike within three hours, three days, or three weeks." Daintily, she expectorated a grape seed into her hand. "Let's hope it won't be something as terrible as what happened to old Dot's friend, Ruby. . . . That's why old Dot had to come home. . . ." Mrs. Ottey paused, scanning my face for a reaction. Knowing that she would curtail her revelation the moment I evinced interest, I lowered my eyes and contemplated the ox vertebrae, which rose from the soup like spiked rocks from a dun-coloured sea. My subterfuge succeeded and Mrs. O. continued.

"Old Dot told me this mornin' it was a put-up job. She said her friend Ruby had no way of knowin' the man was a detective—He told her he was a Member of Parliament and as he talked nice and had an attaché case, Ruby believed him. Thirty days they gave her—poor woman—fancy havin' to spend Good Friday in the clink. Old Dot says the most horrible thing was when ..."

Inadvertently, I looked at Mrs. Ottey. She stopped abruptly. My expression seemed to delight her and, after a portentous pause, she said, blithely:

"I don't think you're strong enough to hear the worst part—You bein' so deathly ill, the shock of it might give you a relapse. Besides, the 'phone's ringin'." She chuckled triumphantly. "You didn't hear it, did you?—I told you you were goin' deaf."

Adroitly plucking another cluster of grapes, she left the room.

The sinister implications in Mrs. Ottey's report horrified me. I sat transfixed, staring at the slowly coagulating surface of my cocoa. I was unaware of Mrs. Ottey's return and not until she nudged me sharply and said, "You in a trance or something?" did I look up.

"Harket's on the 'phone," she continued. "Wants to know why you aren't at the engagement party. He sounds as cross as two sticks. He says why didn't you let him know if you wasn't goin'."

The fact that I had entirely forgotten the important function was a great blow to my self-esteem, for I am justly proud of my meticulosity. Also, I was disturbed. Harket is a sensitive man and I knew with what gravity he would regard so heinous a social sole-cism. Mrs. Ottey tapped her foot impatiently.

"Well?—Don't sit there gawpin'. What shall I tell him?"

The thought that my remissness might result in the rupture of a valued friendship rendered me slightly incoherent and I had difficulty phrasing a message for Mrs. O. to deliver.

"You'd better hurry up and think of somethin'," she said, querulously. "From the way your barber friend carried on you'd think his daughter was goin' to marry a rajah instead of a milkman."

"Tell Mr. Harket that I—Say that as far as you know—Ask if—"I began tentatively.

Mrs. Ottey interrupted with a snort of derision. "I'm not goin' to stand here all night while you splutter—"She picked up the supper-tray and marched across the room. "I shall tell him you're at death's door and that even if you wasn't, you wouldn't be at the party because you forgot all about it."

Ignoring my protests, she began to exit. Then as though struck by an afterthought, she turned and beamed at me.

"By the way—Guess who I saw goin' into DUN ROVIN while I was on the phone—Inspector Coggins. Good night. Sleep tight."

The door slammed and she was gone.

As I turned my face to the wall, I saw that only two grapes remained.

March 28ᵗʰ

Rather than lock the stable after the horse has gone, I have remained in bed. My throat is still painful and although my scalded abdomen no longer incommodes me, its saffron tint is somewhat surprising when glimpsed unexpectedly.

Maude visited me, briefly, this morning. Her mood and thumb were both improved. I learned that she crushed the digit on the 25ᵗʰ inst., while attempting weight reduction by calisthenics on the kitchen floor. Harrison, entering at high speed (he was wearing my old skates), failed to notice his mother's prone position until the damage was done.

That Mrs. Ottey greatly exaggerated Harket's annoyance on the telephone was proven by the letter I received from my good friend today. It contained no word of acrimony—only regret that sickness prevented my being at the party. It must have been a gala affair, for Harket said his family will be enjoying leftover tongue for a least a week. His good wishes for my speedy return to health were unmistakably sincere and most heart-warming. I now realize in what a quandary I would have been had I attended the function. Most assuredly, Harket would have taken umbrage had I appeared without the toupee. On the other hand—had I worn it, Maude would have been badly startled for she is unaware of its existence.

How true are the words of Thomas Tusser (1524-1580):

> Except the wind stands where never it stood,
> It is an ill wind that turns none too good.

Miss Costaine sent me some grapes (black). I am keeping them in the drawer of my bed-table.

March 29th

This morning, when Doctor Triggs called and found me still bedridden, his manner was brusque and his clumsily veiled references to "hypochondriacal mollycoddles" extremely tasteless. At his insistence—and in order to humour him—I arose and spent some hours pacing the bedroom in my dressing gown. This afternoon, just as I had decided to venture downstairs, Mrs. Ottey entered and informed me that Inspector Coggins was below and anxious to discuss a matter of some importance. Not wishing to expose the good fellow to infection, I instructed Mrs. O. to tell him that my state of health precluded an interview. Mrs. Ottey's ability to misconstrue one's motives is extraordinary, for she said:

"What are you afraid of? You'll have to see Coggins sooner or later, so why put it off? Or are you goin' to lock yourself in the bathroom for the rest of your life?"

I ignored the remark and, immediately upon her departure, returned to bed.

As I pen these words the hall clock is striking midnight.

In an attempt to drive discord from my mind, I have been reading avidly since 8:47 P.M. Oblivion is not easily achieved however and, even though I have memorized certain passages from Shakespeare (Boys' Own Expurgated Edition) and also the lengthy directions on my jar of Vicks Vapo-Rub, the benison of Sleep is withheld.

During perusal of the Bard, I realized how strangely applicable to my present crisis is a line from the Scotch play, Macbeth—especially if I substitute one word:

> Methought I heard a voice cry, "Sleep no more:
> Luby had murdered Sleep."

March 30th

Inspector Coggins called again this morning. Unfortunately, I was unable to see him as I am still in bed. He told Mrs. Ottey that he would try again tomorrow.

March 31st

Sixth day of incarceration. I did not realize how small my room is. Inspector Coggins did not call.

April 1st

No sign of Coggins.

On my bedroom wallpaper there are four thousand, seven hundred and twenty-two bunches of brown ivy.

I may go downstairs tomorrow.

April 5th

For one blessed with an unusually perceptive mind, the recording of daily events in a journal is an excellent catharsis. Unfortunately, during the past three days of my convalescence, hypertension has made writing impossible. Also nothing has happened.

Return to my former vigour has been delayed by the prospect of Inspector Coggin's visit, which hangs over me like the naked sword over Damocles. A thick yellow fog has confined me to the house and my days have been spent at the drawing room window watching the front gate through the swirling eddies. Incidentally, I must have the down-spout repaired. I have left my post briefly for meals and, yesterday, while I was enjoying tea, Mrs. Ottey rushed in and told me that Coggins was entering the gate of DUN ROVIN. By the time I returned to the window (I was delayed by having to disentangle my Mother's hearing aid cord from the toast-rack), the Inspector was not in sight and although I kept vigil until dusk, he did not emerge. It has since occurred to me that Mrs. Ottey may have fabricated the incident in order to disturb my equanimity, but

I have not allowed this possibility to lull me into a sense of false security.

From behind the screen of lace curtains, I have seen Mrs. Luby leave and return to DUN ROVIN on several occasions—always unaccompanied. This forenoon the fog lifted a little and, when she passed my window, I was surprised at the improvement in her appearance since her sojourn by the sea. Her form is less obese, her attire less flamboyant and her cosmetics less defiantly applied. She is obviously unaware that the arm of the Law is reaching out to disrupt her life, for she was smiling to herself and her gait was jaunty. The thought of Mrs. Luby living in a "fool's paradise" so depressed me that I could not enjoy my luncheon of cold tongue—a gift from Harket.

Maude's interest in my health seems to have been superseded by the delight she is finding in assisting Miss Costaine with the selection of a trousseau. Shopping expeditions are the order of the day and, in consequence, I see my betrothed fleetingly and never in private. This evening, when the ladies returned from a "fire sale" with four dozen scorched pillow cases and a charred seventeenth-century lute, their enthusiasm was intense. Mine was not, but I attempted to jettison my low spirits by simulating jocularity. I enquired of Miss C. if she intended to take the instrument with her on her honeymoon. Both ladies ignored my merry quip and chattered on as though unaware of my existence. In order to attract their attention, I strummed a desultory chord on the lute. As the instrument is three centuries old, I did not expect it to be in tip-top condition but, even so, the extent of its fragility surprised me. As my fingers plucked the strings, the resonance board crumbled like tinder and the fretted neck parted from the body with an unpleasant splintering sound. Immediately, both Maude and Miss Costaine gave me their full attention. They did not speak and the look in their eyes made it impossible for me to do so. For some seconds I stood helpless. Then while the silence grew more ominous, I tried to hold the broken pieces of the lute together. This proved ineffectual and, having arranged the debris in a neat pile next to the pillow cases, I walked quietly to the door. I could feel the ladies' outraged gaze boring into my back and before leaving the room, I faced them and attempted a friendly smile. From Maude's expression, I fear this was a grave mistake.

While ascending the stairs, I recalled the following lines. I trust that Time will prove them fallacious:

> It is the little rift within the lute,
> That by and by will make the music mute,
> And, ever widening, slowly silence all.
>
> Alfred, Lord Tennyson

April 7th

When Samuel Finley Breese Morse invented the telegraph in 1836, little did he know how emotionally disturbing to mankind would be the ultimate result of his brain-child. Cloddish indeed is the man who can receive a telegram today and feel no qualm. Since attaining my majority, I have been the recipient of two such communications. The first was delivered on June 12th, 1920, and notified me of my cousin Clara Gubbion's death by drowning—the second was adhering to a slice of bread and butter on my breakfast tray, when Mrs. Ottey brought it to me at 9:17 A.M. today. (I have eaten in my room since the 5th inst., in order to avoid Miss Costaine.)

Just as a nettle should be firmly grasped—so should a telegram be instantly opened. This morning I delayed doing this because of the way Mrs. Ottey, agog with curiosity, hovered at my elbow. Her eyes gleamed ghoulishly and, finally, she said:

"Well—aren't you goin' to open it?"

I removed the top of my egg before replying. Then, as calmly as my apprehensiveness would allow, I said:

"The communication is private, Mrs. Ottey. Therefore, if you will excuse me, I should like to be alone."

Sniffing contemptuously, Mrs. O. flounced from the room, making muttered and mystifying reference to something called "a garbo." After the door had slammed, I opened the telegram with buttery fingers. It read:

EMERGENCY MEETING SOCIETY HEALTH
THROUGH SANITATION MY HOME TODAY.
BE THERE 3 P.M.

TISDALE, TREASURER.

Never since my poor Father founded The Society in 1902 has a
Committee Meeting been held anywhere but at our house. Besides
which, a mere "treasurer" is not vested with the authority to all a
Meeting. Tisdale's flagrant disregard of protocol enraged me even
more than the high-handed phrasing of his telegram and, hurrying downstairs, I telephoned his residence. Mrs. Tisdale (Joint
Treasurer) answered. Upon learning my identity, she told me tersely
that her husband was out. Controlling my ire, I informed her that, as
President of The Society, I considered Tisdale's dictatorial communication entirely out of order. My sardonic suggestion that he would
be well advised to read Simple Guide to Committee Procedure, by
E. O. Lambourne (published 1925) was rudely interrupted by Mrs.
Tisdale's saying:

"I don't know what you're shouting about and I haven't got
time to listen. I'm busy feeding the cats." Before I could reply she
replaced her receiver with eardrum-shattering force.

Ever since Miss Throbbitt's musicale—when Tisdale sang those
risqué comic songs and his wife discussed her shingles with such
frankness—I have suspected a certain crudity in this couple. As I
circled the rockery this morning, pondering the problem, I realized
that if my prestige as President was to be upheld, diplomacy was
essential.

Fortunately, my knowledge of human nature enables me to
know when to enforce with temper and when to conciliate with
dignity.

The trip to the Tisdales is tedious and takes two hours by tram.
They live in a neighbourhood whose salubrity has been marred by
the erection of a glue factory. In consequence, the large villas no
longer house the wealthy merchants for whom they were designed,
but have been transformed into lodging houses, maisonettes and
flats which are tenanted by a heterogeneous group drawn from
both middle and lower classes. I reached our Treasurer's abode at
exactly 2:59 P.M. It stands to leeward of the factory chimney and, as

I entered the front gate, I marveled that life could be sustained in so odoriferous an atmosphere. I pressed the bell-push. The resultant chimes were instantly drowned by a chorus of eldritch caterwauling from within. It grew in volume and to the cacophony, angry spittings and scratchings were added. Through a window on my left, three snarling tabby cats regarded me with amber-eyed animosity. Then the front door opened slightly and through a crack, approximately two inches wide, one of Mrs. Tisdale's eyes scrutinized me.

"You'll have to wait 'til I've caught Sultan and Melanie—I don't want 'em running out in the street," she said. The door closed. Five minutes elapsed before it reopened and my hostess bade me enter. To her bosom she clutched two writhing blue Persians and, from her shortness of breath and manner, I deduced that their capture had been arduous. My greeting was interrupted by Mrs. Tisdale's saying, irritably:

"My husband's not back from Gravesend yet. Wait in the drawing room and don't make a noise, because Fluff's in labour." Then she hurried upstairs, calling, "Togo—where are you, Togo? Mother wants you, Togo."

I looked about me, dazed by my reception and also by a feline aroma which, blending with the smell of glue, made respiration tiresome. On the hall-table, supine in a nest of hats, lay a monstrous tom and beneath that hat-rack two attractive kittens frolicked with what once had been a fish-head.

I went into the drawing room.

Crouching on the window ledge were the tree tabbies I had observed from the street. They ignored my entrance and I saw that their attention was focused malevolently on a far corner of the room where, with unnatural rigidity, sat Miss Throbbitt. She gazed at the cats as though hypnotized and, upon nearing her, I noticed that her face was mottled and her upper lip dewy.

"Greeting, fair lady," I said.

"Oh, Mr. Carp—thank heavens you've come," she whispered. "Please—please make those horrid creatures go away."

"Come now, Miss Throbbitt," I said, soothingly. "They cannot harm you. They're only cats."

"Of course they're cats. I know they're cats—can't you see how blotchy my face is? I'm allergic to cats." The note of hysteria in Miss T.'s voice alarmed me.

Surreptitiously withdrawing my poor Father's gavel from my breast pocket, I took a step toward the felines. "Pussy, pussy—nice pussies," I said gently.

"Mrs. Tisdale calls them Winkin', Blinkin' and Nod," whimpered Miss Throbbitt, helpfully.

I moved nearer, repeating the names. The animal on the left yawned, but its companions received my overtures with guttural growls. I put on my gloves. Two more steps brought me within reach of the yawning cat, which I decided was Nod. Picking it up, I hurried to the door and placed it in the hall. Winkin' and Blinkin' proved less amenable and, in spite of my cajolings, all attempts to touch them were fiercely repulsed. Miss T.'s whimpers grew louder and finally I was forced to raise the window and "shoo" the tabbies out into the front garden with the handle of the gavel.

My gloves—the ones Maude knitted years ago for her late husband—had proven poor protection against sharp talons, and my wrist had sustained a disconcertingly deep scratch. Usually I carry a pocket phial of iodine. Today, by some oversight, I had neglected to do so and, perforce, the wound went untreated.

To my surprise, Miss Throbbitt made no attempt to thank me for having evicted the beasts, but continued to sit, unrelaxed, staring into the middle distance. The mottling of her skin seemed a deeper maroon and reminded me of a cirro-cumulus sky at sunset. The tension in the room was electric and, in order to ease it, I said:

"I do think that Mrs. Tisdale might have given us a fire."

Avoiding my eyes, Miss T. pointed timidly to the fireplace. Amidst the dead ashes, curled on a khaki pullover, was a pink-eyed, extremely distended, white cat.

"it's name is Fluff and it can't be moved because—because it's going to have—" Miss Throbbitt did not complete the sentence and, as she wiped the moisture from her lip, her complexion became a uniform crimson.

Providentially, our mutual embarrassment was mitigated by the entrance of Tisdale and Rolfe, the plumber. Although indoors, the latter still wore his hat. From Tisdale's expression and the way he slammed the door, I knew something was amiss. Both gentlemen ignored my greeting and, flinging himself into a chair, Tisdale said, angrily:

"Find President you are, I must say. They've condemned both my houses. Asking you to do something about it did about as much good as stuffing up a rat-hole with a dumpling."

Dispersing Rolfe's cigar smoke from before my face with a wave of the hand, I said, calmly:

"Mr. Tisdale. Let us not forget there is a lady present."

Tisdale leapt to his feet. Before he could speak, Mrs. Tisdale rushed into the room, pushed her husband back into his chair and said, menacingly:

"How many times have I got to tell you not to slam this door? D'you want Fluff to lose her kittens?" She hurried out again calling, "Winkin'—Blinkin', where are you? Mother's got your liver ready."

Under his breath, Tisdale muttered something which sounded suspiciously like, "Bl—dy cats!" and, from the fireplace, Fluff emitted a heartrending "meow." I looked at Miss Throbbitt. Except that her eyes were rolled back, exposing much white beneath the iris, her appearance was unchanged. Rolfe, still wearing his hat, regarded me stonily through the mephitic fumes of his cigar.

In a handbook by John Rigg, entitled How to Take the Chair, the author contends that harmony can be restored to the most discordant Committee Meeting if the President preserves an unflustered mien. Remembering this, I rose, rapped the table lightly with my poor Father's gavel and, ignoring Tisdale's look of disgust, declared the Committee in session. Then, as is my custom, I enquired what subject the Members wished to discuss. Rolfe's eyes became baleful and he said:

"I'd like to discuss why you haven't paid me for mending the leak in your attic."

The question was, of course, out of order but before I could say so, another piercing wail drew everyone's attention to the fireplace. Miss Throbbitt quickly closed her eyes and, during the ensuing silence, the rest of the Committee watched the first of Fluff's progeny arrive.

How great a miracle is birth.

When finally, I called the Meeting to order, both Tisdale and Rolfe ignored the gavel and continued to concentrate on the fructifying feline. Notwithstanding their inattention, I decided to begin the Presidential speech I had prepared on the tram. No one enjoys talking to empty air and so I addressed my allocution to Miss Throbbitt who sat facing me, with eyes closed, moaning softly.

In view of the Sewage Commission's confiscation of the property at Gravesend, the preamble to my memorized speech was no longer apropos. Therefore I substituted some extemporaneous remarks regarding "Progress and its effect upon the individual." With a pithiness deserving of a more appreciative audience, I pointed out that there are times when individual sacrifice may mean great benefit to the community. Such a theme is inspiring and, as the wings of Oratory bore me higher, I quoted King Lear's speech to his daughter at the British camp near Dover:

> Upon such sacrifice, my Cordelia,
> The Gods themselves throw incense.

As any good speaker will tell you, such lines should be followed by a pause. This afternoon, a caterwauling from Fluff ruined this effect and Tisdale said, excitedly, "Here comes another one."

There was a jingle of coins as Rolfe placed money upon the hearth.

"I'll lay you seven to two she has six," he said.

"It's a bet," replied Tisdale and the two shook hands.

From the way Miss Throbbitt rocked back and forth, it was obvious that she found the obstetrical atmosphere oppressive. In order to distract her I continued my speech. I commiserated with Tisdale on the loss of his houses and, at the sound of his name, our Treasurer gave me his attention for the first time. I went on to say that he should derive consolation from the fact that, on the site of his property, the Sewage Commission intended to erect a Horizontal Agitator Type Activated Sludge Channel—and not one of the out-moded Fill and Draw Sedimentation Tanks with Continuous Filter, upon which so much of the taxpayers' money has been wasted. At this point, Tisdale's expression halted my words. He rose to his feet, leaned across the table and thrust his face very near mine. His neck seemed larger and, beneath his jawbone, I noticed a corded artery pulsating rapidly.

"Carp," he said, "you're a damned fool," and Miss Throbbitt squealed.

What followed was a tirade of such abuse that even to recall it makes my palms moist. From Tisdale's vulgarly phrased outburst, I gathered that he was sick to death of the Society and that he had little time for a President who considered a Horizontal Agitator Type Activated Sludge Channel superior to a Fill and Draw Sedimentation Tank with Continuous Filter. Three times I attempted to put forward sound arguments in favour of the process I believed in. I failed dismally, for it is useless to reason with a mind out of control. In desperation, I called upon Rolfe—as Vice President—to restore order to the Meeting. Without taking his eyes from Fluff, he said:

"I second the motion."

"What motion?" I enquired.

"That you're a damned fool," replied Rolfe.

Tisdale continued to shout and Miss Throbbitt's moans became higher in pitch. To this uproar was added the puling of newborn kittens and Mrs. Tisdale's strident tones as she hurried into the room. Her husband paid no heed to the dire consequences with which she threatened him unless he stopped shouting, and the lady turned her fury upon me. She said that the disturbance was entirely my fault and, with arms akimbo, accused me of smugness and several other qualities which I have no intention of recording. The unfairness of these charges stunned me and I stood speechless, while the purple-faced Tisdale abusively consigned The Society, myself, my Mother and Maude to perdition. Then his wife dragged him from the room. As they exited, Rolfe looked up from the fireplace and shouted after him, "What about our bet?" and Miss Throbbitt began to laugh. Her merriment at this juncture caused me some irritation, but upon looking at her closely, I saw that her titters were accompanied by copious weeping. Rolfe regarded the two of us dispassionately and, having retrieved his money from the hearth, walked slowly to the door. With his hand on the knob he turned, expelled a long plume of smoke in my direction and said:

"You know what you can do with The Society."

The door closed and I noticed Miss Throbbitt swaying precariously on her chair. As she toppled toward the floor, I leapt to her side and by grabbing her musquash fur-piece, managed to break the impact of her fall. Slapping her hands proved useless. There being no water, I finally maneuvered her limp form to the window, which I opened. The chill gusts of glue-scented air quickly revived her, but thirty minutes elapsed before she was sufficiently recovered for us to take our leave. During this time, Fluff completed her delivery and I drew a modicum of satisfaction from the fact that Rolfe had lost his bet. The litter was seven in number.

From the kitchen, the Tisdales; voices could be heard, raised in argument, but no further glimpse of them was seen and at 5:32 P.M., with Miss Throbbitt leaning heavily on my umbrella arm, I left the residence of our whilom Joint Treasurers, silently vowing never to return.

En route to the bus terminus, Miss T.'s wan expression prompted me to suggest "the cup that cheers." Choosing a teashop to windward of the glue factory, I ordered a pot for two. Seemingly, the Meeting had sharpened Miss Throbbitt's appetite, for she disposed of a Welsh Rarebit, and Eccles Cake and two Chelsea Buns. The price of the latter was exorbitant and had my dear Maude been present I know she would have questioned the bill. However, Etiquette and the waitress's steely eye forbade my doing so, and I paid with as much grace as I could muster.

Prior to boarding her bus, Miss Throbbitt attempted to thank me for my kindness. Unfortunately, an attack of snorting overcame her and she hurried into the vehicle holding a sodden handkerchief to her mouth. I watched her choose a seat and upon catching sight of me through the window, she nodded primly and tightened the musquash about her narrow shoulders. As I raised my hat in farewell, I saw above her head an advertisement for wedding rings. The radiance of the pictured bird contrasted ironically with Miss Throbbitt's look of withered desolation, and as the conveyance disappeared into the gloom, I pondered compassionately on the countless women for whom Spinsterhood makes Life a sleeveless errand.

I waited twenty minutes for my tram and upon embarking discovered that the costly tea had depleted my cash in hand, leaving only enough for a fare to the Town Hall. This edifice is an hour's walk from Gubbion Avenue and when I alighted, darkness, thick fog and a heavy drizzle had so reduced visibility that I missed my way three times. I reached home at 8:11 P.M. with one foot saturated owing to a puncture in my left galosh. Supper was over and the bowl of lukewarm lentils, which Mrs. Ottey thrust before in the kitchen, neither titillated nor assuaged my appetite. While toying with the repast, I learned from Mrs. O. that, during my absence, my Mother had been "difficult." She had spent the afternoon emptying drawers and cupboards searching for something—the nature of which she would not disclose—and at dusk had gone into the garden, insisting that she had to meet someone by the rockery. Only by promising an extra kipper for supper had Mrs. Ottey induced her to come in out of the fog.

An hour ago, when I entered my Mother's room to say good night, she said:

"Is that you, Tacky?"

"No, Mother, it's Edwin," I answered. Her reply hurt me deeply, for she said:

"Edwin who?"

I have written a letter to The Society of Health through Sanitation, resigning my Presidency. Its succinct phrasing affords me great pleasure.

Unfortunately, I have no idea to whom it should be sent.

April 8th

This morning, while in the hall donning my outer garments prior to visiting the Public Library, the "click" of our front gate sounded. I looked through the letterbox slot (a recently adopted precaution before admitting visitors) and saw Inspector Coggins approaching the portico. Grabbing Vendetta, by Marie Corelli and my umbrella, I made an alacritous exit via the kitchen, the garden and the back alley. Mrs. Ottey was upstairs with my Mother and only Mr. Dimmock—feeding his chickens an MON REPOS—saw me leave. He did not speak, of course, but from the way he gaped, I think he was impressed by—and perhaps a little envious of—the speed at which I ran. Due to recent rains the alley was a morass of mud and when I emerged at the junction of Gubbion and Disraeli Avenues, my brightly burnished boots were sadly sullied. Luckily, I reached the Library without meeting anyone I know.

Behind the desk—replacing the oafish librarian I had previously encountered—was a comely young woman (brunette). Her vivacity so entranced the youth ahead of me in line that, while exchanging his book *Motorcycle Musts for You and Your Carburetor*, he invited her to spend Easter Monday riding pillion on his machine. With a *moué* of her very red, very moist mouth, the damsel explained that she was committed to accompany "Alf" to a Tea Dance at The Regal. Oblivious of myself and others waiting behind him, the young motorcyclist continued to press his suit. This took seven and three-quarter minutes, during which I learned:

- That the young woman was not "too keen" on "Alf" because his work at the brewery made his hair smell "funny."
- That "Alf" was insanely jealous and was always "pawing."
- That the motorcyclist had recently won a cash prize in a Football Pool.
- That the young woman would spend Easter Monday on the pillion, if she was assured there would be no "messing about."
- Having agreed to this condition, the youth took his ecstatic leave and I watched, with fascination, the young woman's rapt expression as she stamped my book without once removing her eyes from the muscular figure of her departing Don Juan.
- Puppy Love—although ephemeral—is interesting to observe.

On my homeward journey I saw Coggins for the second time. He was in conversation with a constable a scant thirty feet from the bus stop where I alit. Fortunately, the Inspector's back was toward me and I quickly sought sanctuary in the nearest shop. It proved to be Feuchtwangler Bros. Fish Emporium. There were no no customers and the younger Feuchtwangler (Ignatz) greeted me effusively and extolled his wares with heavily accented lyricism. Knowing the importance of remaining hidden until Coggins had gone his way, I feigned interest in the fish and hovered undecidedly over the jellied eels and the whitebait. Like others of his nationality, Mr. Feuchtwangler is given to mercurial changes of mood and, after eight or nine minutes, his blandness was replaced by an impatience which brooked no further dalliance on my part. My purchase of a herring (for which I had small use) did little to placate Mr. F. and, as he wrapped it in newspaper, he muttered gutturally. Emerging cautiously from the shop, I was dismayed to see? Coggins had not moved. Fortuitously, a bus halted before me and, without ascertaining its destination, I hurried aboard. The vehicle passed within four feet of Coggins and, as it did so, I buried my face in the library book. It was then I discovered that—instead of *The Sorrows of Satan*, which I had withdrawn for my Mother (she has not read it for nine weeks)—the lovelorn librarian had given me *Les Miserables*, by Victor Hugo.

As the distance between myself and Coggins increased, I reasoned that chance of further encounter would be lessened if I remained away from home as long as possible. When the conductor came for my fare, I asked how far the bus went.

"Wormwood Scrubbs Prison," he replied.

Stifling the qualms which thoughts of penal servitude engender in the hyper-sensitive, I took a return ticket. As the conductor handed me change, he said, sympathetically:

"You goin' to the prison to see a relative, sir?"

I enlightened him with some vehemence.

"No offense meant, sir," he said. "I only asked because it's visitin' day—that's why we're so crowded." He looked round the bus and then whispered, "See that woman across the aisle? She visits 'er 'usband once a week reg'lar. 'E went after 'er with a chopper—be a year before 'e gets out. Poor old girl, she always talks to me. Says the loneliness is the worst part. Makes you think, don't it? Still, that's life I s'pose. Well—'ave a nice ride, sir."

Smiling cheerfully, he continued on his rounds and I made covert inspection of the other passengers. Almost every face bore a look of strain. Behind the lonely woman sat a frail old gentleman holding a baby. On my left a middle-aged lady stared vacantly before her, twisting a handkerchief in her lap. I wondered whom she was visiting—and what his crime. Her pince-nez and the two red roses on her hat made me think of Maude and, suddenly, I found myself envisioning my dear one on a similar mission. In order to banish these depressing thoughts, I began skimming through Les Miserables.

I do not approve of the French or their writings. I have heard Victor Hugo referred to as a classicist, but it was always by the indiscriminate and never, until today, have I delved into his works. His tale of the peasant Valjean's persecution by Javert (a moronic minion of the law) struck me as lugubrious and improbable. I fear its author has an insensitive finger on the pulse of the reading public, for he wishes it believed that a peasant can be sentenced to rowing a large boat for nineteen years—simply for stealing bread with which to feed his niece. The poor man is then hounded for several decades by the policeman Javert. This is poorly conceived character delineation, for no one so loutish as Javert would have sufficient application to remain interested in such a task for more than four or five weeks. The name of the heroine is, also, most unsuitable: Cosette—it sounds more like an insect than the flower of womanhood which the author would have us believe she was. (There is a mealy bug—a single-celled, parasitic protozoan, characterized chiefly by its manner of reproduction—called *Coccidae*.) During the long bus-ride, I found only one thing about this book with which I could not quibble—its title. Mr. Hugo's work is, indeed, miserable.

My recent cold has in no way impaired my olfactory sense and by the time we reached Wormwood Scrubbs, the proximity of the herring had become oppressive. I disposed of it in a convenience at the bus terminus. Having missed luncheon my return journey was marred by acute *borborygmus*—the meaning and correct spelling of which I discovered when I re-read *What to Do until the Doctor Arrives* during my incarceration. It was 3:57 P.M. when I reached Gubbion Avenue and, despite hunger pangs, I made careful reconnaissance for evidence of Coggins. The street was empty, but remembering how Constable Parkhurst had lurked in the laurels, I retraced my steps and entered the house via the alley. I could hear Mrs. Ottey singing in the bathroom and I went into the hall intending to order an egg with my tea. As I placed my hand on the newel-post, a voice behind me said:

"Good afternoon, Mr. Carp."

I turned. On the threshold of the drawing room stood Inspector Coggins. For a moment I was unable to speak. Then, as my umbrella and *Les Miserables* fell to the floor, I said:

"Inspector Javert!"

My inexplicable slip of the tongue added to my consternation and, quite naturally, puzzled Coggins. There was an awkward pause, during which he picked up the book and placed it on the hallstand. Retrieving my umbrella, I entered the drawing room with racing pulse. Coggins followed closely and, having closed the door, stood looking at me. Knowing that tension can sometimes be eased by observance of the social niceties, I said:

"Won't you sit down, Inspector?"

Coggins ignored my invitation and walked to the fireplace. From his manner I could tell that performance of his duty was causing him embarrassment.

"I've been tryin' to see you for some time, sir—I'm sorry you were so ill," he said.

"I had a cold—" I began. My voice seemed unnaturally high and, in order to lower its pitch, I cleared my throat. Before I could continue, Coggins said:

"There's lots of colds about, sir—I've 'ad one meself. But it's no good me stayin' in the bed—there's no one to look after me. I just sweated it out on the job."

A long pause followed, during which we again looked at each other.

"They say there's more colds about now than there 'as bin for years," continued Coggins and, having walked to the window and back, added, "A gent on the wireless the other night said there 'asn't bin so many colds since the flu epidemic in 1918." Another pause. "Did you 'ave it, sir?"

I found myself wondering who would visit Mrs. Luby when she went to prison and Coggins repeated his question.

"Did you 'ave it, sir?"

"Did I have what, Inspector?"

"The flu—in 1918?"

"No, Inspector, I didn't."

"Nor did I, sir."

This verbal fencing was playing havoc with my nerves. Silence fell again and Coggins walked slowly round the room. The strongest mind will reel if the onslaught is great enough and, in an attempt to dam the ebbing tide of my Self Control, I tried to remember the

"Prayer for Indifference," by Mrs. Greville. Unfortunately, I could only recall part of the sixth stanza:

> O! haste—tee tum tee tum tee tum,
> My shattered nerves new-string;
> And for my guest, serenely calm,
> The nymph Indifference bring.

Gripping my umbrella handle, I repeated the lines silently—with frenzied concentration. Coggins circled the room three times, then, halting by the window, blew his nose vigorously. At last—in a flat, businesslike voice, he spoke:

"Well, Mr. Carp, I've beaten around the bush too long already—but what I've got to say isn't easy."

A bead of perspiration trickled from my upper spine to my lower back.

"The last time I saw you, sir, was on the—" Coggins consulted his notebook. "—on the 8th of March. On that date I made certain allegations against your tenant, Mrs. Dorothy Luby. Well, Mr. Carp, what I told you was vile wicked slander. It isn't easy for a man like me to eat 'umble pie, but that's what I'm doin'. I'm apologizing, sir, and I 'ope and trust you'll forgive my 'orrible mistake and let bygones be bygones." He smiled and held out a friendly hand. Suddenly his expression changed to one of concern and he said:

"You orlright, sir? You've gone such a nasty putty colour—'ere, 'ave a nice sit down." He lowered me gently onto the settee. "I'll bet you 'ad the flu and didn't know it, sir—that's 'ow it leaves you—weak as water."

Words cannot limn my utter bewilderment. Somehow I managed to mumble acceptance of the Inspector's apology and allowed him to pump my hand vigorously. He seemed anxious to leave and, having advised me to build up my strength with Guinness's Stout, made for the door. Then he turned and said:

"Anyone but you would have made trouble for me, Mr. Carp. You're a prince—a real prince and I'm not the only one who thinks so. Dorothy—er, I mean, Mrs. Luby thinks so, too."

Coggins' unexpected use of my tenant's Christian name amazed me further. Even more amazing was its effect upon Coggins. Waves of crimson flooded his already florid countenance and, spluttering incoherently, he hurried from the room. Marveling that a man of his age could blush so deeply, I went to the window and watched him leave the house. He made straight for DUN ROVIN and, though my windows were closed, his lighthearted whistling was clearly audible.

How perspicacious was the Bard, when into the Prince of Denmark's mouth he put the words:

> There are more things in heaven and earth, Horatio,
> Than are dreamt of in your philosophy.

April 9th

Life is an exciting business. It is an expedition through uncharted terrain—a safari through virgin jungle. There are no signposts. Man's Intellect is the machete he wilds to hack a path through the matted underbrush of Circumstance and the tendrilled lianas of Illusion. The keener the blade—the swifter the pace. The scenic panorama is ever-changing. From the hills of Hope, we plunge into canyons of Despair, whose boundaries seem to reach the edge of the world. Then the road turns and, suddenly, we are in a garden—a verdant place—an unexpected Eden. Our eyes—so used to gloom—are dazzled by the brightness of the sun and all that charms us is more beautiful, because we are unprepared for it.

So is today more joyous if yesterday was sad.

Unfortunately, the Majority does not appreciate this, for its horizon of thinking is limited. But for those of us who recognize the privilege of belonging to the genus Homo sapiens, the contrast of our days is a never-ceasing wonder.

The foregoing profundities result from a serenity of mind which I am enjoying for the first time in weeks. The hall clock is striking 6 P.M. It has been a wonderful day. My dear Maude, Miss Costaine and Walter Roach have departed after a sumptuous high tea (poached eggs on haddock and two kinds of cake) and I am writing this in the dining room. The fire which I lit to make the occasion more festive is dying and, as the coals collapse, flurries of sparks glow comfortingly. Though my friends are gone (Maude spent twenty minutes alone with me after the others had left), the aura of companionship remains and I am content. I am also immensely proud, for Walter Roach has asked me to be best man at the nuptials in June. Maude will be Matron of Honour.

To be carefree is exhilarating. The problem of DUN ROVIN, one to daunt the doughtiest of men, has inexplicably solved itself and my apology to Miss Costaine for damaging her lute was proffered and accepted during tea. I am certain she bears no rancour, for she did an imitation of my behaviour at the time of the accident which afforded Roach great amusement. Miss C.'s vivacity and abandon since her engagement are remarkable and, though her mimicry left my risiblilties unstirred, I laughed hilariously. Maude did not smile once and later, when the lovebirds had departed, she voiced a resentment at having me ridiculed, which I eventually silenced with a kiss. I learned, with joy, that the shopping excursions are over and that henceforth my dear one's leisure hours will be spent with me.

The street lamps outside have just switched themselves on. I suppose Progress demands their automatic ignition, but I am nostalgically reminded of the friendly lamp-lighter of my boyhood whose nightly rounds set them shining. Mr. McCoombe—or was it McCool? He had a red beard and an inexhaustible supply of Aniseed Balls which changed colour while dissolving in the mouth. I doubt if he is still living. I remember now—his name was Finch.

A loud noise on the stairs has just distracted my thoughts. What Mrs. Ottey is doing I cannot imagine. Now she is wailing in the weirdest fashion. The din makes concentration impossible—I shall resume this entry when I have reprimanded her—

It is 7:14 P.M. Doctor Triggs left the house ten minutes ago. The sedative draught which he insisted upon my taking has calmed my nerves, but still vivid in my mind's eye is the picture of my Mother lying prone before the hat-rack. She has spoken only once since Doctor T., Mrs. Ottey and I carried her to her room. Her words—which passed unheeded by the others—convince me that I am indirectly responsible for her falling down the stairs. As we placed her on the bed, she opened her eyes and said, irascibly:

"Edwin—there's a rat in your collar drawer."

If only I had hidden my toupee more carefully she would never have come upon it.

If only I had cleaned her spectacles after tea she might not have mistaken the hairpiece for a rodent and taken flight a t such break-neck speed.

Doctor Triggs has left Mrs. Ottey in charge of her and has requested that I stay out of the room. He was alarmingly evasive when I demanded diagnosis of my parent's condition. I shall never forgive myself it—

7:35 P.M. doctor Triggs has returned, bringing with him Doctor White. They are with my Mother now.

September 7th

It is five months, one week and four days since last I made an entry which I consider worthy of my pen. Those written during my nervous breakdown I have deleted. Their incoherence and lack of style revealed a state of mind which I prefer to gloss over rather than recall, and though by July 15th my poise was fully regained (I missed the Roach's wedding, alas), not until now have I felt disposed to open this journal.

I can think of no more auspicious day than this on to which to recommence the chronicling of my Life's events. Seven hours ago—in the Ministerial Chamber at St. Jude's—my dearest Maude and I were launched upon the Sea of Matrimony by the Reverend Josiah Moncrieff. Only our intimates attended the ceremony. Doctor Triggs gave the bride away; Walter Roach was best man; Miriam Roach was Matron of Honour and Harrison (in his first long trousers) made a gentlemanly Junior Groomsman despite his head cold. Maude looked beautiful.

The shaky penmanship of this entry is not entirely due to my excitement. Its main cause is the unevenness of The Great Western Railway Company's road-bed. Also, the angular lady on my right is knitting a sock. My dear one occupies the corner seat opposite mine (she likes her back to the engine) and though she looks at me rarely, the little smile playing on her lips tells me that my happiness is shared. She is watching the scudding countryside through the window. There is a soft sheen on the September landscape and in the copse through which we are speeding, a scattering of prematurely coppered leaves prophesies a gaudy Autumn. We have just passed two cows whose proximity to the embankment and obvious contempt for the thundering locomotive disturbs me. I trust their owner is close at hand.

Never before have I ventured on so long a train journey. For this thrill I am indebted to Miriam and Walter Roach, whose high praise of Mrs. Barracombe's Boarding Establishment at Budleigh Salterton is the reason Maude and I are honeymooning in Devonshire. By all accounts, the two weeks our friends spent there last June were idyllic and we have promised them we will visit all the places they did. This will make splendid conversation for the long evenings to spend with them this coming winter (they have leased THE NEST from Maude). The list of beauty spots they have prepared for us makes exciting reading and both Maude and I are anxious to discover for ourselves the wonders of—Clyst Honiton, Bovey Trace, Ottery St. Mary, Polbathick, Pinhoe and Bradninch. Today, at the station, Walter again reminded me that the shrimp teas at Pinhoe are the finest in the world.

The young man next to Maude seems to have forgotten that he is in a "non-smoker" for he has ignited his pipe. I shall give him several minutes to realize his mistake before I complain.

A few grains of rice still nestle in the artificial peony which decorates Maude's new hat. I wonder if others in the compartment have noticed them and realize their significance. I hope they have. So great is my pride that I am tempted to shout aloud that we are newly wed. I shall fight this urge for obvious reasons.

I have just spoken to the young man with the pipe and he has extinguished it with fair grace. My authoritative handling of the matter caused Maude to throw me a look of admiration which set me glowing twice as much as the small glass of Tawny Port which I indulged in at our wedding breakfast. The bottle of Villa Nova da Gaia was a gift from Murke and one of the twelve handsome presents we received from our friends. The plethora of pickle forks (we received five) gave me a moment's concern, but Maude assures me that she can exchange them together with the nutcrackers and the extra hot-water bottle.

Never, within living memory, has 35 Gubbion Avenue known a celebration more gala than our wedding breakfast today. Never have its walls echoed with more good will and never has its table groaned beneath a more Lucullan feast. Maude and Mrs. Ottey spent a week preparing the innumerable dainty viands and the fact that two of the seven days were devoted entirely to the making of blanc mange gives some inkling of the over-all lavishness. The festive board was given an added touch of sophistication by Miriam Roach's hand-painted place card—each one of which she decorated with a real acorn. Both she and Maude were showered with well-deserved compliments and it was a joy to watch the gusto with which the repast was disposed of by the following:

> Doctor Henry Triggs
> Mr. & Mrs. Walter Roach
> Mr. Julius Murke
> Miss May Throbbitt
> Professor Thaddeus Hume
> Mr. Guy Dimmock
> Mrs. Grace Ottey

I am happy that my friendship with Mr. Dimmock has been resumed, for I shall always be indebted to him for his gifts of fresh eggs during my collapse. I am certain that their nutritive value, together with Professor Hume's many visits and sound counsel, helped speed my recovery. Incidentally, one of the finest speeches this morning was delivered by the good Professor. I am still disturbed by his dentures, however. Although months have passed since their installation, I cannot accustom myself to their unnatural symmetry and flashing whiteness. Also, the percussive "clickings" with which they interlard his speech are most districting. Today as he spoke, I was aware of a newly developed "rattle" on every palatalized consonant (especially those following a glottal stop). Harrison, being immature, seemed to find these sad impediments amusing, but with the aid of the serviette which I passed him beneath the table, he managed to hold his hilarity in check and, at the conclusion of the Professor's thirteen-minute oration, I was gratified to see the enthusiasm with which the boy applauded.

Walter Roach's rendition of "O Promise Me" which followed was "par excellence." Not wishing to move the assemblage from the dining room(we were enjoying our Tawny Port), he stood in the doorway and sang, while Miriam Roach accompanied him some distance away on the clavichord in the drawing-room. Despite this handicap I was amazed that she finished only three bars ahead of her husband.

It was during Walter's ovation that I went to the sideboard to get a clean serviette and, in the corner of the drawer, saw my poor Mother's hearing aid. I felt a pant that she was not with us on this momentous day, but it passed quickly, for I realized that the occasion would have afforded her little joy.

By the time it was Murke's turn to say a word, the bottle of Villa Nova da Gaia at his elbow contained no more than a furry sediment and, as I feared, the content of his speech leant heavily upon conjugal innuendo for its effect. Mercifully, he was too weary to remain standing long and, after two and a quarter minutes, reseated himself. Murke is a good fellow and means no harm, but I would have been happier had he left unsaid the extremely pithy remark which caused Maude to blush and Miss Throbbitt to snort. I think, too, that my own speech—which took many evenings to prepare—was robbed of some of its impact by Murke's interruptions. Though I struggled manfully through the first six minutes, his frequent cries of "Cut the cackle and kiss the bride" were eventually taken up by all the guests and I was forced to abandon my peroration and kiss Maude. We are both averse to public demonstrations of affection but, despite this, our embrace delighted all present and evoked rousing cheers. Following this disconcerting moment, I seized the opportunity to thank Mrs. Ottey for her unswerving loyalty during the many difficult days of the past year. I concluded by saying that I knew of no one in whose care I would rather leave my son while my wife and I were at Budleigh Salterton. I think she sensed my sincerity for, as I reseated myself, she raised work-worn hands to her mouth and laughed, self-consciously. It was odd to see the good woman lost for words and I was immensely proud of Harrison who averted what might have been an embarrassing silence by shouting, "Three cheers for Mrs. Ottey." When the noise subsided she thanked me awkwardly, then spoiled the effect by shrieking with laughter and saying to Maude:

"Wait 'til tomorrow morning, old girl, when you see him without his glasses."

Murke laughed uproariously.

Every time doctor Triggs was called upon to make a speech he excused himself good-humouredly and not until we were about to leave for the station was his disinclination explained to me. While we awaited the taxi, the old gentleman led Maude and me into the drawing room. Having closed the door he said, "I've waited a long time to see this day, my boy, and I—" Placing his arms about our shoulders, he drew us to him and embraced us as though we were his children. When he released us his eyes were suspiciously moist. Twice he tried to speak and failed. Finally, pressing Maude's hand into mine, he said, gruffly, "Forgive me—I'm just a damned old fool," and hurried from the room.

We left the house bombarded by a barrage of confetti and rice thrown by the cheering friends who lined the garden path. Despite the speed at which I ran the gauntlet, I could not fail to notice Miss Throbbitt's left heel firmly planted in the heart of my *Dryas Octopetala*. The mishap was, of course, unpremeditated and although I had no time to give Mr. Dimmock instructions (he has promised to tend the garden during my absence), I am hoping that he will see the damage and, if possible, save this prize specimen. I also noticed my second best pair of galoshes among the many old boots attached to the rear of the taxi. Fortunately, I was able to rescue them at the station and Miriam Roach took them home for me.

As we drove by DUN ROVIN there was a slight movement of the drawing room curtains and I am certain that I saw the shadow of a waving hand. It is a relief to know that, at long last, all is well with my property. In my pocket is a reply to the wedding invitation I sent. It reads:

> Dear Old Ed,
>
> You're a real sport to send the invite and I hope you wont be upset Because I wont be there—but I don't really think I'd fit in somehow. You know how noisy I get when I've had a couple Ha Ha.

Well, anyway—lots of luck dear old Ed and if you have as good
a Honeymoon as we did you'll be off to a fine start.
All the best,
Dorothy and Bertram Coggins

The train is pulling into Basingstoke station and from the bustling activity among the passengers, many seem about to disembark. On the luggage rack above Maude's head an errant breeze is stirring the label attached to her suitcase. The inscription reads, "Mrs. Edwin Osric Carp."

If, by some good fortune, Maude and I are left alone in the compartment, I shall kiss her the moment we are again under way.

.

ABOUT THE AUTHOR

RICHARD HAYDN, hitherto best known as a motion-picture actor (*The Sound of Music*) and director, was born in London in 1905. This was his first and only book, based on his signature character, honed in his early stage career. Mr. Haydn lived in London, Paris, New York, Jamaica B.W.I., Los Angeles, and North Africa. He died in 1985. His body was donated to medical science, and his ashes scattered at sea.